Devoured

A HORROR ROMANCE

SEPHYRRA
CORDELIA MIRE

WITHER & RUNE PRESS

Wither & Rune Press

www.authorsephyrra.com

contact@authorsephyrra.com

newsletter@authorsephyrra.com

Author's Note

Devoured was born from a simple truth: the monsters we fear most are often the ones already living inside us.

Depression moved into my head years ago. Anxiety followed. They're not visitors anymore, they're residents. You learn that survival means something different when the threat lives in your own mind. It means negotiation. Boundaries that shift. Some days you win. Some days you just coexist.

That understanding bled into every page. The horror here isn't about things that go bump in the night. It's about the uneasy truce you make with the parts of yourself that want to devour you. About learning that sometimes the only way through is to stop running and start making space for your monsters.

This story won't comfort you. I didn't write it to be gentle. But I hope it stays with you the way real fears do. Not because of the blood or the screaming, but because somewhere in these pages, you recognized something familiar.

The best horror always feels like coming home.

And for all the girls who played Silent Hill and thought Pyramid Head was kind of hot. Yeah, I see you. This one's for us.

Content Advisory

This book contains extremely graphic and disturbing content.
If ANY of the following topics are triggering or unsettling to
you, **PLEASE DO NOT READ THIS BOOK.**

Sexual Violence:
    Graphic non-consensual acts
    Forced physical responses during assault
    Medical boundary violations
    Sexual coercion and harm
    Extreme Violence & Gore:
    Graphic torture scenes
    Live skinning/flaying
    Dismemberment while conscious
    Detailed mutilation
    Extensive blood and body horror
    Domestic Abuse:
    Severe physical domestic violence
    Psychological torture
    Emotional manipulation

Victim blaming
Mental Health & Self-Harm:
Detailed suicide attempts
Self-harm/cutting
Severe mental illness
Psychiatric abuse
Institutionalization trauma
Reproductive Trauma:
Multiple miscarriages
Blame and abuse related to infertility
Additional Disturbing Content:
Child abuse (referenced)
Religious blasphemy/corruption
Body horror and transformation
Captivity and imprisonment

PLEASE PROTECT YOUR MENTAL HEALTH

This is a HORROR ROMANCE novel. This is NOT a dark romance or spicy romance — this is genuine horror with romantic elements woven through extremely disturbing situations. This book is intended only for readers who are comfortable with graphic horror content.

Your mental health and wellbeing are more important than reading this book. Please make an informed decision about whether this content is right for you.

If you choose to proceed, please ensure you have appropriate support systems in place.

Chapter One

Warmth spread across my wrist.

I had dragged my skin across the rough edge of the cot frame where the weld hadn't been finished right, pressing harder until the metal bit deep. The blood was warmer than I expected, pooling in the groove. My vision blurred. It wasn't from pain, but from relief.

Control: after years without it, I had found it in the simplest act of destruction and oh it felt so good.

Behind me, Theo started laughing.

Gone were his dry chuckles when dinner wasn't perfect, the ones that always came right before his fists. This laugh gurgled wet and drowning, as if his throat had filled with bile. I didn't want to look, but from where I lay face-down on the cot, my eyes found the window anyway.

He stood there in the reflection, that blue shirt hanging open. His intestines had pushed through the gaps between buttons, gray-pink coils touching the floor, leaving trails when he moved. Blood ran from his mouth in thick streams. But he was laughing. Laughing like this was the funniest thing he'd ever seen.

"That's my girl." His lips never moved. "Always taking the easy way out."

I pressed harder. The metal bit deeper. There was more blood now, running down my arm, dripping onto the concrete floor. My legs felt strange. Light. Like I might float up to the ceiling if I let go.

"You think this fixes anything?" Theo taunted me and I saw his reflection in the window step closer. A loop of gut caught on something and tore. He didn't even care. "You think bleeding out in a cell makes you less of a murderer? Less of a fat, worthless pig?"

The room swayed, or maybe I did. My face pressed deeper into the mattress, but I could still see him in that window, grinning with those blood-black teeth.

Then I heard footsteps.

"Fuck," I muttered through the haze that was taking over me.

"Jesus Christ." The guard's voice cracked. She was on her radio before she'd even finished unlocking my cell. "Medical to B-Block. Attempted suicide. Heavy bleeding."

Her hands pressed something against my wrist, rough, probably her uniform sleeve. She kept talking into the radio, rattling off codes I didn't understand.

The ceiling started moving above me. No, they were moving me. Lifting, rolling. The lights passed overhead like mile markers on a highway I couldn't get off.

"Come on, Zahra! Stay with me!" I heard the woman's voice again. She kept saying my name over and over again but it sounded far away, like she was calling from the end of a tunnel.

Still, Theo's laughter followed me until everything went dark. Pitch dark.

~

WHEN I WOKE UP IN THE HOSPITAL, MY WRISTS WERE STRAPPED to the bed rails. Not tight, but enough to remind me I'd lost the right to make decisions about my own body. The bandage on my left arm was thick as a club. It throbbed with each heartbeat.

"You're awake." The nurse didn't look at me as she checked the IV. "The doctor just left. But you're stable. Another doctor will come to see you."

Disappointment settled heavy in my chest. I'd failed. Again. Just like I'd failed to leave Theo all those times. Failed to fight back until it was too late. Failed to be the kind of woman who could handle things without falling apart.

The door opened. A woman in a white suit walked in and sat across from me. Everything about her was neat. Pressed clothes, shined shoes, not a hair out of place. When she moved her chair forward, her perfume hit me. White Shoulders, the same Mom used to wear. The scent made my chest tight.

God, when was the last time I'd thought about Mom?

The woman pulled out a leather diary and silver pen. Adjusted her glasses. When she smiled, little lines appeared around her eyes. "Hi, Zahra. I'm Dr. Wang. How are you feeling? Want to talk about it?"

I shook my head. The tears started before I could stop them.

"That's okay." She uncapped the pen but didn't write anything yet. "Take your time. I'd just like to understand what happened. Maybe I can help."

"Why don't you read the medical files? The case files or whatever paperwork they prepare." The words came out rough from crying.

"I know what the report says." She leaned forward slightly. "I'd like to hear it from you."

I studied the water stains on the ceiling. They made shapes if you looked long enough. A dog. A cloud. A burning house.

"There's nothing to tell." I sighed.

"The guards at the County jail said you've been seeing someone. Someone who isn't there."

I pressed my teeth together. Of course they'd told her. Privacy was just another thing you gave up when they locked you in County.

"My husband." The word scraped going out.

"Your deceased husband," she corrected me.

Deceased.

Such a clean word for what Theo was.

"He stands in the window. Talks without talking. Shows me things."

"What kinds of things?"

"What he looks like now." I replied.

Her pen scratched across paper. "These visions started after your arrest?"

I drew a breath before I spoke. "They started when I stopped pretending he was gone."

More writing. More questions. How long had I been seeing him? Did I hear other voices? Had I tried to hurt myself before?

4

She kept her tone neutral, professional, like we were discussing the weather instead of how I'd tried to open my veins with makeshift tools.

"What you're experiencing sounds like trauma manifesting as hallucinations," she concluded. "Your mind is trying to process what happened, the guilt, the violence, the sudden life change. It's creating these visions as a way to cope."

I almost laughed. Cope. Like seeing my dead husband's ghost was some kind of healing mechanism.

"The human mind can do extraordinary things under stress," she continued. "But these visions aren't real. They're symptoms we can treat."

"With pills?" I shifted in the hospital bed.

"Medication can help, yes. Along with therapy. We need to process your trauma in a safe environment."

She prescribed something with a name I couldn't pronounce. Little white pills that would make the visions stop, she promised. Help me sleep without dreams. Let my mind rest from its guilt.

"Will they make him go away?"

She paused. Then said, "The hallucinations should decrease, yes. Eventually stop entirely."

"But will he go away?" I asked the question looking dead into her eyes. My face must have worried her, because she set down the pen. "Zahra, your husband is gone. What you're seeing is a projection of your own guilt and trauma. Once we address those underlying issues, the visions will stop."

I nodded. Let her think I believed her.

I was taken back to County jail a week later. Two months I'd already been in that place before I'd tried to end it. The cell looked different. Bigger somehow, until I realized why. They'd taken the metal cot while I was gone.

I was left with a thin mattress and a scratchy blanket. The pillow was flat as paper, stuffed with something that crunched when I touched it. Everything here was designed to keep me alive, whether I wanted to be or not.

I sat in the middle of the mattress and pulled my knees to my chest. The bandage on my wrist had been changed that morning, fresh white gauze wrapped tight as a shackle.

The first pill came with dinner. A paper cup, one white tablet rolling around at the bottom. The guard watched me take it, then checked my mouth to make sure I'd swallowed.

When he finally left, I lay down and waited for the medication to work, hoping there would be no sign of Theo tonight.

But the bastard showed up right on schedule.

"Miss me?" Theo stood in the window's reflection, picking at the holes in his chest.

"Bet you thought those pills would make me go away."

I kept my back to him, face pressed into the flat pillow. But it didn't matter. He lived in my head now.

"Look at you. Curled up like a fat little grub. Orange really isn't your color, baby. Makes you look like a bloated pumpkin."

The guard's flashlight swept across my floor during night rounds.

"Can't sleep?" The female guard stood in the doorway. Older, with gray streaks in her hair.

"Trying to." I pressed the words into the pillow.

She moved on without another word. I was a husband killer. Not her problem.

Theo chuckled.

"Alone again. Just you and me, like old times."

"You know what's funny? Even here, in County, you're still the ugliest bitch in the cell block. That blonde they brought in for meth? At least she's got a face worth looking at. Not like you. Pizza face. Grease hair. Built like a garbage bag full of cottage cheese."

I pressed my palms against my ears, but he wasn't speaking through the air. He was in my bones. My blood.

"Thirty-six years old, and what do you have to show for it? No kids. No career. No friends. All you had was me. And you couldn't even keep that."

"You're pathetic," Theo whispered. "Poor little victim. But we both know the truth. You're not a victim. You're a murderer. An ugly, worthless murderer who's exactly where she belongs."

I sat up, pulling my knees tighter to my chest. I started counting cracks in the wall instead of listening. One. Two. Three. But he kept going.

"We've got all night, baby. And every night after. Just you and me, and the truth about what a disgusting piece of shit you really are. No one's coming to save you. You're exactly where you belong."

I lay back down. There was nothing else I could do. I was trapped. Trapped between the ghost I'd created and the guilt that fed him, counting the minutes until dawn.

Chapter Two

My mom came to Michigan for college in the early '80s. She was Pakistani. My dad was American. They fell in love fast and got married before either family could talk them out of it. Both families cut them off. But they were happy together.

When I came into the world, my mom named me Zahra, after her grandmother in Karachi. Zaa-hh-ra, the way she said it made it sound like music. Teachers and neighbors called me Sara because they couldn't pronounce it right. I learned to answer to both names. To be both girls. To be neither.

I had Mom's face—Pakistani features: light brown skin, dark eyes, thick black hair that frizzed in the summer humidity. Hair that fought every brush, just like hers. But I got Dad's build. His genes gave me a soft, round body.

I never fit in. I never could. I wasn't white enough for the white kids who saw my brown skin, not desi enough for the Pakistani aunties who clicked their tongues at my broken Urdu. I lived in the space between worlds…never quite belonging to either.

Our house always smelled like cumin and cardamom mixed with apple pie. Mom cooked dal while Dad made grilled cheese for my lunch, cut into triangles, no crusts, because he knew I liked it better that way.

He learned enough Urdu to argue properly. She learned football so she could yell at the TV with him on Sundays. They slow-danced in the kitchen while dinner cooked. Held hands during movie nights with me squished between them on the couch. Dad called me his princess. Mom called me her jaan, her life.

They loved me like I was their whole world.

I was twelve when my life turned upside down. My parents had gone out for an anniversary dinner at the Italian place my Mom loved. A truck driver fell asleep at the wheel and crashed into their car.

The police said it was instant. That I should find solace in knowing they didn't suffer. But how does that help a child who's lost everything? They didn't suffer. I did.

The police didn't even let me stay in my own home. No one came forward to claim me, no family, nobody. So the social workers had to step in. They couldn't figure out where to place me. Zahra Mitchell—Pakistani face, American last name. Foster families looked for children who mirrored them, and I was nobody's reflection.

Eventually, I was sent to a group home that felt like a warehouse for unwanted kids. I hated it. The first night was the hardest. I hadn't even wrapped my head around being an orphan, and here I was in a room full of kids, trying to sleep. I missed my parents so much that first night. I didn't even have a picture of them. Everything was still at our house, which I wasn't allowed to go back to.

Weeks passed at the group home and I realized this was my life now. I told my brain to accept it. Somehow it understood, and I ate the bland food, talked with other kids. Hearing their stories and sharing mine made me feel lighter. But nights were the worst. At night I'd lie in that narrow bed, closing my eyes and pretend they were still with me. Mom knitting a sweater, Dad watching TV, next to her.

It made everything bearable for a while. But one night when it was raining outside, like the night Mom and Dad died, I broke. The grief I had locked away tore loose.

I pressed my face into the pillow. "Give them back." The words just came out in a whisper. I wasn't even sure who I was talking to. "My mom and dad were good people. They slow-danced in the kitchen. They were supposed to get old."

I waited, like maybe God or someone would answer. But the room stayed quiet except for the rain.

"If you can't give them back..." The words broke apart. "Then take me too. Why did you leave me here? Why am I the only one who had to stay? It's not fair!"

I kept whispering through snot and tears. "Take me to wherever they are. I don't want to be here without them. Please. I'll do anything. Just don't leave me alone."

The sobbing made me sick. I swallowed everything down until my stomach burned. When exhaustion finally took me, I dreamed of drowning.

And woke to stone walls that dripped water. The entire place reeked with the smell of rust and pennies. It was cold like our basement in winter but worse. The room was so dark I couldn't see the ceiling, just shadows that seemed to move. In the corner stood something big. Bigger than any person should be. It wore some kind of metal mask with two glowing spots where eyes should be. It just stood there, watching me. Not moving. Just watching like it had been waiting forever.

I tried to run but couldn't move. I tried to scream but no sound came out. The thing in the corner shifted a little, and looked straight at me. That's when I knew it had heard me earlier. Heard me begging to trade places with Mom and Dad.

I woke up gasping, one hand clutching the blanket. I told myself it was just a bad dream. That's what happens when you cry yourself to sleep. Your brain gets all mixed up, makes up scary stuff because the real stuff is too sad to think about.

I completely ignored that nightmare and tried to forget it. I did forget it perhaps but somehow the dark had started to feel different after that. Like something was in it. I started leaving the bathroom light on and told the other kids I needed to see where the bathroom was.

The group home didn't work out. After three months, they found a family willing to take me. That didn't work out either. Then another family. Another. Another.

I bounced between homes for six years, never fitting anywhere, never sleeping right. Every new room had different shadows, but I always found a light to keep on. A desk lamp here, a hallway light there. Some foster parents understood. Some didn't. The ones who didn't, usually sent me back pretty quick.

But then my luck finally changed. Just a bit, even. Annie. My eleventh placement.

Annie made pancakes on Sunday mornings and never flinched when I went quiet for days. On my first birthday at her house, she threw me a small party: a store-bought cake, paper plates, a candle stuck in sideways.

For the first time in years, I felt safe. Like maybe I could stop holding my breath all the time. Annie's house wasn't just another placement. It was almost like having a home again.

But even with things finally going right, I couldn't shake the worry about my future. I wasn't good in school...that was the kindest way to put it. Teachers said I lacked focus, but it felt more like I was underwater, and no one noticed I couldn't breathe. How I got my high school diploma is between me, God, and a guidance counselor who took pity.

Most kids got kicked out the day they aged out of the system. But Annie let me stay through my high school graduation. When I finally found my own apartment, she paid the first month's rent without making a show of it.

Work came next. It had to. I did everything, from morning shifts at a gas station to nights bagging groceries while my feet screamed in cheap shoes. Once, I even worked the floor at a men's boutique, pushing cologne samples while older men stared too long at my ass and left their phone numbers on receipts.

The relationships were all the same story with different faces.

Men loved the idea of me. My exotic features, my dark eyes, they were drawn to me because I was different from their usual type. They called me Jasmine, or Arabian Nights, like I was some fantasy they'd downloaded. But once the novelty wore off, once they saw me in harsh morning light or noticed how my thighs rubbed together when I walked, the texts slowed down. The excuses started.

One told me I had "such a pretty face," then explained he wasn't into "bigger girls."

Another kept asking if I could cook biryani for his friends, like I was some kind of performing monkey. He dumped me after I gained ten pounds over winter.

By twenty-four, I'd stopped trying.

I started working at Kurt's Diner off the highway, six days a week, double shifts when they needed.

After five years, it had become the closest thing I had to safety. To stability.

Mr. Kurt ran the place. Sixty-something, slow-moving. He didn't smile much, but he always made sure the girls got a ride home after late shifts, and the back fridge stayed stocked with free pie slices for the staff.

He called me "kid," even when the lines around my eyes said otherwise.

Sometimes, when it was slow and the only sound was the hum of the refrigerators, I'd sit near the ice machine with a book about starting your own business. Or nursing. Or real estate. Whatever dream felt possible that week.

I wasn't aiming for anything specific. I just needed something that didn't feel like failure. I wanted to be someone but at twenty-nine, working doubles just to pay rent, I wasn't sure I had it in me.

One night, after closing, I was wiping down table six when Mr. Kurt leaned on his mop and said, "You ever think about being a manager? You're good at running things. The way you handle the lunch rush, keep everyone working together."

I looked up, rag frozen mid-swipe. "Me? A manager?" The laugh came out sharp, not believing it.

"You tell people what to do when it's busy. Train the new servers without being asked. See problems before they happen." He set the mop aside. "Community college has classes for restaurant management. Could lead to running a place like this. Or bigger. Hotels, even."

"You're not dumb, Zahra," he added after a beat. "You just grew up in noise. There's a difference. There's no age for learning."

That stuck with me. The way he said it. And the fact that he'd already looked into it.

Two weeks later, he'd brought in books about running restaurants, getting certificates, even hotel management programs. "Look, you already do this." He pointed at work schedules I'd fixed. "You just don't have the paper saying you can."

I stayed after work most nights, studying with him. He'd ask me questions about managing people, show me the diner's budget sheets.

Sometimes he made coffee and we'd sit in that cramped office, going over how to be a boss until the streetlights came on.

I actually thought I had a chance. That maybe I could be something more than a diner waitress pushing thirty.

Then Theo walked in.

He looked expensive. He sat at table seven, ordered the Grand Slam with extra bacon, and smiled at me when I poured his coffee.

The next day, he asked for me again.

The day after that, he left his business card folded under the receipt with a fifty-dollar tip. Theodore Quinn, Attorney at Law. Beneath it, in neat blue ink: Let me take you to dinner. A real one.

I met him a few days later at a restaurant where the napkins were cloth and the water came with lemon slices. He shook my hand like he was sealing a deal. He ordered my drink for me, some white wine I didn't know how to pronounce, and told me I had sad eyes. Brushed the tip of his thumb under my left one. Said, "Let me fix that."

I didn't know then what I know now, that men don't say things like that unless they already see you as broken. Unless they're shopping for something they can shape.

Six months later, I was wearing a dress that cost more than anything I'd ever owned, walking down an aisle in heels that pinched my toes until they went numb. Annie sat in the third pew, dabbing at her eyes with a handkerchief.

"You did it," she whispered when I passed. "You finally found someone who sees you."

Mr. Kurt came too. When he hugged me afterward, he told me quietly, "If you're happy, I'm happy. But you have so much potential. Don't forget about those studies after all this settles down."

I promised him I wouldn't. I meant it then.

But life had other plans.

Theo expected a perfect housewife. He'd get mad over small things, the dishes not stacked right, the laundry folded the wrong way. But he always apologized afterward. Said he was tired. Said he didn't mean it.

I knew he looked up to his mother. He was an only son, raised like something delicate, and he wanted everything to look perfect. Be perfect. Feel perfect.

But as the years passed, I started to see it. Theo wasn't just difficult. There was more to him than I let myself believe.

I WAS LYING IN THE HOSPITAL AFTER MY FIRST MISCARRIAGE when his mask completely slipped.

"You lost the baby because of your weight, Zahra." He dug his nails into my arm. "If you weren't so fat, maybe our child would have lived."

The cruelty was so casual, like he'd been thinking it the whole time I was bleeding and just decided to finally say it out loud.

After that, everything changed.

He'd wanted a child, an heir, really. Someone to carry on the Quinn name. Now he looked at me like I was defective merchandise he couldn't return.

The second miscarriage came eight months later. He didn't come to the hospital.

The last time, I sat in a hospital gown that didn't close in the back, dried blood still caking my inner thighs. He stood in the doorway, checking his phone.

"Three strikes." He didn't even look up. "You can't even do the one thing women are supposed to do."

I stopped thinking about education or a future after that. There was no point in dreaming when I couldn't even perform the basic function of being a wife. I was exactly what Theo said I was, broken, useless, worthless.

He could have divorced me, but his mother would never forgive him. "The Quinns don't divorce," she'd announced at once, at a family dinner when Theo told her about a friend of his divorcing his wife, completely oblivious to how her son looked at me like something stuck to his shoe.

Besides, Theo liked owning things. Even broken things. Especially broken things he could blame for his unhappiness.

We could have tried again for a baby. The doctors said

there was no reason we couldn't. But Theo had already decided I was defective, and that gave him permission to find what he wanted elsewhere.

The first lipstick stain showed up four weeks after the last miscarriage. Coral pink on his collar, nothing like the nude shades I wore. Then came the hotel receipts. The late-night texts he didn't bother to hide. Different women sending pictures, making promises, arranging afternoon meetings.

He left the evidence where I'd find it, like a cat leaving dead birds on the doorstep.

One night, I'd had enough. The words came out before I could stop them. "I want a divorce."

He heard me loud and clear but didn't answer. Didn't even frown. Just stepped forward and hit me so fast I didn't process the movement until I was already falling.

I didn't hit the ground. I caught myself against the wall. The plaster cracked where my shoulder landed. Then he hit me again.

And that was just the start.

From that night on, he only needed an excuse. A towel on the floor. A look he didn't like. Silence when he wanted to talk.

Summer came and I wore sweaters in ninety-degree heat. Covered the bruises with makeup two shades too light that fooled no one.

My neighbors stopped meeting my eye.

Annie stopped calling after I made too many excuses for missing Sunday dinners.

Mr. Kurt would text me sometimes, asking if I was okay, if I needed anything. I always said I was fine. Eventually, he stopped asking too.

And still, I stayed. Seven years of this. Seven years of covering bruises and making excuses.

Until August 2024. My thirty-sixth birthday. I woke up with a black eye because the previous night's dinner wasn't to Theo's liking.

I looked at myself in the bathroom mirror and something just... changed. I don't know where the courage came from. I told myself that I was a grown-ass woman, and I had to—I needed to stop taking his shit and get my life together!

I'd been planning for days. Skimming grocery money. Checking bus schedules on the library computer.

That evening, while Theo was at a partner's dinner, I finally did it. Packed a bag with one change of clothes, my birth certificate, two hundred dollars in small bills, and the gold bracelet his mother gave me that I could pawn.

I made it to the bus station. I was just about to get on the bus to anywhere-but-here when a black Lexus pulled up to the curb, I knew it was him before the window came down.

Theo sat behind the wheel, not even looking at me. Just waiting. Like he'd known exactly where I'd be.

"Get in," he growled.

I had one foot on the bus step. The driver was watching me. Other passengers were shifting in their seats, impatiently. I could've just climbed up. Sat down. Gone to Cleveland.

Then Theo smiled. Not big, just that little twist at the corner of his mouth that meant he was done asking.

My legs turned to water. I stepped back down onto the sidewalk and walked to his car like I was sleepwalking. Like my body remembered what happened when I made him wait.

We drove through empty streets. He kept one hand on the wheel, his wedding ring scraping against the leather with each subtle turn. His other hand rested on the gearshift, thumb tapping out some rhythm only he could hear. Waiting.

"You really thought you could leave?" he finally asked.

I said nothing. What was there to say after seven years of this? He laughed once. It was short and mean, like I was a dog that had tried and failed some pathetic trick.

Outside the house, he killed the engine. Got out first, then came around to open my door like a gentleman. I followed him up the walkway, knowing what was coming. My legs felt like they belonged to someone else.

He unlocked our front door and held it open for me. I walked past him into the house. The lock clicked behind us.

Everything shifted.

His hand shot out and grabbed my hair, yanking me down hard. My knees cracked against the tile.

"You ungrateful bitch." His fist connected with my face. Once. Twice. Blood filled my mouth. When I curled up, his boot found my ribs. A crack went through me. I couldn't breathe after that.

I went still. It wasn't the numbness I'd learned to wrap around myself like armor. This was different. This was the quiet that comes before lightning strikes. Seven years of this. Seven years of blood in my mouth and bruises hidden under sleeves. Seven years of being small, being sorry, being whatever he needed me to be to survive another night.

I was done.

He was halfway up the stairs when I managed to push myself up on my elbows. Blood dripped steadily from my nose.

"Coward!" I shouted. I managed to stand up, despite the excruciating pain running through my body.

He stopped. Turned. Came back down slow.

"You think beating women makes you tough?" My throat felt raw, torn. Each word cost me. "You're nothing. Always were nothing. Just another weak little boy playing dress-up."

His feet stopped moving.

The house went quiet except for my ragged breathing. He stood there on the landing, looking at me like I'd lost my mind. Maybe I had.

"What's wrong? Can't handle the truth?" I taunted.

He laughed, but there was nothing funny in it. That fake smile spread across his face, the one he wore when he was about to hurt me worse. He stopped right in front of me.

"You done running your mouth?"

I wiped blood off my lip with the back of my hand. "Kill me or let me go."

Then I spat. Right at his boots. The red splattered across the cracked leather.

Before I could blink, his hand was around my throat. He slammed me into the wall so hard the picture frames jumped. My spine screamed. All the air rushed out of me at once, and when I tried to pull more in, his fingers just squeezed tighter.

He leaned in close, breath hot against my ear. "I think I'll kill you." He stayed calm, like he was working through a math problem. "Break the back door after. Mess up the living room. Take some jewelry. They'll think it was a robbery gone wrong."

His fingers adjusted their grip, finding better purchase. "Poor Theo comes home to find his wife dead. I'll cry for the cameras. Maybe offer a reward for information."

My nails dug into his forearm. Black spots bloomed at the edges of my vision. My mouth opened and closed, gaping.

He was going to kill me. He was really going to kill me. The thought floated through my mind, strangely peaceful. No fear anymore. No panic. Just... relief. My hands fell away from his arm. My body went slack.

Let it happen. Let it finally be over.

The darkness swept in from all sides. But it didn't take me where I expected.

I fell through a cold that burned. When I hit the ground, it was wrong. Everything was wrong. The walls of my house were still there, but covered in something that moved like veins. Black rot crept up from the baseboards. The ceiling dripped something viscous. Everything seemed familiar but twisted.

My breath caught. I knew this place. The stone walls, the smell of rust and pennies, the way the shadows moved wrong. It was the same place from my nightmare all those years ago in the group home. The night I'd begged to be taken too. The night something had listened.

And in the corner, where nothing should have been, something massive waited.

Eight feet of muscle, bare chest scarred and gleaming, leather pants clinging to massive legs. A huge blade dragged behind him, scraping grooves into the blood-filled floor. His helmet was crude iron, just slits where eyes should be. Red light burned through those slits, watching me.

He stepped forward, and when he spoke, the sound came from everywhere and nowhere, grinding like metal on stone. "What you do next will condemn you to hell."

I looked at him, into his red eyes. At the twisted version of my home around us. "Good," I whispered, and meant it.

Then everything snapped back.

I gasped, eyes flying open. The living room ceiling stared down at me. My throat burned where Theo's fingers had been, but I could breathe. Air moved in and out of my lungs.

I sat up slow. My body felt different. Heavier. Like someone had filled my bones with lead and my veins with ice water. When I touched my neck, the skin was tender but whole.

But I remembered dying. Remembered the relief of it, the welcome dark.

And I remembered what I had to do.

I sat there, trying to breathe through the blood. My ear rang high and tinny. Blood tickled as it ran from my nose, pooling on the white tile he insisted I keep spotless.

Upstairs, he was humming in the shower. Actually humming "My Way," like he hadn't just killed his wife in the living room. Like this was any Tuesday night. The sound crawled under my skin and nested there with all the other nights, all the other songs.

I got up. Everything hurt. My face, ribs, the spot where my knees had hit the tile. My vision swam, the walls tilted at strange angles. Red footprints marked my path to the kitchen, not neat drops, but smeared half-moons from my bare feet sliding in my own blood. The knife block stood under the cabinet lights like it always did. I grabbed the carving knife, the German one with the heavy handle, the one he used at dinner parties to show off while he carved the roast.

The stairs whined under my weight. I knew which ones creaked, had memorized them over seven years of trying to move silently through my own home.

In the bedroom, steam leaked from under the bathroom door, carrying that mint soap scent I'd grown to hate. Light spilled through the gap. I heard the shower shut off. The curtain rings scraped against metal.

He walked out with a towel around his waist, another in his hands as he rubbed it through his hair. When he saw me, he stopped dead. "What the fuck!" His eyes narrowed, water dripping from his hair. "Guess I didn't choke you hard enough, huh? Should've held on a little longer, made sure you stayed down."

He spread his arms wide, still dripping, still smirking. "What're you gonna do? Cry on me? We both know you don't have the balls. Put it down before you embarrass yourself even more than usual, you pathetic cunt."

I don't know why, but I laughed. Blood poured from my mouth as I laughed at his question. How was I supposed to tell him that I think I chose hell just to come back and kill him?

"Oh no, that's not how you should be talking to me, Theo. Ask me nicely and I'll tell you what I intend to do with this very serrated knife."

"Zahra! Put it down." He shifted into that executive tone, the one that expected instant obedience. He stepped toward me, hand out, like he was approaching a skittish animal. "Put the knife down and we'll forget this happened."

I felt the break happen. Not in my mind, but somewhere deeper, in whatever part of me had been holding my spine straight all these years.

I lunged forward and drove the knife into his stomach, just above the towel. The blade stuck at first, resisting against skin and muscle, then slid in with a sound like puncturing a watermelon. He made a noise which was half grunt, half gasp and stared down at the handle like it was some impossible thing that didn't belong in his world.

I twisted the knife and ripped sideways. His skin split with a wet, tearing sound. For a second, nothing happened, then his insides bulged out like they'd been waiting their whole lives to escape. Guts slithered through the opening in wet, purple-gray ropes. He dropped to his knees, hands scrambling to stuff everything back in, making small, desperate sounds.

"Call someone," he wheezed. "Call a fucking ambulance."

I stepped closer and opened his throat with one hard slash. Blood sprayed the white walls in a wide arc, hit the mirror, hit my face. He clutched at his neck, eyes bulging with that special terror reserved for people who never imagined they could die. His legs gave out and he collapsed backward, towel falling away.

He was still half-hard. Fucking figured.

I stood over him, watching him gasp the way I had only moments ago. His chest jerked in smaller and smaller movements. His eyes rolled back, then fixed on mine with the last of his consciousness, pleading for something... mercy, maybe. Or just understanding.

I knelt beside him in the spreading pool of blood and grabbed his cock in one hand.

"This doesn't belong to you anymore."

I sawed through it with the same knife. The sound was gristle and meat. He convulsed once, violently, and went still.

I sat there in the warmth of his blood. The knife dripped between my fingers. Blood seeped into the floorboards beneath our bed. His eyes stayed open, staring at the ceiling, finally seeing something I couldn't.

Then I stood.

My legs worked fine. My hands were steady. I went through the door to the garage, a place I rarely entered. This was Theo's domain: his tools, his projects, his escape from me. The gasoline sat behind his workbench. The red container was heavier than I expected, still half full.

I turned to leave and bumped the wall button. The garage door groaned to life, lurching upward on its tracks.

Shit.

Through the widening gap, I saw Mrs. Landon on the sidewalk, walking her terrier. She stopped when the garage light spilled onto the driveway. We'd done this dance before, me pretending not to know about Tuesday afternoons, her pretending she wasn't fucking my husband.

"Zahra?" She stepped closer and saw me standing there with the gas can. Saw the blood on my clothes, on my face. "Is everything..."

She stopped. We both knew what she wasn't asking.

"Everything's fine." I forced the words flat.

She looked at me for a long moment. Then at the gas can. Then back at my face. Her dog whined, pulling at the leash.

I hit the button. The door shuddered down between us.

Back in the bedroom, I poured gasoline over our bed. The comforter we'd picked out during our first month of marriage. The pillows that still smelled like his aftershave. I doused his body last, watching the fuel pool in the hollow of his stomach where the knife had gone in deepest.

One match from the fireplace set. The whoosh of ignition. Heat that felt like absolution washing over the bedroom walls.

I walked outside and sat on the concrete steps. Blood had dried on my hands in rust-brown crescents beneath my nails. My lip was split where he'd punched me. I didn't cry. No tears. No shaking. No horror at what I'd done. Just a hollow space where guilt should've been, and the distant sound of sirens growing louder through the night.

There was simply nothing left in me to drain. I was empty as a gourd, hollow all the way through.

Smoke rolled from the windows upstairs. Glass shattered in the heat, and I could hear the house eating itself from the inside out.

Headlights curved up the street. Mrs. Landon stood at the edge of our driveway with her terrier. She must've called them. Her face was pale in the flashing lights as she pointed, at me, then at the house.

An officer walked toward me. "Ma'am? Can you tell me what happened here?"

I looked up at him from the steps and said, "I killed my fuck of a husband."

Chapter Three

White. That's what I remember most about the day they condemned me

Theo's mother, Agnes Quinn, wore it to the trial. She sat in the front row, hands folded in her lap, a rosary coiled tight between her knuckles like she might strangle God if He didn't give her the right answer.

I saw her before I saw anything else...the way she refused to look at me, even as I was led in, shackled at the wrists and ankles.

They called it murder with extreme cruelty and arson.

The stabbing alone might have been second-degree murder, but the things I did to his body... The stomach wound that I twisted the knife in, wanting him to feel what I'd felt all those years. The throat cut, so he couldn't use that voice to hurt anyone again. What I did to his dick. The way I burned the place down after, erasing our hell together. The way I sat on the porch when it was over, patient as a saint, finally free to breathe.

That screamed premeditation. The prosecution wanted life without parole.

Three of Theo's colleagues took the stand, lawyers in thousand-dollar suits painting me as unstable, volatile, obsessed. They claimed I'd threatened Theo at a firm dinner, that he was afraid of me, considering having me committed.

No one mentioned the bruises shaped like fingers. The ER visits. The nurses who asked quiet questions when Theo stepped out.

Mr. Kurt testified, hands trembling as he swore the oath. He spoke about my work ethic, how I never missed shifts. When pressed about witnessing abuse directly, he admitted he hadn't, but said he knew the signs.

Mrs. Landon testified about the garage door, the gas can, and the blood on my hands. She'd called the police before I'd even left the front steps.

Annie came next, walking slowly with her cane, her hair now completely white. She talked about raising me, how the light in my eyes had dimmed by the wedding and disappeared entirely six months later. When the prosecutor suggested she'd "failed" as a foster mother, her spine straightened.

She hadn't failed me, she insisted. Life had failed me.

The court-appointed psychiatrist, Dr. Wang, laid out my diagnosis in clinical terms: severe PTSD, major depression, dissociative episodes, visual and auditory hallucinations. She described my psychological break and how sustained trauma had fractured my mind. I wasn't operating from rational thought, but from pure survival instinct.

The defense presented the medical records. Multiple ER visits. Photos of holes punched in walls. A paper trail of violence.

When I testified, I explained why I hadn't left, how he controlled everything, how he isolated me, how he told me daily no one else would ever want me. I described that night. The bus station. The beating. I told them everything.

The jury deliberated for two days and finally the verdict came. "We find the defendant not guilty by reason of insanity."

Theo's colleagues erupted in angry murmurs. His mother clutched her rosary, tears sliding down her cheeks.

The judge—a woman with silver hair—looked at me for a long moment.

"Mrs. Quinn." She let the words come slowly. "You have been found not guilty by reason of insanity for the murder of Theodore Quinn. Given the severity of your mental illness and the risk you pose to yourself and others, I hereby order your indefinite commitment at St. Dymphna Secure Psychiatric Facility."

She paused, studying my face. "This court recognizes that you are a victim as well as a perpetrator. You will receive the treatment you need."

The bailiff approached to escort me out. As I stood, I turned toward Agnes and really looked at her. She was seventy-eight years old. Theo had been her only child, her miracle baby, born when she was forty-one.

"Agnes." The courtroom went still. "I'm sorry. Not for defending myself, but for taking your son from you. For making you bury your baby."

She looked up at me then, her face streaked with tears, twisted with grief and rage.

"Burn in hell," she whispered, breaking on the words. "Burn in hell for what you did to my boy."

And I knew she was right. I knew I was going to burn in hell.

Chapter Four

T he transfer order came on a Thursday. Just a few days after the verdict.

"St. Dymphna," the guard announced, sliding the paperwork through my cell slot. "It's a fun place."

Months in County had been hell, but at least it was familiar. This was totally different. This was a place for the broken ones. For the crazies.

Rain lashed the transport van windows as we drove along the coastal cliffs. The female guard had been kind during the drive, offering water, adjusting my shackles when they cut too deep. But her whole body tightened when she said, "Almost there." As if she was scared of what was ahead.

Through the windshield, I saw it.

St. Dymphna rose from the cliff's edge like something clawed up from beneath. Gothic spires twisted toward storm clouds. Stone walls seemed to breathe with the wind. Above the entrance, carved deep into the stone: SANCTA DYMPHNA ORA PRO NOBIS.

"Saint Dymphna, pray for us," the guard translated. "Patron saint of the mentally ill."

I nodded, though I didn't really want to know the meaning.

We crossed a narrow causeway with no railings, just crumbling asphalt between us and the black water below. Iron gates swung open to reveal a cobblestone courtyard.

The van stopped.

My legs were numb from the ride. When I tried to get out of the van, I slipped on the wet stones, the shackles making it impossible to catch myself. My knee hit hard enough to split the skin through the thin cotton pants.

The building loomed, its windows dark despite the midday hour. A woman waited at the top of the steps, somehow dry despite the downpour. She stood under the entrance overhang like she'd been expecting us, hands clasped in front of her. A white lab coat over a blue dress, blonde hair in soft waves to her shoulders. Everything about her seemed too clean for this place.

"Mrs. Quinn? I'm Dr. Alan," she greeted with a forced smile.

"Mitchell." The correction came out sharper than I'd intended. "Zahra Mitchell. My husband is dead."

This was going to be a problem. I should've never taken Theo's last name. Now it followed me everywhere. On every document, every introduction, every file someone read—Mrs. Quinn. The husband killer.

Dr. Alan's smile didn't falter, but something flickered in her eyes, interest, maybe. Or calculation.

"Of course. Ms. Mitchell." She made a small note on her clipboard. "Let's get you inside and out of this weather."

I nodded and followed her.

The entrance hall was massive, old stone, high ceilings the lights couldn't quite reach. Our footsteps echoed wrong, like the sound was bouncing off more walls than should be there. The yellow bulbs in the antique fixtures gave everything a sickly hue. Made the shadows look thick.

A staircase curved up to the second floor. The stone railing was carved with hands, reaching, grasping, holding things. I tried not to look too closely, but my eyes kept catching on them. They looked like they moved when you weren't watching.

Once the guards removed my restraints and departed, Dr. Alan's smile widened. "I know this must be overwhelming, but I assure you, we're here to help."

The sound echoed strangely, bouncing back distorted.

Here to help... help... help...

A tall, thin nurse emerged from a side corridor. Wire-rimmed glasses perched on her nose. Gray hair pulled into a severe bun. Her fingers were long and pale, almost translucent beneath the lights. A permanent scowl had etched deep lines around her mouth. She looked to be in her late fifties. Perhaps she was younger, but she looked the kind of woman who'd been worn down by years of hard shifts.

"This is Nurse Sela," Dr. Alan explained. "She'll handle your intake."

"This way," Nurse Sela ordered, pulling a ballpoint pen from her pocket. She clicked it. Unclicked it. Click. Unclick. The sound followed us down the hall like a metallic heartbeat.

We passed through double doors marked INTAKE. The temperature dropped instantly. The air smelled of bleach and something bitter that burned my nostrils.

Click. Unclick. Click. Unclick.

"Could you not do that?" I asked, keeping the shake out of the words.

She looked at me over her wire-rimmed glasses, and for the first time, her mouth twisted into something that might have been a smile on someone else's face. On hers, it looked like a wound.

"Why should I listen to you?" A dry, mirthless chuckle escaped her throat. "You're the patient. I'm the nurse. You don't make requests here."

She clicked the pen one more time, deliberately slow, then clipped it to her clipboard with a sharp snap.

"Strip." She pulled on latex gloves. "Everything off."

I froze, arms wrapped around myself. The room was cold, cold enough that I could see my breath.

"Don't be modest," she huffed. "I've seen it all before. We need to document any self-harm or injuries."

Slowly, I peeled off the soaked transport clothes. The jumpsuit clung to my skin. My undergarments were nearly transparent from the rain. The air bit at my damp skin, raising goosebumps everywhere. I kept my arms at my sides, not from confidence, just exhaustion.

Her gaze moved over me with complete detachment. Then she saw my wrist.

"Self-harm scars," she noted, grabbing my arm and turning it toward the light. The tissue was still raised and pink, not fully flattened. "How recent?"

"Months ago. I don't remember exactly."

"In County?" Her tone was bitter. Or maybe she was. She looked like someone who'd been bitter her whole life.

"Yes."

She scribbled furiously. "Suicide attempt?"

"The psychiatrist called it a trauma response." I told her.

"I'm asking you. Not the psychiatrist." She looked at me with an expression that said, don't bullshit with me.

I met her eyes. "I wanted it to stop."

"It?" She asked.

"Everything."

She rolled her eyes hearing my reply, like she heard it every day from patients. Maybe she did.

The exam continued. Samples drawn with needles that felt too large. Weight recorded: 194 pounds on my 5'2" frame, down from 212 before arrest. I'd barely eaten in County. Couldn't stomach the food when everything was falling apart.

She handed me pale blue scrubs that hung wrong on my frame. Too tight across the hips and chest. Too long in the legs. I knelt and rolled the hems.

The door opened again. Dr. Alan entered, carrying a tablet and a small paper cup. She'd removed the lab coat, her blue dress looked expensive, out of place.

"How are we doing?" she asked, her tone rehearsed.

"I don't know," I answered honestly.

She nodded. "Understandable. This is a lot to process. The transition from county to treatment can be jarring."

She swiped through her tablet. "Depression. PTSD. Dissociative episodes." Her gaze met mine. "The court found you not responsible due to mental illness exacerbated by long-term abuse."

I said nothing.

"I'd like to adjust your medication," she continued. "Sertraline for depression. Trazodone for sleep. They'll help with the... adjustment."

She handed me the cup, two pills, one white, one blue.

"These will help." She held out the pills. "Take them."

I dry-swallowed both. They stuck in my throat. Dr. Alan smiled, satisfied.

The door slammed open, hitting the wall with a bang. A massive man walked towards us. Everything about him was oversized, barrel chest straining his uniform, thick neck blending into his shoulders, hands like sledgehammers at his sides. A scar ran from his left eye to his mouth, pulling his face into a permanent sneer. His eyes were too close together, small, intense, predatory.

"Tobias." Dr. Alan's tone cooled. "Ms. Quinn needs escorting to Room N-17 in the North Wing." Quinn. Not Mitchell. She knew exactly what she was doing.

Tobias's gaze swept over me, lingering where the scrubs pulled tight. His tongue flicked out, wetting his lips.

"Fresh meat for North, huh?" he sneered, the pitch surprisingly high for such a massive man. "What's a thick little thing like you in for? Suffocate your husband between those thighs?"

Heat flooded my face. "I—"

"That's enough," Dr. Alan snapped, though she didn't sound particularly upset. Then she turned to me. "I'll check on you tomorrow. Try to rest. The first night is always the hardest."

Tobias grabbed my upper arm, his fingers digging deep into the flesh, hard enough to leave bruises. "Let's go, princess. Time for the tour."

He dragged me from the intake room, not walking so much as hauling. We passed back through the double doors into the older part of the building. The temperature dropped again. The walls changed, no longer painted concrete, but old stone darkened by moisture and time.

"See, this place used to be something else." Tobias spoke like we were old friends. "Before it was an asylum for cuckoo people like you, it used to be a monastery. Others say a prison. Me? I think it was always meant for keeping things that shouldn't be let out."

We descended a narrow staircase, the steps worn smooth from centuries of feet. The lights grew dimmer, spaced farther apart.

"North Wing," Tobias grunted as we reached a heavy door plastered with warning signs. "Home of the special cases."

He swiped his keycard and shoved the door open. The corridor beyond was narrower, older. Our footsteps echoed as we walked.

Halfway down the hall, he shoved me against the wall, his massive frame pinning me in place. His face loomed close, breath hot with cigarettes and something sour, old food, maybe, or just rot that lived inside him.

"You know what happens to new girls here?" he whispered, one hand sliding into my hair, fingers tangling in the wet strands. "Even ones built like you can make special friends. Friends who make things easier... or harder."

I turned my face away, heart hammering against my ribs. His other hand planted on the wall beside my head, caging me in.

"The pretty ones, they learn quick. The smart ones, quicker. But the ones like you?" He laughed, low, cruel. "The ones who think they're tough because they killed someone? You learn the hardest lessons."

"Please," I whispered, hating the sound of it in my own mouth. "I just want to go to my room."

"Please," he mocked in a falsetto. "That's better. That's how you should talk to me. With respect."

He stepped back, just enough for me to breathe, then grabbed my arm again, yanking me along.

We passed more doors. One had a narrow window, and I glimpsed a woman inside, standing in the corner, facing the wall. She was naked, skin pale as paper, and drawing on the wall with something dark.

"That oldie is Margaret. Don't look at her," Tobias warned. "She doesn't like being watched."

She kept her back to us, one arm moving in slow, ritualistic loops across the plaster. Like she was trying to summon something.

"Why's she here?" I asked before I could stop myself.

Tobias ground his back teeth. "She stayed with her husband. Serial killer. Took little girls. Carved 'em open like Sunday roasts. Buried their teeth in the garden." He didn't blink. "She knew. Slept beside him while he cleaned the blades. Said love means loyalty. Loyalty means silence."

I blinked hard. The hallway tilted slightly, like the floor wasn't sure it wanted to stay level.

"She waited. Kept quiet for decades. Then, after he died of old age, she walked the cops through the house. Room by room." He paused. "Should've done it while he was alive."

Then suddenly, he brightened. Like a switch flipped behind his eyes.

"But don't worry." His tone went sing-song, almost cheerful. "She'll be free soon."

My breath hitched. "What does that mean?"

He didn't answer. Just yanked me forward again, his grip tightening. "Don't ask questions. Walk."

We reached Room N-17 at the very end of the corridor. The door was metal, the number barely legible beneath layer after layer of flaking paint. Rust bled through in jagged streaks, patterns that almost looked intentional.

He swiped his card. The lock clicked.

"Home sweet home." He shoved me inside so hard that I hit the ground on hands and knees. The floor was stone. Cold enough to burn.

"Dinner's at six. But you won't get any."

"Why not?" I asked, voice barely above a whisper as I pushed myself up.

His grin widened. "Because you need to learn to be grateful for what you get. Besides, fatties like you could stand to miss a few meals anyway."

The door slammed shut. The automatic lock engaged.

I was alone.

The room was small and made of stone. No warmth. No welcome. A metal bed frame with a thin mattress. There were no sheets, just a rough blanket that looked like it had never been washed. An exposed toilet in the corner. No privacy screen. A cracked porcelain sink that dripped in a steady rhythm, already burrowing into my brain. There was one window, wire-reinforced and narrow as a mail slot.

This was it.

This was where women like me ended up.

The ones who fought back.

The ones who burned it all down.

The ones who chose fire over fear.

Chapter Five

How many women had sat on this bed before me? How many had stared at these same stone walls, counting water drops from the same leaking sink? St. Dymphna had to be old. Everything about it felt ancient, from the stone floors to the way sound echoed weirdly in the corridors. Decades of women who'd done things they couldn't take back. Who'd crossed the line that separates the broken from the dangerous.

I wondered if any of them had gotten out. Really out. Not just transferred. Not just buried.

I stood and walked to the window that showed me nothing but rain and darkness. Night had fallen while I sat, mind circling the same questions. The storm was getting worse. Wind rattled the reinforced glass, and somewhere in the distance, thunder rolled across the sky.

Then suddenly the lights went out.

The darkness hit as if it had weight. Complete. Total. Not even a strip of light under the door. My chest seized immediately, that old childhood terror slamming into me full force.

I couldn't breathe. I couldn't think. I couldn't even remember where the bed was. My hands shot out, searching for the wall, for anything solid. My knee hit something hard, the bedframe. I grabbed it and pulled myself onto the mattress.

The panic was everywhere now, crushing my lungs, making my heart slam against my ribs. In foster homes, I'd learned to sleep with the lights on because darkness meant eyes watching from the corners. It meant whispers that might or might not be real. This darkness felt alive in the same way, like it was full of things waiting just out of sight.

The trazodone was pulling at me, trying to drag me under, but I fought it. I kept my eyes open even though there was nothing to see. But the medication was stronger than my fear. Despite the strange building, despite the dark, my eyes finally closed.

The mattress turned to water beneath me. I plunged through it, through the floor, through earth that split open. I fell past terrible things in the dark, a woman's face with empty eye sockets, hands reaching from walls that breathed, doors that led nowhere. My hair streamed upward. The scrub fabric flapped against my skin. Strange voices whispered in my ears.

I hit stone hard enough to knock the air from my lungs and landed flat on my back, my head cracking against the floor. For a moment I just lay there, trying to breathe, trying to understand where I was.

A circular chamber stretched around me. Torches burned in iron holders on the walls, throwing shadows on the ancient walls. I pushed myself up, palms slipping on the wet floor.

Oh God. No. Not again.

But I was back. The third time now. First when I was twelve, begging to die in that group home. Then when Theo strangled me and I chose hell. And now here I was again, like this place had hooks in me I couldn't shake.

That awful smell was everywhere, stronger each time. What I'd thought was rust and pennies as a kid, what I'd tried to ignore when Theo almost killed me—I couldn't pretend anymore. It was blood. New blood mixed with old, soaked so deep into the stones that it would never come out.

The center of the room drew my attention. Figures stood in a circle there, robed in brown cloth stiff with old stains. They swayed together, synchronized, chanting words that made my teeth ache:

"Dolor purificat. Sanguis mundus facit. In dolore, veritas."

"Pain purifies. Blood makes clean. In suffering, truth."

In the center of their circle stood the woman I had seen earlier through the door window—Margaret. She was older than I'd thought, maybe seventy-five, with stringy white hair that hung to her waist. Her pale, wrinkled skin was covered in scratches, some old and scarred, others fresh and weeping.

She stood perfectly still, arms at her sides, staring at nothing. Her lips moved, mouthing words I couldn't hear over the chanting. Then her hands rose to her face. Her long, ragged fingernails dug into the skin at her hairline. She pulled, and the skin came away like wet paper, peeling down in strips, revealing the red meat beneath. Blood ran down her neck, pooling at her feet.

The chanting grew louder. Faster. The robed figures rocked back and forth like wheat in wind.

Then came the scraping. Metal on stone, getting closer.

I knew that sound.

He walked out of the shadows. As big as I remembered, but clearer now. He was strong and muscular. His bare chest was riddled with scars. The helmet looked like rough iron bolted together, with slits cut for eyes. Red light flickered behind those slits. His blade dragged behind him, carving lines in the floor. When he lifted it, the thing looked heavy enough to split the world in half.

The chanting stopped cold.

In the silence, I heard the woman speak for the first time, calm despite her ruined face. "I am ready for judgment."

The blade came down.

It split her perfectly in half, from crown to crotch. For a moment, she remained standing as if the two halves had not yet understood they were separate. Then she fell, opening like a book. Scarlet fountained out, spraying the robed figures, painting the walls. I wanted to scream, but my voice was locked in my throat.

The robed figures erupted in celebration. Not cheering exactly, something more primal. They threw back their hoods, revealing faces hidden behind masquerade masks. Gold and silver, some with feathers, others studded with what might've been jewels or glass. The masks covered everything above their mouths, which were open, gasping. They fell to their knees in the spreading blood, pressing their faces to the stone, tongues out, lapping at it like animals at a trough.

And from somewhere—everywhere—came a sound that made my bones ache. A moan of deep satisfaction, of hunger finally fed. It vibrated through the walls, through the floor, through my teeth. Whatever had made that sound was pleased.

The figure with the blade, the figure from my nightmare, stood over the split corpse. I thought I was invisible here. Just awareness. Just witness.

Then his head snapped toward me.

Those crimson points of light found me, piercing through dimensions to where I shouldn't have existed. Everything froze. Not slowed. Stopped. His regard pinned me. Just that hellfire gaze through the iron mask. But whatever consciousness burned behind the metal recognized me. Knew me. The way he studied me wasn't carnal. It was worse. Like a creditor coming to collect an ancient debt written in my bones before I was born.

I felt naked in a way that had nothing to do with clothes. Every thought, every memory, every piece of myself laid bare. I tried to look away but couldn't. My body just froze there, pinned by his gaze.

He kept staring until I felt like I was dissolving. Coming apart piece by piece. Not dying. Just... unraveling under that gaze.

Then those red slits closed. Just for a second. A blink, maybe, if things like him could blink.

When they opened again, the whole dream shattered like glass.

I woke up gasping in my cell, all sweaty. I looked around. The lights were back on. I thanked God and tried to calm myself.

My hands wouldn't stop shaking. The mattress beneath me was soaked through, and when I pressed my palm against my chest, I could feel my heart hammering so hard it hurt. The dream clung to me like wet clothes, the screaming, the blood, those red eyes cutting through dimensions to find me.

I pulled my knees to my chest and bit down on my wrist to keep from sobbing. The pressure helped, grounding me in the pain of here and now instead of there and then. But even with my eyes wide open, even with the lights blazing overhead, I could still feel him out there. Waiting.

Those burning slits had marked me somehow. Tagged me like prey.

My skin crawled with the certainty of it—I'd been seen by something that shouldn't exist, in a place I shouldn't have been able to reach. And now there was nowhere left to hide.

Chapter Six

First morning at St. Dymphna. The sky through the narrow window had gone from black to gray to pale yellow while I lay there, too afraid to close my eyes again. I still felt those red eyes looking at me, even though I was alone. But I wouldn't tell anyone about the nightmare. Not on day one. I knew they'd mark me down as hallucinating, up my meds, make me easier to control. Better to keep quiet and figure out the rules first.

The door made a sound and opened, and Nurse Sela entered.

"Up."

She stood with a chart in one hand, pen in the other. Click. Unclick. Her hair was scraped into a bun so tight it dragged the corners of her eyes upward.

"Go get a shower. Breakfast is in twenty."

Click. Unclick. Click.

Then she was gone.

No greeting. No eye contact. Just the next task on her list and that damned pen keeping time. I wondered if she'd always been like this, or if St. Dymphna had worn away whatever softness she'd once carried.

I swung my feet down. The stone floor was ice cold, shocking up through my soles. I sat there for a minute, waiting for feeling to return to my legs. When I could walk, I shuffled to the exposed toilet in the corner. Afterward, I moved to the sink. I splashed cold water on my face, fingers finding puffy skin and a sore cheek.

The door to my room wasn't locked from the inside. I pushed it open slowly, peering into the hallway. Other women moved past in pale blue scrubs with their heads down, silently. They knew where they were going. I didn't, so I followed them, staying close to the wall. At the end of the corridor, I found the showers. A row of stalls with no doors, no curtains. Nothing between you and whoever walked by.

Two women were already washing, steam curling around their bodies like ghosts. The hiss of the water echoed sharply against the tiled walls. I waited until one left, then peeled off my clothes and stepped beneath the spray.

The water struck me like punishment, first scalding, then icy, then scalding again, in cruel rhythm. I bit down on my lip, hard, to keep quiet. The taste of blood mingled with steam.

My fingers fumbled with the slick soap. It slipped from my grasp and hit the floor with a wet thud that echoed too loudly. I snatched it back immediately, spine pressed to the cold tile, unwilling to expose my back to the room.

Then I saw it.

Near the drain. A stain.

Dark. Coiled. Dried at the edges, but the center gleamed, viscous and sticky. Blood.

I reached out before I could stop myself. Just one finger.

It was still soft.

The air changed. The steam grew heavy, charged, like static before a lightning strike. The thick liquid clung to my fingertip, strangely warm, wrongly warm.

And suddenly I wasn't in the shower anymore.

I was in that stone chamber again. Watching Margaret stand perfectly still. Watching the figure with the blade raise it high. Watching her body split from head to hips, falling open like a zipper unfastened too fast. The sound. The spray. The impossibility of her silence.

I jerked my hand back, gasping.

This is just a shower stall. This is just a stain. My mind is mixing nightmares with reality.

I scrubbed myself until my skin screamed. Let the scalding water burn away everything soft. Let the soap strip away the memory, the smell, the stain. But nothing could erase the feel of those hellfire eyes finding me in the dark or the sense that they were still watching.

When I was done with the shower, I found fresh scrubs waiting on a bench outside. Same pale blue. Same thin fabric that clung to damp skin. I dressed fast, still wet, still shaking, and bolted from the showers.

The hallway stretched in both directions with no markings. No signs, just endless stone walls. An orderly passed by, arms crossed, eyes narrowed.

I kept my head down.

I followed the only sound that made sense, dishes clattering, voices murmuring somewhere up ahead.

Two corridors later, I found the cafeteria. Wide doors propped open, breakfast smell drifting out, eggs and toast on the edge of burning. Inside were white tables in neat rows under harsh lights that turned everyone's skin gray. Women sat scattered throughout, some alone, some in small clusters. Orderlies lined the walls with their arms crossed, watching everything.

Nurse Sela stood near the food line with her clipboard, ticking off names as patients shuffled past. She glanced up when I entered, her expression shifting from bored to annoyed.

"You're late." She looked at me like I'd had a choice. "Get in line."

I joined the queue behind a woman who kept scratching at her neck, leaving red marks. Nobody talked. There was just the scrape of trays, the thunk of ladled food hitting plastic, the shuffle of feet on linoleum.

The woman behind the counter didn't speak either. Just pointed with one gloved hand.

Oatmeal. Toast. A green apple that looked waxy enough to bounce if dropped. A carton of milk with the date rubbed away by handling. I took my tray and moved to an empty table near the back, instinct pulling me toward a wall. I didn't know if that was safer, or if it just gave me fewer directions to be surprised from. This was an old habit I had developed from living with Theo, always know your exits, always keep your back protected.

The chairs were bolted. Everything in here seemed fixed in place.

I started with the oatmeal. It tasted like wet cardboard, but I kept eating anyway. On the third bite, something metallic and bent cut into my tongue. I spat into my hand. A staple pin fell out, bent and gray, streaked with red. My tongue found the cut it left and tasted copper. I put the staple on my tray. Seriously, I didn't even feel mad. Just worn out. Too tired to care about one more shitty thing.

This was it. My whole life now. St. Dymphna until I died. No getting out. Just this place, these people, swallowing staples and counting days until my body quit.

I stared at the staple sitting next to my toast when suddenly, someone touched my shoulder. I jerked away without thinking.

"Sorry." The voice was male but soft. "Didn't mean to startle you."

I turned to find a young nurse in white scrubs, but everything about him seemed different from the others. Where Tobias had been all predatory bulk, this one was lean, almost careful in how he held himself. Ginger hair fell across his forehead, and behind wire-rimmed glasses, brown eyes held something I'd almost forgotten existed, genuine concern.

"I'm Isaac." He stepped back to give me space. "Dr. Varnar wants to see you now."

He didn't say it like a command. More like a request.

I stood, leaving the contaminated breakfast behind. As I pushed back the chair, his gaze flicked to the staple on my tray. His mouth pressed into a hard line.

"You should report that." He kept his tone low. Then, under his breath: "Not that it would help."

We walked through the corridors, Isaac beside me instead of ahead. He wasn't herding me like Tobias had, just walking with me.

Near the rec room, I heard humming. Through the doorway, I saw a woman sitting cross-legged on the floor, rocking slightly. She had dark skin and black hair cut in uneven chunks. When she looked up, her face was thin, with big brown eyes and hollow cheeks.

"That's Marion." Isaac's tone warmed, almost protective. "She's been here about a year. Marion, this is Zahra. She's new."

Her head tilted, studying me. Then her eyes lit up with recognition, her mouth curling into a grin that was equal parts friendly and unsettling.

"Oh shit. You're her." She scrambled to her feet with movements quick and birdlike. "The firestarter. I saw you on the news. Well, once—TV time's a fucking luxury here, and we only get twenty minutes on Sundays if we're good little psychos."

She laughed at her own joke. Isaac shifted slightly, and I caught something in his expression, the way his eyes tracked her movements, ready to steady her if she stumbled.

"I'm Marion." She thrust out her hand. "Marion B. Jordan. Haven't figured out what the B stands for yet... maybe Beautiful? Blessed? I'll ask my husband Michael B. Jordan when I see him." She said it completely straight-faced, like it was fact. "They probably got me down as Marion Washington or some other boring shit in their files."

Her hand hung between us.

That's when I noticed: her nails were bitten down to the quick, dark grime packed underneath like soil in cracked earth. Old track marks dotted the inside of her arm, faded but still visible.

I looked at her hand. At the story it told.

I didn't take it.

Her grin faltered, then snapped back, sharper this time. "Oh, okay. I see how it is. Too good to touch the crazy girl?"

She glanced at her fingers. "That's cool, that's cool. Give it a week though. You gonna have dirt under your nails too. Nobody stays fresh in here. The showers be cold, the soap feel like rocks, and after a minute? You just stop caring."

"Marion." Isaac's voice came soft, like handling glass about to shatter.

She turned toward him. The manic glint in her expression faded. Her shoulders dropped slightly, something almost tender ghosting across her face. "I'm being good, Isaac. Just making friends." Then she turned back to me, lowering her hand. "Though apparently our new celebrity prefers to keep her distance."

"Come on, Marion. She's just careful. It's her first week." A British accent softened the quiet words. He adjusted his glasses and gave Marion a gentle look that seemed to calm her slightly.

"We're all careful at first," Her eyes pinned mine. "Then this place teaches you that careful don't mean shit. But hey, you burned your husband alive, right? So maybe you already knew that."

"We should go." Isaac touched my elbow lightly. "Dr. Varnar doesn't like to wait."

Marion's expression went dark. "No, he doesn't." She looked at me with something like pity. "Word of advice, firestarter? Whatever he asks, whatever he wants to know, lie. Lie like your sanity depends on it. Because it does."

Isaac's grip on my elbow firmed, guiding me forward.

As we walked away, I glanced back. Marion had returned to her place on the floor, but she wasn't watching me.

She was watching Isaac.

Her expression was bare, something vulnerable and raw I

recognized. Not quite love. More like the desperate hope that grows in places starved of kindness. And Isaac kept glancing back too, quick guilty flickers he tried to bury. He ran a hand through his ginger hair, trying to look casual about it, but the gesture gave him away. He liked her... and she liked him too.

After the whole Marion thing, the silence between us felt jagged. I needed to break it.

"There was a woman in the North Wing last night when they took me to my room." I leaned forward. "Margaret, I think the orderly called her. How is she?"

Isaac's expression tensed. "Margaret... she's not here anymore. She got released, I think. I'm not around night shifts, but that's what I heard."

"At night?" Even as I asked, the vision slammed into me— Margaret standing perfectly still while that blade came down. The gore. The way she hadn't even tried to run.

I staggered, and Isaac caught my arm.

"Are you alright?"

I shook my head, trying to clear it. "She's dead, isn't she?"

He didn't answer. Just quickened his pace and reached a large wooden door.

At Varnar's office, he knocked twice.

Dr. Alan opened the door, but she looked different from yesterday. Her hair was mussed, lipstick smudged, blouse untucked on one side. She smoothed her skirt with jittery hands. Behind her, I saw Varnar moving away from his desk, adjusting his tie.

"Zahra." Her smile was off today. All the maternal warmth from yesterday was gone. "Right on time."

She looked at Isaac, and something passed between them. Cold. Heavy. Like shared secrets kept under duress.

"Thank you, Isaac. I'll take her from here."

He hesitated, then his shoulders dropped. "Take care," he murmured, to me, not to her.

Then he was gone, and I was left with Dr. Alan's Cheshire-cat smile.

"Shall we?" She stepped aside.

I crossed the threshold on my own. My feet slowed, not from fear, exactly but more like instinct. The body knowing when to brace, even if the mind isn't ready.

Behind me, the door clicked shut.

Chapter Seven

D r. Varnar's office looked nothing like the rest of St. Dymphna. No plastic furniture or scent of bleach. Instead, it was all dark wood and leather, with a Persian rug on the floor and black-and-white photographs of empty beaches on the walls. Real books lined real shelves, and heavy curtains blocked the window completely. The door behind me had a frosted glass panel with a long diagonal crack running through it. On the far wall, a second door stood slightly ajar, through the gap I could see white tile, an examination table, and a metal cabinet full of instruments.

He stood when I entered, and I immediately understood why Marion had warned me. He had that particular kind of handsomeness that made you want to look away, a well-sculpted face, pale eyes that seemed to strip you bare with a glance. His hair was dark, silvering at the temples, cut short. The charcoal suit he wore was tailored so perfectly it barely moved when he did. When he smiled, the skin around his eyes stayed perfectly still, like the muscles there had been trained not to participate. I felt it, the same way I did with Dr. Alan.

That careful, practiced charm. Like they'd both learned how to appear human without ever quite being it.

"Mrs. Quinn," he greeted. "I'm Dr. Varnar. Please, sit."

"Ms. Mitchell," I corrected. "Or just Zahra. My husband is dead."

A flicker crossed his face, interest, maybe, or amusement.

"Of course. My apologies, Ms. Mitchell."

The leather chair he indicated was positioned slightly lower than his, so once we were both seated, I had to tilt my head to meet his eyes. I recognized the tactic. Some men needed that angle to feel superior.

"Water?" he offered.

I shook my head. My throat was desert-dry, but taking anything from him felt like accepting a collar.

He lifted a folder from his desk. My name was printed in black ink on the tab. His fingers were long, manicured. He didn't open the folder right away, just let it rest on his palm like he was weighing it. Weighing me.

"How did you sleep?" The question sounded casual. It wasn't.

"Fine." The lie came easily. I wouldn't tell him about the hooded figures, the ritual blade, the chanting that still echoed in my skull. Dolor purificat. Sanguis mundus facit. In dolore, veritas. The words had carved themselves into my brain.

"No nightmares? No... disturbances?"

The way he said disturbances made my skin crawl. Like he already knew what had happened in my room. Like he'd been watching somehow as I lay curled on that mattress, too terrified to close my eyes.

"I don't remember my dreams." Another lie.

"Interesting." He made a note without looking down. "First

night is usually difficult. This building has a way of... welcoming new arrivals. The walls here have seen so much over the years. Sometimes new patients report strange experiences. Visions. Sounds."

He paused, watching my face. "But you don't believe in such things, do you?"

"No." I lied again.

"Good. We deal in reality here."

He finally opened the folder, scanning pages he'd clearly already memorized.

"Tell me about your marriage."

"It was normal." I kept my eyes on the ceiling.

"Normal." He repeated the word like he was tasting it. "Such an interesting choice. You know what I find fascinating, Zahra? How women like you—intelligent, capable women—can normalize years of pain. It's actually quite remarkable."

My vision blurred at the edges, and suddenly I wasn't in his office anymore. I was back in my house, Theo's hands around my throat, squeezing until the world went gray.

"Zahra?" Varnar called my name and I looked at him.

I blinked. He was watching me with interest, not concern. Like I was a specimen doing something unexpected under a microscope.

"Sorry. I was just..."

"Taking a moment to reflect. Perfectly natural."

His smile was understanding in a way that wasn't.

"This process can be overwhelming. Confronting our past. Our choices."

He leaned back, fingers steepled.

"Let's return to your marriage. You adapted to his violence. You survived. That takes incredible strength. To wake up every morning knowing what was coming and still make breakfast, still smile. That is not weakness. That's dedication."

The words sounded like praise, but I heard the mockery underneath. He was congratulating me for staying. For taking it. For being the kind of woman who let herself be destroyed piece by piece rather than walk out the door.

"Tell me about the physical abuse." He said it casually, like asking about my favorite book.

"When you killed him, did you feel powerful?"

"I felt nothing." I told him the truth.

"Nothing?" He snapped. "You stabbed your husband multiple times and felt nothing?"

"Just... empty."

"What about his mother?" His tone shifted, softer now, probing. "She lost her only son. Have you thought about her grief?"

My chest tightened. Theo's mother in court, wearing white, her face destroyed by grief. She'd loved him. Really loved him. But she didn't know what he was.

"A mother's love is quite something." Varnar watched me closely. "Unconditional. Eternal. Something you never got to experience yourself."

They hit exactly where he'd aimed them.

"Three miscarriages." He glanced at my file and spoke gently, like a scalpel going in. "That must have been devastating. Perhaps if you'd been able to give Theo a child, things might have been different. Men often settle down when they become fathers."

I wanted to tell him to go fuck himself.

But the tears were already coming.

"Some women just aren't meant to be mothers." He spoke

softly, as if he were being kind. "But the inability to fulfill that basic biological function can create tremendous psychological strain. Perhaps that's what really broke your marriage. The empty nursery. The silence where children's voices should have been."

My hands clenched in my lap. He was twisting everything, making it my fault. Making me the reason Theo had hurt me.

"His mother will never have grandchildren now. Another loss you gave her."

I wiped my eyes quickly, hating myself for breaking in front of him.

That's when everything shifted.

Behind Varnar, something massive loomed in the corner. The figure from my nightmare, just standing there like it had always been.

The walls started to weep black.

The Persian rug dissolved into wet stone beneath my feet. The air stank of rot, copper, things gone bad. Varnar's face stretched wrong, his professional smile pulling wider and wider until I could see teeth all the way back to where teeth shouldn't be.

I fell backward off the chair. Hit the floor hard. Suddenly, I couldn't breathe.

"Zahra?"

Varnar was beside me instantly, his hand on my arm. Normal hand. Normal face. Normal office. Everything had returned to how it should be.

I blinked hard. No figure. No bleeding walls. Just Varnar, looking down at me with clinical curiosity, like I was a puzzle he'd just found a new piece to.

"What did you see?" he asked, helping me up.

"Nothing. I just... lost my balance."

"You were staring at something behind me." His eyes searched mine. "What was it?"

"Nothing." I let him guide me back to the chair. "I guess, I'm just tired."

But he knew I was lying. I could see it in the way he studied me, like I'd just become infinitely more interesting.

"One last question." His tone shifted, becoming almost intimate. "Do you still see Theo? Your previous reports mentioned visions."

I shook my head.

"In these visions, did he ever forgive you?"

I shook my head again.

"No."

"Smart man." The words were light, almost joking, but they landed like stones. "Forgiveness isn't really the point, is it? The point is living with what we've done. Carrying it. Some people call that justice."

He stood, signaling our session was over. I made it to the door before he spoke again. "Zahra."

I turned.

He was there, too close, moving with that terrible grace. His hand settled over mine where it gripped the doorknob.

"You're going to do wonderfully here." He dropped his tone. "I can see it in you, that desire to be better. To be... clean again. We're going to work on that together."

His eyes dropped to my mouth, cataloging me. Then his other hand moved, fingers brushing the length of my ponytail.

"Such lovely hair," he murmured. "Theo must have enjoyed it."

They sliced through me. Theo had loved my hair. Had wrapped it around his fist when he'd fuck me, or hit me.

I pulled away from Varnar and yanked the door open. But as I stepped into the hallway, the words followed.

"Have a good day, Zahra," he called. "And try to get some sleep tonight. Since you couldn't last night."

I didn't turn back. I didn't need to. I could hear it, he was smiling.

The door closed with a soft click.

I stood in the hallway, shaking as his words echoed in my head.

Try to get some sleep tonight. Since you couldn't last night.

The way he'd said it, like he knew. He knew what I saw. Or imagined.

No. That was impossible.

I was just tired. Stressed. Seeing things that weren't there. The medication, the new place, this fucked-up session digging up old wounds, it was all messing with my head. Making me paranoid.

I pressed my back against the wall and tried to breathe normally. I just wanted to get back to my room. Take the meds. Sleep. Stop imagining things that couldn't be real. Stop giving Varnar more ammunition to use against me.

But as I walked back through those stone corridors, I couldn't shake the feeling that something was watching.

Waiting.

Chapter Eight

Two weeks at St. Dymphna.

Two weeks of oatmeal that formed a skin on top, no matter how fresh it was.

Two weeks of showers that scalded you one second and froze you the next, no matter how you adjusted the handle.

Two weeks of lying awake at night, wondering if what I saw was real, or just my mind cracking.

It was the same routine every day.

Wake up to the click of the magnetic lock releasing.

Choke down breakfast.

Sit through group therapy where everyone lied.

Except the sleeping part was getting worse.

Fourteen nights lying on that narrow mattress, staring at the ceiling. The red eyes from that first night hadn't come back. But Theo had.

He showed up after lights out, when the hallway went quiet except for someone crying a few doors down. Sometimes he looked normal. Sometimes he had holes where I'd stabbed him.

"Getting fat, aren't you?" he had said the previous night, standing in the corner. Blood dripped steadily from his chest. "Look at those thighs. That belly. No wonder I had to fuck other women."

I had pulled the blanket up higher.

He was right. I had gained weight since coming here. The food was bad, but it filled something in me. Stress made me eat even when I wasn't hungry, just to have something in my mouth, something to do with my hands. My scrubs were tighter than when I arrived.

"Nothing to say?" He walked around my bed, no footsteps, even though dark liquid pooled wherever he stood. "You always were pathetic. But at least when you were just plump, you were pretty pathetic. Now you're just fat and disgusting."

I didn't answer anymore.

If I told anyone about seeing him, they'd up my meds. The current ones were already making everything blurry and far away.

I'd rather hurt than feel nothing at all.

In these two weeks, I'd had three more sessions with Dr. Varnar. Each one left me feeling like he'd taken something from me that I couldn't name.

The second session, he stayed behind his desk. But his questions cut deep anyway.

"Tell me about your childhood." Smooth. Interested. "Were you always so accepting of pain?"

The third session was different He left his desk and walked around my chair while I talked. I couldn't see him, but I could hear his footsteps circling me. Then his hand settled on the back of my neck. His fingers pressed into the flesh there, almost like a massage, but not quite. The pressure made me want to lean away, but I stayed still.

"You have a remarkable capacity for endurance." He circled behind me. His thumb moved along my spine. "Most people would have broken. But not you. You just absorbed it all. Like a sponge."

I had wanted to throw up when he said it.

The fourth session was two days ago. He pulled his chair close to mine. Our knees almost touched. When I talked about cutting off Theo's dick and watching the house burn, he leaned in and put his hand on my knee.

"You must have felt so broken, so forced to do that." His fingers pressed through the thin scrub fabric. His thumb moved in little circles. It was supposed to feel comforting, but it didn't.

"Carrying that weight by yourself. No one to confess to. No one to absolve you."

I knew this game. Theo had played it too.

Touch that pretended to be kind but was really about control.

I sat still and answered his questions and let him think he was getting somewhere. Better to be his success story than his special project.

Now I stood in the breakfast line, trying not to think about any of it.

Same gray trays as always. Same plastic spoons that couldn't hurt anyone. Same oatmeal that looked like cement.

I took my tray and found my usual corner table, away from the clusters of women who still seemed to care about things like conversation and companionship.

Dr. Alan passed through the cafeteria, her blonde hair

perfect as always. She stopped at a table of younger patients, bending down to talk to them. She spoke softly, asking about their medications, their sleep, how they were feeling. She touched one girl's shoulder gently. Smiled at another.

Everyone loved Dr. Alan. She was warm where the other staff were cold. She remembered names, asked about families, seemed to actually care.

But something about her bothered me in a way I couldn't explain.

Maybe it was the way she leaned in too close, like she was feeding off whatever you gave her.

Or how she always seemed to appear right when patients were at their worst, like she could smell desperation.

Last week, she came into my room during one of the bad nights. I hadn't heard the door open. One second I was alone with Theo telling me I was worthless, the next she was standing there in her white coat, watching me shake.

"Oh, sweetie." She moved to sit on the edge of my bed. No other staff did that. They kept their distance. But Dr. Alan touched, hugged, got close.

"Having a hard time?"

I nodded, not trusting myself to speak.

Theo had vanished the moment she entered, but I could still hear his words echoing.

She pulled me into a hug that felt wrong somehow. Her hands were cold through her coat, and her perfume was too strong. I didn't like it.

"Poor thing. Your mind is trying so hard to process what happened." She pulled back to look at me, still smiling. "It must be so difficult, carrying all that guilt. But you know, sometimes we get exactly what we deserve in life. Don't we?"

The words were gentle, but they cut deep.

"The mind has ways of punishing us when we've done something truly terrible," she continued, stroking my hair. "These visions you're having? That's just your conscience trying to balance the scales. Your husband is visiting you even in death. How devoted he must have been."

"He beat me," I whispered.

"And you killed him by stabbing him." She stayed soft, sympathetic. "Multiple times. That's quite a lot of anger, isn't it? Quite a lot of rage for someone who was just defending herself."

She tucked me back into bed, smoothing the blanket with those cold hands.

"We should definitely increase your medication. Help quiet that guilty conscience of yours. Though sometimes, sweetie, the punishment fits the crime.

And sometimes we need to feel it to heal from it."

Then she stood in my doorway for a long moment, silhouetted against the hallway light.

"Sweet dreams, Zahra. Try to forgive yourself. Though I understand if your husband can't."

The door closed with a soft click.

I still didn't know why she had been doing rounds at that hour, or how she had known to check on me specifically.

I pushed the memory away and focused on my oatmeal, drawing shapes in the gray mush. Across the cafeteria, Marion sat with a few other patients. She caught my eye and waved. Even from here, I could feel the restless energy radiating off her. I looked back down at my tray.

I had been avoiding her since that first day. Something

about her was too much, too intense. But you couldn't hide from people here. Not really.

Marion didn't understand boundaries.

She came bouncing over like it was recess and we were kids. Her scrubs looked different on her than on the rest of us, tied at the waist with what looked like a shoelace. She had given herself another haircut, perhaps, because it looked shorter and more uneven than before. It made her look wild. Untamed.

"Two weeks and you're still sitting alone." She plopped into the seat across from me without asking. "That's dedication to being miserable. I'm almost impressed."

I didn't respond. Just kept pushing the oatmeal around.

"Silent treatment? Really?" She leaned forward, studying my face with uncomfortable intensity. Her eyes were too bright today, pupils dilated despite the harsh lighting. Manic phase, probably. "You know what your problem is?"

I looked down. "I have several," I muttered, still not meeting her eyes.

"Ha! She speaks!" Marion clapped her hands together, the sound sharp as a gunshot in the quiet cafeteria. Several people flinched. "But no, your specific problem is that you're disappearing. Every day a little more invisible. Pretty soon you'll just be an outline where a person used to be."

"Maybe that's what I want," I replied, finally looking into her eyes.

Marion's expression shifted. The playful spark in her eyes hardened.

"No. Fuck that. You don't get to just fade away. Not on my watch."

"You don't even know me."

"Of course I know you, firestarter!" Marion's voice rose. "I even gave you a nickname. I know what you did. Cut his dick off and burned the house down."

She stood, shifting on her feet, restless.

"You're just like me." Her eyes locked on mine. "We kill bad men."

"We're not the same."

"No?" Marion's hand shook as she reached for her water cup. "The difference is, I'm not pretending it didn't change me. I'm not sitting here acting like I'm still the person I was before."

Before I could respond, she lunged across the table. Her fingers went straight for my mouth. I tried to pull back, but she was faster, shoving two fingers past my lips. They tasted like dirt and metal. I gagged, tried to bite down, tried to get away.

"What, too dirty for you?" Her face was inches from mine, eyes wild. But they weren't angry. They were desperate. Pleading. "Too real? Too much?"

I jerked my head back hard, finally breaking free. I spat, wiped my mouth with the back of my hand.

Before I could process what had happened, she slapped me. Hard. My head snapped to the side, ears ringing. I tasted copper from where I'd bitten my tongue.

"There we go!" Marion laughed. "Color! Finally, some color in those cheeks."

She hit me again, this time with her fist. I didn't fight back. Couldn't. I just sat there, blood trickling down my chin, staring at nothing.

"What the fuck is wrong with you?" The words cracked, the manic edge giving way to something like desperation.

"Fight back! Scream!" She grabbed my shoulders, shaking me. "Do something!"

She hit me again. Wild now. Uncoordinated. But I was already gone, retreating to that safe, gray place in my mind.

"She likes it!" Marion screamed, looking around at the audience that had gathered. "Look at her face! She fucking likes it! She wants to die!"

Orderlies came running. Marion fought them, kicking and scratching as they tried to pull her away. They had her arms pinned, dragging her backward. She twisted in their grip and spat. The glob hit my cheek.

"Spineless," she hissed. "You're fucking spineless."

A wire snapped in me. I stood up and drove my fist into her stomach as hard as I could.

The air rushed out of Marion. The orderlies still had her arms, so she couldn't double over, just sagged in their grip, gasping. Then she started laughing. She seemed delighted like I'd finally given her what she wanted.

"There she is," she wheezed. "There's the woman who killed her husband."

Nurse Sela appeared, face pinched with irritation. She looked at Marion, who was still laughing, then at me, blood on my face, drool sliding down my cheek.

"Solitary." Flat. Final. "Both of you. Now."

They marched us to the isolation wing. Marion went willingly now, still grinning. They shoved us into cells next to each other, concrete walls between us but metal mesh near the ceiling that let sound carry through.

The door slammed. The lock clicked.

Then the darkness hit me. Complete. Total. There was not even a crack of light under the door.

I froze. My split lip throbbed. The cell had already felt small, but in the pitch black, it was a coffin.

"No," I whispered. Then louder: "No, wait—"

I stumbled forward, hands outstretched, and hit the door harder than expected. There was no handle on this side. I felt along the edges for light. A gap. Anything. Nothing.

My chest started to tighten. That old panic from childhood began to rise, climbing up my throat like smoke.

I pressed my back to the door and tried to breathe slowly, but it was already getting away from me.

The darkness wasn't empty. It was full. Full of things I couldn't see. Couldn't name. Just like those nights in foster care.

"Marion?" The word came out small and scared. "Can you hear me?"

She didn't answer.

I slid down until I hit the floor. The concrete was cold through the thin scrubs. I pulled my knees to my chest and made myself as small as possible.

But there was nowhere to hide from this kind of dark.

Chapter Nine

I must have been in there for hours. Maybe I slept. Maybe I just floated in that space between awake and unconscious. Time didn't exist in the dark.

Then Marion's voice came through the wall. "Hey. You alive over there?"

"Yes." My throat was dry, the word scraping out.

"Good." Relief bled through. "I was starting to worry I might've actually broken you." A pause. "Well, more broken."

I touched my split lip. "Why did you do it?"

"Had to see if you were worth saving." I could hear her shifting on the floor. "Had to know if there was still someone in there."

"And?"

"Jury's still out." Her laugh was hollow. "But you're talking to me, so that's something."

Silence stretched between us.

"I'm sorry about your lip," the words came through softer now. "That was... me having an episode. I get like that sometimes. Like there's this noise in my head that just builds and builds until I have to let it out. Make somebody else hurt so I stop hurting. You ever feel like that?"

"Just felt it once," I admitted quietly. More than I wanted to think about.

"You've been here a year?" I asked after a beat, just to change the subject. I didn't want to think about Theo, about the past. Especially not here in the dark.

"A year," she replied. "Twelve months of this place crawling under my skin."

"That's a long time."

"Time doesn't mean shit here. Could be a year, could be ten. Every day feels the same." Marion's voice turned bitter. "Varnar and Alan run this place like their own personal kingdom. And we're just... entertainment."

"They're just doctors." The words came out hollow, unconvincing, even to me.

Marion laughed harshly. "Doctors. Right. That's what they call themselves. But there's something wrong with them. Something evil. I can't explain it exactly, but you feel it too, don't you?"

I thought about Varnar's hands. Alan's cold embraces. The way the walls seemed to breathe at night.

Those damning red, glowing eyes.

"Maybe when our treatment is done, we can—"

"Get out?" Marion cut me off. "Nobody gets out of St. Dymphna. Not really."

"But people must leave. Get discharged. Go home."

"You really believe that?" She went flat. "This place is all levels of fucked up. Take Nurse Patricia. She worked here for years. Started getting... creative with patients. They'd find these strange cuts, thin red lines that made no medical sense. Took them months to figure out she was using surgical thread to stitch patterns under their skin. Called it 'art therapy.' After they caught her?" She paused. "Nobody saw her again. Not as staff. Not as a patient. She was just...gone."

The silence that followed was nerve-wracking.

"St. Dymphna is a slaughterhouse with fluorescent lights," Marion continued. "I know you can feel it. The wrongness in the air. This place gives me the creeps."

I wanted to argue, but the words died in my throat. She was right. There was something off about St. Dymphna, beyond just bad dreams and dead husbands showing up at night.

"You want to know what I've heard?" Marion's voice came through the wall, barely louder than breathing. "This place wasn't always a hospital. Used to be something else. A castle or some shit, way back. Some rich family built it on bad ground."

"Bad ground? I think Tobias mentioned something about that."

"Tobias." I could hear the disgust. "That piece of shit is part of whatever's wrong here. Of course he knows. But he's not gonna tell you the truth."

"What truth?" I asked.

There was a pause. I heard her shift on the floor, moving closer to the wall.

"Margaret was an old patient here. Real old. She told me stuff." She spoke even more quietly. "The family that built this place, they brought something with them. Or maybe it was already here. A demon, she said. Something that needs to be fed."

Margaret. The name sent a chill through me.

I saw her again in that chamber, standing still while the blade fell. Red, thick liquid everywhere. Those robed figures on their knees.

"You okay over there?" Marion asked.

"Yeah." The word shook. "Keep going."

I pressed my ear against the cold stone.

"Margaret said the family tried to contain it. Built special rooms. Performed rituals. But it got out. Killed all of them in one night. Since then whoever owns this place... has to make sacrifices to please that entity, demon or whatever it is."

"That's just stories." I lied to her, and to myself.

"Is it?" Marion sounded tired now. "You've seen things. I know you have. We all have."

"I haven't seen anything." The words stuck in my throat. "Just bad dreams. The medication—"

"Right." She laughed, short and bitter. "Keep telling yourself that. See how far it gets you when—"

"Why are you here?" I asked, cutting her off. The whole history of the place was really freaking me out.

Marion was quiet for a moment.

"You sure you want to know? Once you hear this, you can't unhear it." She chuckled.

"We're stuck in solitary together. Might as well," I answered.

"I was seventeen when I had her. Emma. My baby girl." She softened. "I was messed up back then. Using, bipolar but nobody knew yet. Gave her up for adoption. Thought I was doing right by her."

I stayed quiet, letting her talk.

"Ten years later, I got clean. Got my head somewhat straight. And this... this need hit me. To see her. To know she was okay." Marion's voice cracked. "Took me months to find her through the system. When I finally did..."

She stopped. I could hear her breathing get ragged.

"I knew the signs," she whispered. "I had lived them. The way she flinched. How she walked. The bruises she tried to hide. Her adoptive father was... he was doing things. Things nobody should ever do to a child."

"Marion..." the word shook out of me.

"I followed them for weeks. Watched. Made sure. Then one night, I climbed through her bedroom window. Caught him in the act." She went flat. "I killed him right there. First with my bare hands. Then with a knife from their kitchen. Made sure he felt every second of it."

The confession shocked me. And somehow it didn't.

"After that, it was like something woke up in me. A thirst." She let out a short, joyless laugh. "I found others like him. Men who hurt kids. Killed eight more before they caught me." Marion laughed again, bitter and broken. "They said it was the bipolar. Said I was delusional. But I knew exactly what I was doing. Every single time."

"You were protecting the kids." I kept my tone gentle.

"Was I? Or was I just feeding something dark inside me?" Marion's voice was barely audible now. "Either way, here I am. And here I'll stay."

Neither of us spoke after that. Her words left me with nothing to say.

Then a huge yawn broke the quiet.

"Shit. Sorry," Marion muttered. "They gave me something new this morning. Some blue pill with breakfast." Another yawn. "Makes me so fucking tired."

I heard her shifting, probably lying down.

"Marion?"

"Mmm. Gonna sleep now. Can't... can't keep my eyes open."

Within minutes, her breathing deepened through the wall. Whatever they'd given her had knocked her out cold.

I sat there alone, thinking about Margaret. About demons. About all the things I wished were just stories.

Some time later, the temperature in my cell began to drop. My breath fogged in the air, and I knew what was coming.

"Miss me?" Theo stood in the corner, blood still fresh on his shirt.

"Because I've missed you. Missed reminding you what a cunt you really are."

He stepped forward, and I saw all his wounds, the hollow where his penis had been.

"Look what you did to me. And for what? Still ugly. Still worthless. Only now you're crazy too."

I pressed myself against the wall. This was the ritual, he would appear, torment me, list my failures, and eventually fade when the sun came up.

But this time I didn't flinch.

The door to my cell exploded inward with a sound like metal screaming as it bent and tore. Two massive hands reached through and grabbed Theo by the shoulders. His fingers sank deep into the ghost's flesh.

"No," Theo gasped and I saw real terror on his face for the first time since the night I had killed him. "You can't—I'm already—"

The hands pulled in opposite directions, and Theo screamed as he tore down the middle. Not blood inside, something worse. Darkness that writhed and tried to escape. His face split last, that cruel smile finally turning to horror.

Then the figure stepped into my cell.

The same massive form I'd seen before: bare chest marked with ritual scars and old wounds. That iron helmet with red light burning through the slits. He crushed what was left of Theo between his palms until nothing remained. Not even shadow.

Then he turned to me, and pure terror flooded my veins.

This thing—whatever it was—had just destroyed a ghost with its bare hands. Those same hands could crush my bones to powder.

He took a step toward me, and I scrambled backward. My breath came in short, panicked gasps. My heart pounded so hard I thought it might burst.

What did he want? Why wasn't he leaving?

When he raised one massive hand, a sound escaped my throat. Part whimper, part sob. I was shaking now with violent tremors that made my teeth chatter.

He stopped.

His hand lowered slowly, and he stepped back. My terror made him retreat.

Then he vanished, without any warning, without any sound. One moment he was there, the next he wasn't. Like he'd never existed at all.

The cell was empty and silent. The door was whole and locked as if nothing had happened. I slumped against the wall, gasping. The corner where Theo had stood was empty. But I could still smell burnt metal and old leather, and somehow, I knew: whatever had just happened—Theo was gone for good.

And after years of sleeping with the lights on, I finally lay down in complete darkness. There was no hallway light bleeding under the door. There was no checking the corners of the room before closing my eyes.

Theo was gone.

And somehow, impossibly, I slept. The darkness didn't feel like it was waiting to swallow me whole anymore.

Chapter Ten

"**R**ise and shine, Quinn." Tobias's annoying voice bounced off the concrete walls. "Solitary's over."

"It's Zahra. Or Mitchell." I ground my teeth, and he laughed.

Light flooded in as the door opened, harsh overhead lighting that made me squint after hours of near-darkness.

Next door, another orderly unlocked Marion's cell. She stepped out slowly, dark hair tangled. The moment she saw me, Marion rushed forward and wrapped her arms around me in a fierce hug, like we were long-lost sisters instead of two people who'd been beating each other just yesterday.

"Move it," Tobias barked. "Back to gen pop."

I stepped out, bare feet freezing against the tile, my split lip throbbing in the bright light, still holding onto Marion.

"Fucking lunatics," the other orderly muttered behind us. "Fighting like animals yesterday, now they're best friends."

"That's how the crazy ones work," Tobias chuckled. "Never know which way they'll swing."

We reached the junction where solitary met the main corridor. That's when Marion spoke, still close beside me.

"Didn't think you'd last the night."

I smiled, despite the swelling in my lip. "I actually slept. Had a very, very weird dream, but yeah, I slept. I feel... weirdly fresh, if that makes sense."

Marion smiled back, something genuine and warm flickering in her eyes.

Tobias overheard and leered at me. "Oh, you slept good, huh? Maybe next time you can sleep under me. I'll make sure you get real comfortable."

The disgust must have been clear on my face.

"In your fucking dreams, asshole."

His expression darkened. Before I could react, he slammed me against the wall, pressing his forearm against my throat.

"What did you just say to me, you fat bitch?"

"Leave her alone!" Marion stepped forward.

Tobias backhanded her across the face, the sound echoing off the concrete. Before she could recover, he grabbed her by the hair and slammed her into the opposite wall, pinning her with his body.

"Time someone taught you bitches some respect," he growled, his free hand roaming over her chest as she struggled.

Marion tried to shove him away, but he pressed closer, his hand sliding lower.

"Maybe you'll learn to keep your mouths shut."

"Get off her!" I lunged forward, but the other orderly's panicked voice rang out behind us.

"Tobias, man, this is too far. I'm getting Sela."

His footsteps echoed as he ran.

Tobias leaned in close to Marion's ear, whispering something that drained the color from her face. She squeezed her eyes shut, tears streaking down her cheeks, while his hands continued their assault.

"Really, Tobias?" Nurse Sela cut through the chaos.

I looked up. She stood at the end of the hallway, hands on her hips, more annoyed than concerned. "It's not even ten AM and you're already tormenting patients?"

Tobias stepped back, letting Marion fall like she meant nothing. She hit the ground with a soft, broken sound. I dropped beside her, wiping the tears from her cheek with the edge of my sleeve.

Tobias turned to Sela, lifting his hands.

"They were being difficult." He shrugged. "Resisting."

"Uh-huh." Sela walked over, her shoes clicking sharply on the tile. That pen was already going. Click. Unclick. Click.

What was with her and that damned pen?

She looked down at me and Marion with thinly veiled disgust, like we were something she'd scraped off her shoe.

Click. Unclick.

"Get up. Both of you. Now."

I helped Marion up. Her body shook all over. A trickle of blood ran down from where her head had hit the concrete, and her shirt was torn where Tobias had grabbed her.

"Breakfast line's already started." Sela didn't bother hiding her irritation. "You'll be lucky if there's anything left. And I suppose I'll have to hear complaints about that too."

Tobias was already walking away, whistling like nothing had happened.

"Move," Sela snapped, her patience frayed. "And next time, try not to provoke him. Some of us have better things to do than babysit problem patients who can't follow simple rules."

She stalked off, muttering under her breath about how much she hated this job.

We stood there for a second, stunned.

"Welcome to St. Dymphna." Marion's mouth twisted into something that might've been a smile, if it wasn't so bitter.

We made it to the main ward as breakfast was winding down. The cafeteria had that after-rush feel, trays cleared, staff already cleaning. I thought we'd missed it, but the kitchen worker took one look at Marion's face and scraped together what was left. Small mercies came when you looked broken enough.

I got my tray, rubbery scrambled eggs, dry toast, apple juice in a tiny cup, and found a table near the back wall where I could watch without feeling exposed. My stomach was too empty to care that the eggs were cold.

"Tuesday special." Marion slid into the seat across from me, favoring her left side.

"This is food?" I asked her with a sad face.

She laughed, quick, surprised, then cut it off.

"Careful." Marion grinned. "People might think you're human."

That's when Dr. Alan appeared beside our table. Her smile stretched too wide, and her lipstick had bled into the fine lines around her mouth. "Zahra, darling, how are we feeling this morning? I do hope you managed some rest after yesterday's excitement."

"I am... fine." I stuttered as I replied.

"Wonderful. And the medication? No dizziness, no strange dreams?"

She tilted her head, studying my face like I was something growing in a petri dish. Her eyes swept over my bruised face but didn't linger, as if she was cataloging damage without concern.

"Nothing stranger than being locked in solitary overnight."

Her laugh tinkled like breaking glass, like it belonged to someone who'd forgotten how real laughter sounded.

"Oh, that was just a little misunderstanding. These things happen when patients get... overexcited." She aimed the words at Marion, who was trying her best to avoid her gaze.

She pulled out a folded note, her pink-polished nails gleaming under the harsh lights as she clipped it to my tray with a crisp snap.

"Now, I have some lovely news. Dr. Varnar would like to see you tonight. 10:30."

Cold dread washed through me. "At night?"

"He keeps special hours for special patients." Dr. Alan leaned closer, her perfume wrapping around me in a cloud of sickly-sweet vanilla. It clung to my throat like syrup. "You should feel honored. He doesn't offer evening sessions to everyone."

Across the table, Marion's fork scraped against her tray, ugly, harsh, metal on plastic. Her shoulders had gone rigid like someone had flipped a switch and turned her into stone.

"Is something wrong, Marion?"

Marion stared down at her untouched eggs.

"No, Dr. Alan." She clipped the words short.

"Good."

Dr. Alan straightened slowly, smoothing her white coat with a long, deliberate stroke, like she was brushing something dirty off herself.

"Dr. Varnar is so looking forward to your session, Zahra. He has such wonderful plans for your treatment."

She walked away, heels clicking sharply on the linoleum.

I turned to Marion, who hadn't moved a muscle. She looked carved from marble.

"What was that about?"

Marion poked at her eggs with the tip of her fork, eyes far away.

"Nothing."

"You're a terrible liar." I pursed my lips.

"And you ask too many questions." Marion huffed.

She pushed her tray away like the food had turned radioactive.

"I've got group therapy. See you at lunch."

The morning dragged like time itself was reluctant to move.

Group therapy with Dr. Alan was the worst part. We sat in a ring of ancient chairs, their metal legs uneven and creaky, while she lobbed questions no one wanted to catch.

But she kept looking at me.

She wasn't glancing. She was staring.

Every time I lifted my head, there she was, blue eyes locked on mine, her lips curled into that unreadable little smile.

When I caught her staring, she'd shift smoothly to another patient, ask them about their childhood or nightmares or whatever, but within seconds, those cold eyes would slide right back to me.

It made my skin itch. Made me want to crawl out of it.

By the time it ended, my shirt clung damply to my back, and my scalp felt clammy.

Recreation wasn't much better.

We played checkers with missing pieces in a room that smelled like sweat and lemon-scented cleaner.

Dr. Alan moved through the space without sound.

She'd stop just behind my chair, so close I could feel the heat of her body and her watching pressed close behind me, then vanish again before I could say anything.

Like she was just letting me know: she was there. Always there. Always watching.

During med check, the nurses moved like clockwork, asking the same questions in the same order, like they were reciting a script. But Dr. Alan stood in the doorway the entire time, her gaze fixed on me like she was memorizing the slope of my face, the shape of my hesitation.

Lunch finally came. The tension in my chest refused to ease. The thought of tonight's appointment throbbed at the back of my mind like a bruise you can't stop pressing.

Marion found me at an empty table and dropped into the seat across from me. She looked on edge, worried. We sat in silence for a moment. I could tell she was barely holding on. Like there was a secret she had to tell me.

"This appointment with Varnar." She finally spoke.

"What about it?" I asked.

Marion leaned forward, her hands gripping the edge of the table so tight her knuckles went bone-white.

"He usually waits. Gives new patients time to... settle in." The way she said settle in made something crawl down my spine. Like she meant something far more sinister.

"What happens at these night appointments?" I asked.

"Listen to me." Marion leaned in, urgent. She looked around the cafeteria, nervous and jittery. Her eyes bounced from table to table like someone might be listening.

"Fake sick. Tell them you're throwing up, having a panic attack, anything. Just don't go," she insisted.

"You're scaring me," I admitted.

"Good. Be scared." Her eyes went wild, wide and shimmering with something unspoken. "For real though, trust me on this. Find an excuse. Any excuse."

"But why? What does he—"

"Marion?"

Isaac stood beside our table. His face was open and kind, a contrast to the plastic warmth the other staff wore like masks.

"Art therapy's starting. Don't want to be late." His tone stayed gentle.

Marion changed the moment she saw him. The fear melted from her like fog under sunlight. She even smiled. A real one.

"Coming, Isaac." Her tone softened.

"Wait." I reached out and grabbed her sleeve. "You didn't answer me."

She looked at Isaac, who stepped back a little to give us space. Then she leaned in, her breath warm against my ear.

"Just don't go. Please. I'm begging you," she whispered.

She straightened before I could ask more.

"Ready," she told Isaac.

Isaac placed his hand on her shoulder, gentle, guiding. Protective. They walked away together, his body subtly shielding hers, like he could feel the danger I'd only just begun to sense.

I sat alone with my cold food. Marion's words kept playing in my head. The cafeteria noise faded into a low, buzzing hum.

Whatever happened in Varnar's office at night, Marion had been through it. And whatever it was, had scared her so badly that she was begging me not to go.

Chapter Eleven

Evening came too fast, curling around the asylum. The dayroom emptied slowly, patients shuffling back to their rooms in hunched silence, moving like they'd forgotten where they were going. Some muttered nonsense under their breath, others stared into empty corners as though something was watching them.

Back in my room, I sat stiffly on the edge of the bed, spine straight as a wire, Marion's warning playing in my mind on a loop, like a song I couldn't stop humming no matter how much I hated the lyrics. My hands wouldn't stop trembling. I pressed them into my thighs, but that only transferred the shaking to my arms, my shoulders. I felt hollowed out.

There was no clock in the room, no way to measure the time leaking by. Could've been an hour since dinner. Could've been three. The room had gone heavy with that muffled, weightless quiet that always came before something bad happened. My mouth felt like it was stuffed with dust, but I couldn't make myself drink the lukewarm water beside my bed. The air was wrong. It knew before I did.

Then I heard footsteps.

Heavy boots on the tile. Slow. Deliberate. A predator's rhythm. Each step landed like it was being savored. Whoever was coming wanted me to hear them. Wanted me to wait.

Tobias.

The door clicked open, and he filled the frame with his bulk. His hand was already moving at the front of his uniform pants, adjusting himself like he'd been waiting for this moment all night. His eyes, small and slick like oil, crawled over me and stalled at my chest. When he smiled, I saw teeth the color of old corn, yellow, irregular, like something that should have been pulled out years ago. This was a man who probably had to pay women to touch him. Or worse.

My skin prickled, every nerve suddenly too close to the surface.

"Time to go, princess. Doctor's waiting."

"I'm not feeling well." I forced the words past the dryness in my throat. Somehow, the words came out steady. "I think I might throw up."

"Save it." His hand gripped himself through his pants with more intention now, like the threat turned him on. The bulge was clear and disgusting. "Unless you want to puke on my shoes. I'll have a reason to punch your face. That'd be fun."

This man was diabolic.

I rose on unsteady legs. The floor was ice beneath my bare feet, a cold that climbed up my ankles. Tobias's eyes dropped instantly, and a new hunger darkened his face.

"No shoes tonight," he muttered. "Good. Doc likes them barefoot. Says it helps with the therapy." He laughed, an ugly, wet sound like something caught in his throat.

The hallway stretched ahead, endless and dark. We

walked in silence, Tobias staying close enough that I could feel the moist heat of his breath against my neck. Every exhale reeked of rot, coffee, onions, something sour. Once, his fingers grazed my back and then slipped lower to cup my hip.

I jerked away.

"Jumpy little thing. That's good. Makes it more fun to watch." He chuckled.

We passed the nurses' station, and it was deserted. The med cart sat abandoned, drawers yawning open like crooked mouths. Papers fluttered on the counter from some unseen draft. The whole area felt... evacuated. Like they knew.

"You know." Tobias's hand drifted again toward his crotch. "We had another new girl last month. Rebecca? Rachel? Something with an R. She was jumpy too. Cried the whole time. Doc had to gag her eventually."

My insides clenched. "Gag her? What happened to her?"

"Transferred." The word came out too fast. Reflexive. Practiced. "That's what happens to all of them eventually. Transferred to better facilities." But his grin said otherwise.

When we reached the thick wooden door of Dr. Varnar's office, Tobias knocked once, then pressed his face to the door like he was listening to a lover. His hand started rubbing slow, obscene circles at the front of his pants.

"Oh yeah. Started early tonight." He dropped low and thick. "Can hear someone in there already."

Inside, I heard the sounds too. Wet. Repetitive. Rhythmic. Flesh meeting flesh. Muffled grunts. Groans. The unmistakable cadence of violence dressed in sex.

"Come closer." Tobias grabbed my wrist and yanked me toward the door. "You gotta see this."

"What's happening in there?" I asked, barely able to form the words.

He was rubbing himself harder now, breathing through his mouth like he couldn't get enough air. His grip on my wrist was bruising.

"Someone came by earlier. Real worried about you. Said she needed to talk to the doc about your medication. Something about side effects." He grinned wider. "Doc decided she needed an emergency session."

I pulled against him. "Let me go."

"Not yet. First you watch. Need to see what kind of therapy we provide here."

He shoved me toward the glass panel in the door. It was frosted, but a long crack ran diagonally across it, the glass clear along the fracture line. I didn't want to look. But the inner treatment-room door stood open too, leaving a narrow sightline straight through. And I saw everything.

The image struck me like cold metal driven into my lungs.

Marion. Naked. Forced to her knees on the tile. Her wrists and ankles were bound with IV tubing in cruel knots that bent her body backwards in an impossible, agonizing arch. Her skin was a galaxy of bruises. Blood oozed from long, shallow cuts across her shoulders, dripping steadily to the floor.

Varnar knelt behind her, also naked. His pale body moved rhythmically, thrusting into her with animalistic force. In front of her stood Dr. Alan, legs wide, Marion's face forced between them. One hand twisted in her hair. The other held a scalpel, its blade catching the light.

"Count them," Dr. Alan commanded, dragging the blade along Marion's shoulder again. "That's eight. We're going for twenty tonight."

Marion trembled but made no sound. She took it in silence, endured with a resilience that made my heart ache and my stomach revolt.

"The quiet ones last longer," Varnar grunted, slamming harder. The sound was unbearable.

Behind me, Tobias panted faster. His hand moved frantically in his pants. "Jesus Christ, look at her take it."

Dr. Alan's breath hitched, her movements growing jerky. "I'm close. I'll cut her when I finish. I want to feel her scream."

She dragged the scalpel down Marion's spine. Marion's body arched, a muffled cry vibrating from her throat. Dr. Alan gasped, shuddered, and collapsed slightly.

"Perfect," she sighed, stepping back. She let go of Marion's hair, and Marion's head dropped, coughing and spitting blood and spit onto the tile.

They swapped places like they'd done it a hundred times. Dr. Alan moved behind Marion, grabbing something from a tray that gleamed silver. Varnar walked to her front, yanking her head forward by the hair.

"Your turn to use your mouth properly." He forced himself past Marion's split, bloodied lips.

She gagged violently. Behind her, Dr. Alan was doing something with the metal tool, twisting, widening. Marion bucked forward, gasping.

"The speculum opens them up nicely," Dr. Alan chirped, cheerful. "Let's see how wide we can go."

Behind me, Tobias choked out a moan. "Fuck, gonna—"

He finished with a grunt, hand buried in his pants. The sharp, sour smell of semen filled the hallway as he wiped himself off on his uniform without shame.

The noises from inside the office got worse, slapping, choking, the raw percussion of power and cruelty.

"They'll go for hours," Tobias murmured, eyes glassy. "Sometimes all night."

I staggered back, the floor tipping beneath me. I was going to be sick. My mouth filled with acid.

Sela was suddenly beside me, like she'd stepped out of the shadows. Her expression was calm, but her eyes held a strange flicker, something that might have once been empathy. Or survival.

"Seen enough?"

"They're torturing her—" I gasped.

"Yes. They are." Sela took my elbow. Her touch was steady, grounding. "And if you burst in there playing hero, they'll do the same to you. Maybe worse. Tonight was supposed to be your turn, but Marion went to Alan with a fake medication crisis and offered herself instead."

"Why?" I asked, voice breaking.

"Because she's an idiot who thinks she's protecting you." Sela's grip tightened as she steered me away. "Don't waste what she's giving you by getting yourself thrown in there too."

She guided me down the hall, but not before I heard Marion scream again. Real this time. Raw.

"How—" My throat scraped rough. "How can you work here? How can you let this happen?"

Sela's expression hardened. "Because someone has to be here when girls like Marion need patching up afterward. Someone who actually knows how to set bones and stitch wounds without asking questions." Her grip remained on my arm. "I can't stop them. I tried that my first year here. You know what happened? They made me watch while they worked on a nurse I'd trained. Six hours."

"But Marion—"

"Marion made a choice. She went to them knowing what would happen. She's been here long enough to know their patterns." Sela paused, choosing her words carefully. "They won't kill her tonight. That room isn't where they finish people. Death ends the fun too quickly."

"That's supposed to make me feel better?" I let out a mirthless laugh.

"It's supposed to make you smart."

We reached my room. As she unlocked the door, she met my eyes. "Every patient here gets their turn in that room. Some sooner, some later. But everyone goes eventually. The only choice is whether you go on your feet, or get dragged."

"So you want me to just accept it?"

"I want you to survive," she replied.

She pushed me inside, but her hand lingered on my arm. "That's all any of us can do. Survive. And remember that this place... it's older than it looks. And some things that happen here aren't what they seem."

Before I could ask what she meant, she closed the door.

I stood there shaking, not with fear, but with rage so pure it felt like fire under my skin. Marion was being torn apart just because she cared for me. Because in this place, caring about someone was a weakness they exploited.

The helplessness hollowed me. I lay on the bed, staring at the ceiling, worry for her gnawing through my chest.

At some point my eyes grew heavy. The pull came slow at first, then sudden, like an undertow. Only this time it wasn't sleep. It felt like being dragged backward through time itself.

The room around me flickered. My cell. Then stone. Then my cell again. The walls seemed to argue about which century they belonged to. My head spun violently, and then,

I stood in a stone chamber.

My feet were bare on stones worn smooth by countless footsteps over countless years. I was still in my hospital scrubs, but no one looked at me. No one saw me. I was there, but not there. A ghost watching the past.

People in brown robes filled the chamber. Hundreds of them, packed against the walls. Their hoods hid their faces, but I could feel their fear.

I saw him.

The creature from my nightmares stood by the altar. His bare torso looked more damaged here, scarred with deeper wounds. The blade in his hand was pitted with rust, or maybe old blood. Those red eyes swept across the room and passed over me. They paused. Just for a heartbeat.

He saw me. I knew he did. But he gave no sign. Just continued his slow scan of the room like I wasn't there.

"The third offering this month," someone whispered in Old English, but I understood. "The Judge sends his Executioner to take. He grows hungrier."

The Executioner. So that's what they called him. The name fit perfectly. He was death made flesh. Judgment given form.

Suddenly, the crowd parted.

A young woman was dragged forward, fighting and screaming. Maybe sixteen. She had tangled dark hair and her white shift was already torn and bloody. They had to force her onto the altar, five people holding her down while she thrashed.

"Please!" she screamed. "I don't want to die! Please!"

A figure stepped forward, tall, wearing robes darker than the others.

When she pushed back her hood, I saw a face that looked carved from ice. Utterly beautiful.

"The Judge requires feeding." Simple as breath. "Or he will take us all."

That's when I saw him.

A young man near the altar, watching with familiar hunger. Not Varnar, but his ancestor, the resemblance was sickening. Dressed in rough wool, centuries before our Varnar was born. Same sharp cheekbones, same thin mouth. The family had been breeding this cruelty for generations.

Family.

"Mother." He stepped forward. "Let me do it this time."

The woman—the heir's mother—turned to him with something like pride. "Not yet, my son. Watch. Learn. Your time will come."

She raised her arms, her black eyes reflecting torchlight. "By blood and binding, we offer this guilty flesh. Let her sins be meat and her remorse be wine. Let the blade divide body from spirit. Let this guilty one pass through death to feed our Lord, our King."

The Executioner lifted his massive blade. That terrible thing looked too heavy for anyone to wield. The girl's screams got higher, more desperate. He raised it over his head with both hands, the metal scraping against the stone ceiling.

Then he brought it down in one brutal motion, splitting her from head to pelvis.

The blade went through her like she was made of paper, cleaving everything in its path. But the blood didn't spray outward. Instead, it flowed up from both halves of her body, defying gravity, forming symbols in the air.

The symbols grew more complex. Swirling. Building.

Then the Executioner slammed his blade down into the altar. The stone cracked.

The blood symbols exploded outward.

And then everything went wrong.

From the spreading gore rose something horrifying,

The Judge. Massive and terrible. Fifteen feet of chains and exposed flesh. A skull too long. A jaw that hung open with endless rows of teeth. Rotted bat wings spread from his back like torn leather, dragging wet sounds when he moved. The left wing had holes eaten through it. Where eyes should be, there were only pits weeping black tar. Bone horns erupted straight from his skull.

He was angry.

"This is not enough!" He roared.

The sound shattered stone. Several cultists fell to their knees, blood running from their ears.

"You call this guilt? she stole bread to feed her sister!"

Black tar poured from his eye sockets.

"This pathetic guilt does not satisfy! Where are the murderers? the betrayers? the ones who destroyed lives?"

He swept one massive arm across the room.

Bodies flew, hitting walls with wet cracks.

A woman near me—through me—was torn in half. Her scream ended in a gurgle. Blood painted the walls.

"We offer what we can find!" the heir's mother cowered. "Please, Lord Judge—"

"petty thieves! small sins!" The Judge grabbed two more

cultists, crushing them in his fists like grapes. Gore dripped between his fingers.

"I hunger for true guilt! souls heavy with unforgivable acts!" He moved through the crowd like a tornado of meat and chain.

Every swing of his arms sent bodies flying. The floor became slick with blood, and worse things.

I pressed myself against the wall, even though I hoped the monster couldn't see me, couldn't touch me. But the horror of him was so complete it felt like he might break through time itself.

The Executioner moved then, just a small step that shifted his huge body between me and the blood. To anyone watching, he simply stood there, indifferent to the carnage around him. But something about where he stood felt intentional. He blocked the exact spot where I hid, a wall of black leather. Like he knew I needed protection, even if no one else could see me.

"Enough!"

The Judge's voice made the entire chamber shake. Bodies littered the floor, maybe fifty dead, torn apart. The survivors huddled against the walls, drenched in their friends' blood.

"You will learn to feed me properly or I will devour you all!"

the heir's mother, blood-soaked but alive, fell to her knees. "How? Tell us how!"

"Build the feeding ground," the Judge commanded. "Create a place where suffering flows like water. Where guilt and pain never end."

"Where?" she gasped.

"Here. on these stones. build your human cage here."

Black tar dripped faster from his eye sockets.

"Make it a place of healing above, but below it will be mine. Every cry, every fear, every moment of suffering will flow to me."

"We will," she promised. "We will build it."

"And one day," the Judge continued, dropping to something almost worse than a shout, "when the stars align, when the guilty one comes, one whose guilt burns bright enough to feed me forever, she will be mine. my feast. my bride of sorrows."

At those words, the Executioner shifted his weight slightly. A tiny movement that brought him more fully between me and the carnage. Protecting me across centuries.

The Judge began to sink back into the blood-soaked floor. "Fail me again and I will wear your skins as decoration. I will make your children into furniture. i will—"

He stopped mid-threat. Those weeping black pits turned toward the heir's mother. "Actually." The Judge softened into something almost gentle, worse than the screaming. "A demonstration."

He moved faster than something that size should. One massive hand closed around her waist, lifting her.

"Mother!" The young heir lunged forward, but other cultists held him back.

"I gave you a lifetime of service." She stayed calm even as the Judge's grip tightened. "I kept my bargain."

"Yes. and now your son will keep it better." The Judge's other hand closed around her head.

"He has your hunger, but without your weakness."

The sound she made when he pulled wasn't a scream. It

was wet and final. Her body tore in two. Blood rained down on the survivors.

The young heir collapsed to his knees, soaked in his mother's blood. But instead of grief, I saw something else in his eyes. Understanding.

Acceptance.

Hunger.

"I will serve better," he whispered to the gore-soaked floor. "I will feed you properly."

"Yes." The Judge tossed the pieces aside like trash. "You will."

Then he vanished, dragged back to whatever nightmare realm waits between feedings.

The Executioner lingered a moment longer, perfectly still. Then he turned. Not just his head. His entire body pivoted to face me directly. His crimson eyes stared straight at me. And in that gaze, I saw something impossible.

Recognition.

Like he'd been waiting for this moment.

Like he'd always known I would be here, watching from the future.

He held my eyes for a heartbeat that stretched forever. Then he too faded, drawn back into whatever hell he served.

The survivors stayed on their knees in the gore, trembling. An older man in robes approached the young heir and helped him to his feet. "We must do something." The man barely held back hysteria. "Before he returns. Before this happens again."

"Build what he wants." The young heir wiped blood from his eyes. "But more than that. We trap him."

"Trap the Judge?" someone gasped. "Impossible."

"Not his body. His hunger." The young heir's eyes gleamed. "Mother had books. Ancient texts. There are ways to... fold reality. Create spaces that exist between."

A woman stepped forward, pulling a leather-bound book from her robes. It was soaked in blood, but the pages still turned.

"The Inversions. I've studied them." She met their eyes. "We could create a reflection. A place where death isn't final."

"Explain," the old man demanded.

"We build here, on these stones. A place of healing. A religious sanctuary for the mad." She glanced around the blood-soaked chamber. "But beneath it, or beside it, or within it, we build something else. A place where the dead don't stay dead. Where those who die in guilt and pain are... recycled."

"An endless feast," the young heir breathed. "The same souls, dying over and over."

"But that's not enough," the woman continued. "The Judge spoke of a bride. The guilty one. We must keep offering him new souls. Fresh guilt. Until he finds her."

"So we sacrifice and search." The old man's words came slow. "Every mad woman brought here for prayers and healing, we test. We break. We offer."

"Generation after generation, if needed," the young heir added. "Until one of them is the one he wants. His bride of sorrows."

"How will we know her?" One of the cultists asked.

"The Judge will know," the woman replied, looking around at the corpses. "When we send the right one, he'll recognize her. He'll want her. Until then, we offer every guilty woman. The men we silence ourselves."

They began drawing symbols in the blood on the floor.

Ancient geometries that hurt to look at. The woman chanted in a language older than speech while others arranged the corpses into specific patterns.

"We'll call it a holy place," the young heir announced as they worked. "Dedicated to Saint Dymphna. Patron of the mad. The Church will send us their possessed, troubled women."

The air began to shimmer and reality folded.

Even across the centuries, I felt it, the moment they created that other place. The Realm Beneath. The reflection where suffering never ends.

"Every madwoman, a potential bride," the young heir murmured. "Every confession, a test."

"And if it takes centuries?" Someone asked.

The young heir's smile was cold. "Then we feed him for centuries. What else do we have but time?"

The scene dissolved. Time yanked me back.

But I understood now. Every woman who had been brought to this place for healing had been tested. Broken. Offered. All of them auditioned for a role only one could fill.

I crashed back into my own time, gasping on the narrow bed. My whole body shook with what I'd seen.

We were all just meat for something ancient and hungry, waiting to see which one of us would finally become the Bride of Sorrows.

Chapter Twelve

In the morning, when the door opened and I saw Isaac, I
ran to him and gripped his shirt. My whole body trembled with anxiety, with a desperate need to know what
happened to Marion. Tears were already streaming down my
face, and I couldn't stop them.

"Zahra?" He sounded alarmed, like he was trying to understand why I was falling apart in front of him. "What's wrong?
You're shaking."

The concern was real, genuine in a way that few things
were in this place. But he didn't know. Of course he didn't
know. Isaac worked morning shifts, came in when the sun was
already up and the worst of the night's horrors had been tucked
away behind closed doors.

"Isaac, where is Marion?" The words tumbled out
between sobs, barely coherent. My hands twisted in his shirt,
holding on like he was the only solid thing in a world that had
tilted off its axis. "They hurt her last night. They hurt her so
bad—"

His face changed instantly, the color draining until he

looked almost gray. His hands came up to grip my shoulders, not hard, but firm enough to steady me.

"What? What do you mean, 'hurt her'?"

I didn't have time to explain. Couldn't find the words to describe what I'd seen through that frosted glass—Marion on her knees, the scalpel, the speculum, Dr. Alan's delighted face, Varnar's casual cruelty. The images were burned into my brain, but my mouth couldn't shape them into sentences. Instead, I just grabbed his hand and pulled, nearly stumbling in my desperation to move.

"Show me." Sudden fear pulled him tight. "Where is she? Zahra, where is Marion?"

We ran down the corridor together. Patients scattered out of our way, pressing themselves against the walls like prey animals avoiding predators. A nurse called out for us to stop, but neither of us even slowed down. Isaac's breathing grew harsher with every step, and I could hear him muttering under his breath, prayers or curses, I couldn't tell which.

"The medical wing," I gasped as we turned another corner. "She has to be in the medical wing."

The medical wing was just another large room with beds lined up against both walls, separated by thin curtains that offered only the illusion of privacy. Some curtains were drawn, hiding whatever misery lay behind them. Others hung open, showing empty beds or patients too sedated to care about visitors.

I searched frantically, checking each bed, yanking aside curtains. Behind one, an old woman moaned in her sleep. Behind another, someone had knotted their sheets and was muttering about spiders.

Then I saw her.

Third bed from the end.

When Isaac saw Marion, he made a sound I'd never heard from a human being before. It came from somewhere deep in his chest, raw, animalistic, like something inside him had been torn apart. His entire body went rigid for a moment. Then he was moving, crossing the room in long strides to reach her bedside.

"No," he whispered. Then louder, more desperate: "No, no, no—"

Marion lay unconscious on the narrow bed, and the damage was so extensive I could barely recognize her. Her face had swollen beyond human proportions. Her left eye was entirely hidden behind purple-black tissue. Her lips were split in multiple places, crusted with dried blood. Fresh bandages wrapped her arms, but they couldn't hide the dark stains seeping through the white gauze. Her breathing came in tiny, pained whimpers, like even unconsciousness couldn't protect her from what had been done.

Isaac's hands hovered over her broken body, shaking violently. He seemed afraid to touch her, afraid he might cause more damage to something already so ruined. When he finally let his fingers brush her swollen cheek, the gentleness of it made my chest ache.

"Marion?" He broke completely on her name. He leaned closer, his forehead nearly touching hers. "Baby, can you hear me? It's Isaac. I'm here."

She didn't respond. Just that terrible, labored breathing that sounded so wet. I could see Isaac cataloging each injury with professional eyes, even as tears ran down his face, the defensive wounds on her hands, the precise cuts that spoke of deliberate torture rather than simple violence, the bruises in the shape of fingers around her throat.

"What did they do?" He wasn't asking me. He was asking the universe, asking God, asking anyone who might have an answer that could make sense of this. "What did they fucking do to her?"

His professional composure, which was usually steady and reassuring, completely shattered. He dropped to his knees beside the bed, took her limp hand in both of his, and pressed it to his face. I watched his shoulders shake with silent sobs, this strong man reduced to nothing by the sight of Marion's destruction.

"Isaac."

Sela appeared in the doorway, her face carefully neutral despite the scene before her.

"You need to step back." She commanded.

Isaac's head snapped up, and the look in his eyes was dangerous. Wild. Nothing like the gentle nurse I'd come to know.

"Don't. Don't you dare tell me to step back from her." He warned Sela.

"She needs medical attention. Real medical attention." Sela swept into the room with her usual efficiency, but I could see the concern in her eyes. "Let me work."

Isaac stood slowly, his body coiled with barely controlled violence. When he turned to face her fully, I saw murder in his eyes.

"Where were you last night? When they were doing this to her, where the fuck were you?"

"Saving her life, probably." Sela moved past him to check Marion's vitals, her movements quick and professional. "She was worse when they brought her to me. Much worse. You should be thanking me instead of looking like you want to tear my throat out."

"I'll kill him." Isaac spoke quietly, and the calm was more terrifying than if he'd screamed. "I'll fucking kill Varnar. I'll make him suffer like she suffered. I'll—"

"No, you won't." She cut him off, flat.

Sela didn't look up from Marion. Her fingers checked pulse points and examined Marion's wounds with care. When she spoke again, she dropped to a whisper, forcing Isaac to lean in to hear her.

"You think Varnar is some simple sadist? Just another sick doctor who gets off on hurting women?"

She glanced toward the door, then back at Isaac, her whisper urgent. "He's connected. Protected. I've seen staff try to report him, good people, brave people. They get transferred. Fired. Sometimes worse. One nurse tried to go to the police..." She shook her head. "Car accident. Very convenient."

Her hands kept moving, professional and steady, but she dropped lower. "He has people everywhere. The board. The police. Maybe higher. You can't fight someone like that with your fists, Isaac."

She finally met his eyes. "You want to help her? Then be smart. Stay alive. Keep slipping them extra pain meds. Keep documenting injuries where he can't find them. Keep being the one person here who actually gives a damn."

She dropped to almost nothing. "Because if you get yourself killed or fired trying to be a hero, who's left? Who protects the next Marion? We need you here, not dead, not blacklisted."

Isaac's whole body shook with the effort of holding back. He pressed his forehead against Marion's hand, whispering things too quiet for me to hear, promises, apologies, declarations of love that should have been said when she was conscious to hear them.

That's when Tobias appeared in the doorway, already wearing that ugly grin that made me hate him so much. He took in the scene—Isaac on his knees beside Marion's bed, me crying in the corner, Sela working with grim efficiency, and his grin widened.

"Well, well. Nurse boy found his girlfriend," he mocked. "Touching. Really. Like something out of a romance novel. Man, you should've seen how they broke her. It was so good!"

Isaac removed his glasses, placing them next to Marion's pillow and then moved so fast I didn't see it coming. His fist cracked against Tobias's jaw. Tobias went down hard, blood spraying from his mouth in a bright arc.

"Isaac!" Sela snapped, but it was too late.

Isaac was already on top of Tobias, hitting him again and again, each punch punctuated with a word: "You—watched—you—fucking—watched—while—they—"

Tobias fought back with dirty tactics, fingers clawing for Isaac's eyes, a knee aimed at his groin. They rolled across the floor, crashing into medical equipment, scattering supplies. Isaac had rage on his side, but Tobias was bigger, meaner, more used to violence.

"ENOUGH!" Sela snatched a syringe from the tray, holding it like a weapon. "Both of you, stop, or I sedate everyone in this room!"

They froze mid-grapple, bloodied and panting. Tobias's lip was split, blood running down his chin. He had bruises on his face, while Isaac's eye was already swelling shut.

"Get out," Sela ordered, carrying the kind of authority only earned through years of dealing with chaos. "All of you. Out of my medical wing. Now."

"I'm not leaving her." Isaac kept trying to untangle himself while still guarding.

"Yes, you are. Because if security finds you here after assaulting staff, you'll be fired. Never work in healthcare again." Ice edged every word, but beneath it, something else: understanding, maybe even respect. "Please listen to me and leave."

Isaac stood slowly, his eyes locked on Marion's unconscious form. "This isn't over," he told Tobias, who was using the wall to pull himself upright.

Tobias spat blood and grinned through red teeth. "Looking forward to round two, nurse boy. Maybe next time I'll show you what we did to your girlfriend. Give you a play-by-play."

Isaac lunged again, but Sela stepped in, surprisingly strong for someone so thin. She physically pushed us all toward the door, herding us like unruly children.

"Out. Now. Before I call security!"

In the hallway, after Sela slammed the door in our faces, Isaac leaned against the wall like his legs might give out. His whole body trembled, maybe from adrenaline, maybe from grief. Blood still dripped from his lip, and his left eye was starting to swell.

"She took my place." I needed him to understand. "Varnar was supposed to see me last night. Marion went instead. She volunteered, knowing what would happen."

Isaac looked at me with haunted eyes, and I saw years of accumulated horror in his gaze. All the patients he'd tried to protect and failed. All the damage he'd witnessed while staying professional, staying employed, staying useful.

"She was always too brave for this place." His tone had gone hollow. "Too willing to take someone else's pain."

We stood there in the hallway, united by our love for someone who'd sacrificed herself for a near stranger.

"What do we do now?" I asked.

Isaac wore his glasses again, careful not to press on the black eye. When he looked at me, something had changed in him. The gentle nurse was still there, but underneath, there was steel.

"Now?" He almost laughed. "Now we get careful. And we find a way to get her out of here."

Chapter Thirteen

I couldn't get Marion's broken face out of my head. The image kept replaying, blood, bruises, the way she'd struggled to breathe. I needed somewhere quiet to think, somewhere to process what I'd just witnessed.

The rec room was mostly empty. I found the corner chair with the broken spring and curled into it. My hands wouldn't stop shaking. She'd taken that beating for me.

An orderly appeared in the doorway. The same one who'd let Marion out of solitary that morning, who'd gone to fetch Sela when Tobias was harassing her. He scanned the room until he found me.

"Zahra Quinn?"

"Mitchell," I corrected automatically. "Zahra Mitchell."

His face stayed blank. "Dr. Varnar wants to see you."

My whole body went cold. This had to be a mistake. I'd just seen what he did to Marion last night. She'd taken my appointment. She had suffered for me.

"Now?" The word came out cracked.

"Now." He nodded with a serious look. Maybe even he knew what was going to happen. "I'm sorry. Doctor's orders."

I stood on unsteady legs, scanning the hallway as we walked, looking for Isaac. Maybe he'd see me. Maybe he'd stop this somehow. But the corridors were empty, save for a few patients shuffling past. There was no sign of him anywhere.

Anxiety coiled tighter with each step. Part of me wanted to run, to fight, to scream. But the bigger part—the exhausted part—knew it wouldn't matter. They'd drag me there anyway.

We stopped at his door. The orderly knocked once, then backed away fast.

"Come in."

The office looked exactly like it had before. Clean. Organized. Everything in its place. The curtains drawn shut tight against the morning sun. The desk polished to a shine that hurt to look at. Like nothing had happened here. Like Marion hadn't bled on the tile beyond that inner door just hours ago.

Varnar sat behind his desk, hands folded, watching me with that calm expression he wore like a second skin. I didn't sit at the edge of the chair this time. I threw myself into it, legs spread, arms crossed. Staring him down like I had something to prove.

"Good morning, Zahra." Soft, professional. "How was your night?"

"You already know."

A ghost of a smile touched his lips. "I'd like to hear it from you."

"I didn't sleep." The words came out steadier than I felt. "It's hard to sleep when you know what kind of monster runs this place."

He tilted his head, studying me. "Monster? That's quite an accusation."

"It's not an accusation when I saw what you did to Marion. When I watched through the glass."

"Ah." He leaned back in his chair. "So you were watching. How... voyeuristic of you."

I stood up so fast the chair rocked back. "You're disgusting."

The smile vanished. He stood too. His face didn't change, but his body had gone tense, coiled. Ready.

"Sit down, Zahra," he ordered.

"Go to hell."

I grabbed the first thing I could reach, a heavy glass paperweight from his desk, and hurled it at his face. He ducked, but it caught his shoulder hard. I used the distraction to lunge across the desk, my hand finding his cheek, nails digging in as I dragged them down.

Three red lines opened on his skin.

He caught my wrist and yanked me forward, using my momentum against me. I crashed into him and we both staggered back. His free hand found my throat, slamming me against the wall hard enough to knock a frame loose. It crashed to the floor, glass shattering.

"You think you're strong now?" His breath was hot on my face, fingers tightening on my windpipe. "Think you're different from all the others?"

I clawed at his hand, black spots dancing at the edges of my vision. My knee came up, aimed between his legs, but he twisted away.

The door opened.

He didn't let go.

Dr. Alan walked in carrying her clipboard, taking in the scene with the same expression she'd wear checking inventory. Me pinned against the wall. Him bleeding from fresh scratches. The broken glass glittering on the floor.

"Starting early today?" She closed the door behind her with a soft click. "You always get too hands-on, Varnar. We've discussed this."

Varnar's grip loosened just enough for me to suck in air.

"She attacked me."

"Of course she did." Dr. Alan set her clipboard on a chair and stepped closer, her heels crunching on broken glass. "She watched us work on Marion last night. Stood right outside that door like a little peeping tom."

She reached out and ran her fingers through my hair, gentle at first, like she was comforting a child. Then her fist closed and she yanked my head back, forcing me to look at her. "Did you enjoy the show? Watching your friend break?"

I tried to spit, but my mouth had gone dry as sand.

She smiled and let go, wiping her hand on her coat like I was something dirty. "This one needs more intensive treatment. We were too gentle with Marion."

"The gathering—" Varnar started.

"I moved it to tomorrow." She glanced at her watch, then back at me. "I told them we need more time to... prepare properly."

The way she said 'prepare' made my skin crawl. Her tone caught me—the slight pause before the word—sent goosebumps racing up my arms. There was weight behind it, meaning I couldn't grasp yet.

Varnar released my throat. I dropped, catching myself on

my hands and knees, coughing. The broken glass bit into my palms, but I barely felt it past the burning in my throat.

"Get her on the table." Dr. Alan was already moving to the medical cabinet. "And this time, let's make sure she understands her position here."

Varnar grabbed my upper arm, hauling me to my feet. I swung at him with my free hand, but he caught that too, twisting both arms behind my back. Pain shot through my shoulders. "Stop fighting." His breath was hot against my ear. "It only makes this worse."

"Fuck you."

He dragged me through the inner door into the tiled treatment room and marched me toward the examination table. My feet dragged, trying to slow our progress, but he was stronger.

"No." The panic leaked through. "No, you can't—"

He shoved me forward. My stomach hit the edge of the table hard enough to bruise. I was bent over it, face down, trying to push back, but he had both my arms pinned.

"Hold still," he grunted.

He grabbed the back of my scrubs with one hand, keeping my wrists pinned with the other. I heard fabric tear. The sound froze me for a second, just long enough for him to yank harder. The cheap material split down the middle. Cool air hit my back. He let go of my wrists to grab the sleeves, and I tried to twist away, but he was faster. More tearing. The top fell away in pieces.

"Stop!" The word cracked out of me. "Please—"

He went for the pants next. I kicked backward, caught his shin, heard him grunt. But his hands found the elastic waistband and pulled. The fabric gave way with a sound like surrender.

"Subject shows significant resistance." Dr. Alan's pen scratched on paper somewhere behind me. Taking notes like this was just another procedure. "Elevated stress response. Visible trembling."

Varnar flipped me over, lifting and turning me so I landed on my back on the cold metal. I tried to sit up, but he planted a hand in the center of my chest and pushed. My head hit the table hard enough to make my vision swim.

Now I was on my back, exposed, with Varnar standing at my right side. He grabbed my wrists with one hand and pinned them above my head. The position made my back arch slightly, made me even more vulnerable.

"Observe the physical response." His professional tone was slipping. His eyes tracked over my body with something hungry.

"Accelerated breathing. Pupil dilation."

"Get clinical distance. You're repeating what happened with Helena Wolfe," Dr. Alan warned. She'd moved to stand at the foot of the table where she could see everything.

"Oh no, she's no Helena Wolfe. She's better." His free hand moved to my throat, not squeezing, just resting there. "She's different from the others."

Helena Wolfe? Who was she? Another patient? The way Dr. Alan said the name made it sound like a warning, like something had gone wrong before.

"They're all different until they break." Dr. Alan went cold. "Continue the examination."

His hand started moving down from my throat, tracing over my collarbone. I turned my head away, staring at the wall, trying to disappear inside my own skull. But every touch registered. Every inch of skin he claimed with his fingers.

His hand moved lower, over my hip. "She's fighting even now."

"Of course she is." Dr. Alan sounded bored. "They all fight at first."

His fingers reached between my legs. I clamped my thighs together, but he used his knee to force them apart, his hand still pinning my wrists above my head.

"Don't." The word came out small, broken.

"Shh." His fingers found me, touched me in ways that made my whole body go rigid.

"Let's see what you're really made of."

I bit down on my lip hard enough to taste blood. I tried to think of something else—Marion's laugh, the way morning light looked through the rec room windows, my mother singing in the kitchen years ago. My dad watching TV and doing his running commentary on the game.

But my body betrayed me. He knew exactly what he was doing, where to touch, how to move his fingers. Each stroke built something I didn't want. My breathing changed.

"There we go," he breathed, leaning closer. I could feel him watching my face.

"Your body knows the truth, even if your mind won't admit it." Varnar breathed, enjoying seeing me twist.

"She's responding," Dr. Alan noted from the foot of the table. "Involuntary muscular contractions. Increased lubrication."

I squeezed my eyes shut, tears leaking from the corners. This couldn't be happening. Not this. Not my body proving him right.

His fingers moved inside me with practiced skill, curling, stroking, finding rhythms that made my hips twitch without permission. My back arched off the table, building toward something I fought with every cell in my body.

"Almost there," he murmured, his face close to mine now. "I can feel it."

When it happened, when the pleasure crashed through me against my will—I screamed. Not from pain, but from rage and humiliation so complete it felt like dying. My whole body convulsed, clenching around his fingers.

Varnar went perfectly still. Then he laughed. Soft. Amazed. Like he'd discovered something wonderful.

"She came." He sounded almost reverent. "My God, she actually came."

Dr. Alan's pen stopped moving. The room filled with a silence that felt dangerous.

"That's never happened before," she muttered.

"Never." Varnar was staring at me like I was something miraculous. "Not with Marion. Not with any of them. But she—"

"—Is still a patient." Dr. Alan's voice could've cut glass. "Still a subject. This changes nothing."

"Doesn't it?" He was still inside me, fingers no longer moving but just... there. Possessive.

"You hate me. I can see it in your eyes. But your body—" He smiled.

"Her body is responding to physical stimuli." Dr. Alan moved to my left side. "Nothing more. You're assigning meaning where there is none."

"Am I?" His fingers moved slightly, and my oversensitive body jerked.

Real anger crept into Dr. Alan's voice. "She's not special.

She's not different. She's a sacrifice, Varnar. Remember your place."

Sacrifice? What the fuck was she talking about?

"My place?" He finally pulled his fingers out, and I curled onto my side as much as I could with my wrists still pinned. "I know exactly where—"

Dr. Alan slapped me. Hard. My already split lip burst open again, blood filling my mouth.

"Still resistant," she observed, like she hadn't just hit me. "The orgasmic response doesn't indicate submission. If anything, it's increased her hostility."

She grabbed my breast and twisted until I cried out. "You think you've won something?" She leaned in, close enough that I could smell her perfume. "You think making him obsessed with you gives you power? You're nothing. Less than nothing. And we're going to prove it."

She moved back to the foot of the table, selecting instruments from the medical tray with careful precision. I saw the scalpel's silver gleam, and my whole body tried to curl tighter.

"Turn her over," she instructed.

"Alan—" He resisted.

"Turn. Her. Over."

Varnar hesitated for just a moment. Then he released my wrists and grabbed my shoulders, flipping me onto my stomach despite my struggles. My cheek pressed against the cold metal, my arms now pinned beneath me.

"Hold her down." Dr. Alan's order came flat.

Varnar pressed one hand between my shoulder blades, keeping me flat. I could feel him beside me, his weight holding me still.

"Inner thigh first." I could hear her moving behind me. "Shallow cuts. We want her to feel everything."

She was at the foot of the table. I felt her hand on my ankle, pulling my leg to the side to expose my inner thigh. The blade touched my skin like ice.

Then fire, as she drew it down in one smooth motion. I screamed into the table, my leg jerking involuntarily.

"Beautiful," she murmured. "Look how the blood wells up. Like tears."

Another cut. Then another. Each one precise. Deliberate. Turning my thigh into her canvas.

"My turn." Anticipation thickened the words.

I felt him shift, his hand still pressing me down, moving now to my upper back. The scalpel touched my lower back, just above my right hip.

"I'm going to mark you." He reached for the scalpel. "So everyone knows what you are."

The blade bit deep. Curved down and to the right. Cut again, back up at an angle. I realized he was carving a letter. V. His initial, in my skin.

The pain was clean compared to everything else. Simple. Honest. I screamed until my voice gave out, then just shook as he finished his work.

"Perfect." He leaned down and I felt his lips press against the wound, tasting my blood. "Now you're mine."

"She's not yours," Dr. Alan snapped, and something went strange in the words.

For one second, the mask slipped. She looked at me like I had stolen something promised to her.

I turned my head just enough to see her at the edge of my vision. She was moving closer with something in her hand. A speculum. My whole body went rigid. I knew what that was for. She was going to spread me open, force it inside while I couldn't move.

"Remember, Varnar, she's nothing but a sac— I mean case study," she continued. "A particularly interesting one."

Then she raised the speculum high and brought it down hard against my temple. The metal connected with a sickening crack, and white stars exploded across my vision.

That's when I saw him.

Standing in the corner of the office that shouldn't have been dark but was. The Executioner. Massive and still. That metallic helmet. Burning coals where eyes should be, watching. Waiting.

He'd been there the whole time.

The last thing I heard was Varnar saying my name. Possessively. Like I was something he'd claimed.

But as consciousness slipped away, I could have sworn I saw the Executioner's head tilt. Just slightly. Like he was disagreeing. Like Varnar was wrong about who I belonged to.

Then everything went black.

Chapter Fourteen

Pain brought me back. The deep kind that sits in your bones and won't let go, spreading through every fiber of your being until you can't tell where the hurt begins and your body ends. I tried to breathe normally, but each inhale felt like someone was peeling my skin off, layer by layer.

The medical ward lights were on, those awful white ones that never really turn off. Just dim enough to make you think you're dying, but bright enough to keep you from finding peace in the darkness.

My mouth tasted like copper and something worse. Bile, maybe. Or the metallic tang of blood dried on my tongue. When I turned my head, my neck hurt so bad.

Marion was in the next bed. Awake. Staring at nothing with the hollow expression of someone who'd been taken apart and didn't know how the pieces fit back together.

Her face had gone past purple into colors that didn't have names, deep blues and greens, like a bruise on the world itself. One eye was still swollen shut, the lid stretched tight over what had to be incredible pain. The other moved slowly, like it hurt to look at things. Like seeing was just another form of suffering. New gauze wrapped her arms from wrist to elbow, already spotted through with pink that would be red again soon.

"You awake?" The question scraped out of her like she'd been screaming for hours. Maybe she had. Maybe we both had and just didn't remember.

"Yeah." I croaked.

The word felt strange in my mouth, like I'd forgotten how to make normal sounds. How to pretend I was still human after what had been done to us.

We didn't say anything else for a while. Just lay there, listening to machines beep in the ward, counting out heartbeats that felt borrowed.

Marion's hand moved on top of her blanket. Just her fingers at first, tapping against the thin fabric like she was testing if they still worked, if the nerves still connected to something that could be called herself. Then her whole hand slid sideways, toward the edge of her bed. Toward me.

I reached out too, even though it hurt, but I kept reaching until our fingers touched in the space between beds.

Her hand was hot. Fever-hot. Swollen so badly I could see the skin stretched tight over bones that might be cracked. Two fingers were taped together with medical tape already coming loose at the edges, stained with something brown. I wrapped my fingers around hers anyway, careful not to press too hard on what had to be incredibly tender flesh.

That's when I started crying. Not loud. Not dramatic sobbing. Just water leaking from my eyes like a broken faucet. Marion's hand squeezed mine, and I felt her shaking too.

"He did the same thing to you." It wasn't a question. She

knew. We both knew. We'd been marked by the same monster. Claimed by the same nightmare.

"Yeah." The word barely made it past my throat.

"The V. I saw it when they brought you in. You were naked. Sela fixed you as best as she could and dressed you in scrubs." Marion's voice was tight with anger.

Sela. Thank God for her. I nodded against the pillow that crinkled with every movement. The carved letter on my lower back throbbed in time with my heartbeat, each pulse sending fire through damaged nerves. Varnar had taken his time with that mark, making sure it would hurt for a long time. Making sure I'd never forget who I "belonged" to.

"Did he mark—" I started, but Marion cut me off.

"Don't." Her tone turned panicked. "Just. Don't. I can't... if I think about it, I'll lose what's left."

We held hands and cried without sound. Two women who'd been taken apart by the same man, trying to remember how to exist in our bodies again. Bodies that had been violated, marked, damaged in ways that might never heal.

"I can't stop seeing it," I whispered. "When I close my eyes, I'm back on that table. I can feel his hands. Smell his breath. It's like it's still happening."

"Me too." Marion sobbed. "I've faced him one too many times already. But this one was different. This one broke something in me."

"It's not your fault," I whispered, squeezing her hand harder. "None of it. We survived. That's what matters."

But even as I said it, I wondered if survival was the right word for what we were doing. Breathing wasn't the same as living. And existing wasn't the same as being whole.

Suddenly, the door opened, and we both flinched like

gunshots had gone off. Our hands gripped each other so tightly I felt Marion's bones shift under her skin.

But it was Isaac, carrying a medical tray with hands that shook just enough to make the instruments rattle. He stopped when he saw us both awake, and his whole expression crumbled, like he'd been hoping we'd stay unconscious, that he wouldn't have to see what we'd become.

"Jesus," he breathed, setting the tray down hard enough to make everything jump. "You're both—I didn't think you'd be awake yet. The sedatives should have kept you under for a few more hours."

He sounded rough, like he'd been crying. Or screaming. Or both. There were dark circles under his eyes and stubble that said he hadn't left the hospital since Marion was brought in.

He went to Marion's bed first, moving slowly like he was approaching a wounded animal. His fingers ghosted over her face, never quite touching, like he was afraid she'd break more than she already had. "Can I check your bandages? The ones on your arms need changing."

She nodded, but I saw her whole body tense. Even gentle touch was going to hurt. Everything was going to hurt for a long time.

Isaac peeled back the gauze with infinite care, but Marion still hissed through her teeth. The wounds underneath were deep. Precise cuts designed to cause maximum suffering without death. Some were starting to go bad at the edges, red and swollen with the beginning of infection.

"These need cleaning." The words came thick with something that might have been rage. Or grief. Or both. "Marion, why didn't you call for someone when you woke up? You must've been in incredible pain."

"What's the point?" She stared at the ceiling, tears leaking from her eyes. "What's the point of healing? They'll do it again. They'll keep torturing. If not me, then Zahra. If not Zahra, then someone else."

Isaac's mouth worked like he was chewing words he couldn't say, like there were things in his throat that would cut him if he let them out. He finished with Marion and walked around to the other side of my bed. I was lying on my side, facing her.

"I need to check your dressing." Quiet, careful. "Is that okay?"

I nodded against the pillow.

His hands were gentler than any I'd ever felt in this place. He carefully lifted the hem of my scrub top and lowered the waistband of my pants just enough to expose the wound. When he removed the dressing from my lower back, he sucked in a sharp breath.

"He marked you." The words came out strangled.

"Said I was his now." The taste of ash filled my mouth.

Isaac's hands stopped moving entirely. He just stood there, staring at Varnar's signature, and I could tell something was happening behind his eyes. Something breaking. Or building. Or both.

When he finished with my bandages, he sat on the edge of the bed and put his head in his hands. His shoulders shook once, then went still, like he was forcing himself to hold together through sheer will.

"I can't do this anymore," he whispered, voice quivering. "I can't keep pretending this is normal. That what happened to you both is just... treatment. That this is medicine."

Marion turned her head toward him with effort, wincing at the movement. "Isaac—"

"No. Listen to me." He looked up, eyes red-rimmed and hollow with exhaustion, and something darker. Something like self-hatred. "I've been here two years. Two fucking years. Told myself I was helping people. That the screams were just... part of recovery. That sometimes healing has to hurt."

He stood up and paced to the window, then back again, like the energy inside him wouldn't let him stay still. "But seeing you both like this, seeing what he did... This isn't a hospital. It's a killing floor. And I've been mopping up the blood."

"You didn't know." The words felt hollow even as they left my mouth.

"I did know." Flat, brutal with honesty. "I just didn't want to see it. Didn't want to admit that I was part of something evil. That every day I came to work, I was complicit in torture."

Isaac sat again, leaning forward like the realization was too heavy to carry upright. "But I'm seeing it now. All of it. And I'm getting you out of here."

Marion's eyes snapped into focus. She was suddenly alert despite the medication. "Out?"

"Tonight. Both of you. I don't care what it takes."

"We can barely walk," I pointed out, though some part of me was already reaching toward the possibility of escape like a drowning person reaching for air. Everything below my waist felt like hamburger meat, torn and ruined in ways that made every movement agony.

"You'll have to try." Isaac pressed in, almost desperate. "Because if you stay here much longer, if you give him time to plan whatever comes next..." He swallowed hard. I saw his throat working around words too terrible to speak aloud. "I think Varnar's planning something worse. The way he looked at you both when they brought you back. Like he was just getting started."

A chill lodged deep in my bones. What we'd endured had already been horrific. But the idea that it was just the opening act in a longer nightmare was almost too much to process.

The door opened, and we all tensed, but it was just Sela doing rounds. She stepped inside and closed the door behind her, pausing to take in the scene. Her eyes missed nothing, our red faces, Isaac's agitation, the way we were all leaning together like conspirators planning revolution.

"Problem here?" she asked, though her tone suggested she already knew the answer.

Isaac straightened, trying to look professional. "No, just checking their—"

"Cut the shit." Sela stepped closer, clipboard tucked under her arm like a weapon. "You three are planning something stupid, aren't you?"

We said nothing, but silence was its own answer.

Sela sighed like she'd been expecting this moment for years. Then she pulled up a chair and sat beside Marion's bed.

"Twelve years I've been here." Sela's mouth twisted. "Twelve years of patching up girls just so they can be broken again. Of pretending the screams are from nightmares, not torture chambers. Of mopping up blood and asking no questions about where it came from."

She looked older suddenly, worn down by a thousand compromises.

"You think I haven't noticed the patterns? Girls who ask too many questions disappearing into isolation wards that don't appear on any official hospital map. Patients who fight back getting 'special treatment' until they stop fighting altogether."

"Then why stay?" Marion asked, voice rough with accusation.

"Because someone has to keep the ones still breathing alive long enough to maybe escape." Sela's smile was bitter with guilt. After a long pause, she added, "But I'm done now. I'm done being complicit. I'm tired of going home every night and washing other people's blood off my hands."

Isaac leaned forward. "You'd help us?"

"I'd help me sleep at night for once." Sela pulled a small notebook from her pocket and flipped to a page filled with precise handwriting and what looked like architectural diagrams. "But if we're doing this, we do it right."

She unfolded a hand-drawn map of the hospital. Every corridor. Every hidden passage. Every secret artery beneath the floors.

"Shift change is at 2 a.m. For about fifteen minutes, the skeleton crew is doing rounds and paperwork. Security's focused on the main floors and patient wards. That's our window."

Her finger traced a path through narrow hallways and unlabeled shafts. "Service tunnel system. Runs under the whole building. Connects to the loading dock where they bring in supplies. The tunnels are old, from when this place was built, but they're still functional."

"What about alarms?" Isaac asked.

"The loading dock has an exit that leads directly to the parking lot. No alarms on that door, it's considered internal infrastructure." Sela looked at Marion and me, assessing our condition with cold precision. "Question is, can you two move? Really move, not just pretend?"

Marion struggled to sit up, face going gray with the effort. Every inch she gained seemed to cost her something. But she got upright. "I can move. It'll hurt like hell, but I can do it."

I tried the same, bracing myself for the explosion of pain in my back. It felt like someone was hammering nails into my spine, like the carved V was on fire beneath my skin, but I stayed upright. "Yeah. I can do it too."

"Pain medication will help," Isaac murmured. "I can get you enough to function for a few hours. Not enough to make you numb, you'll need to stay alert, but enough to move without passing out."

"Then we go tonight." Sela snapped the notebook shut. "Get some rest. Try to eat something if you can keep it down. You'll need every ounce of strength you've got."

The rest of the day crawled by in a haze of preparation and pain that felt like waiting for execution. Isaac brought food that tasted like nothing, but we forced it down, knowing our bodies needed fuel. He snuck extra medications from the supply closet, not just painkillers but antibiotics for the infections blooming in our wounds, anti-inflammatories to dull the swelling, stimulants to keep us awake and sharp.

Marion practiced sitting up, then standing, then taking a few steps around the narrow space between our beds. Each movement drained the color from her face, sweat beading on her forehead despite the cool air, but she kept going. Kept pushing herself past what should have been possible.

I did the same, gritting my teeth against the fire in my lower back every time I put weight on my leg. The carved V felt like it was splitting open with each step, but I forced myself to keep moving. To prove I could. To prove I had to.

"Your fever's getting worse," Isaac murmured, checking my forehead for the tenth time that evening. "The infection is spreading faster than the antibiotics can fight it."

"I'll make it." I had to. The alternative was staying here for whatever Varnar had planned next, and that wasn't an option. Death was preferable to that.

As darkness fell outside the barred windows, the ward settled into its nighttime routine. Nurses made final rounds. Patients were medicated into compliance, their moans and cries gradually fading into drugged silence. The lights dimmed to that murky half-brightness that made everything look like a bad dream you couldn't wake up from.

Isaac brought us clean scrubs and real shoes, because we might need to run. "Twenty minutes," he whispered, glancing at his watch. "I signed on for emergency overtime after Marion was brought in, so I can clock out at two without anyone questioning it. Make everything look normal. Act like I'm going home for the night."

After he left, Marion and I changed in silence. The clean scrubs hurt going on. When I pulled up the pants, the waistband pressed against the carved V, and I had to bite my lip to keep from crying out. Marion couldn't lift her arms high enough for her shirt. I helped her, both of us moving slow and careful, like we might break if we weren't gentle.

Sela appeared at exactly 2:00 AM. "Ready?"

We nodded, though ready felt like the wrong word for what we were. Marion gripped my hand as we started walking, both of us swaying but upright, held together by determination, medication, and the desperate need to escape.

"Remember," Sela whispered as she led us toward the door, "walk normal. If anyone sees us, we're going for emergency tests. Standard procedure. You're patients. I'm staff. Nothing unusual."

We passed the nurses' station, where a single staff member sat reading, not even looking up. Down one hallway, then another, each corner a disaster waiting to happen. Any moment could bring security, staff, or someone who'd raise an alarm and drag us back to face consequences that would make our current injuries seem merciful.

But the building felt like it was holding its breath. Like the hospital wanted us to escape.

Sela led us to a maintenance door I'd never noticed, tucked between two patient rooms and marked with a sign: AUTHORIZED PERSONNEL ONLY. She swiped her card, and the lock clicked open with a sound that seemed loud enough to wake the dead.

Beyond was a narrow staircase, plunging into darkness.

"Service tunnel," she whispered, pulling a small flashlight from her pocket. "Stay quiet and stay close. These tunnels connect to every part of the hospital, but it's easy to get lost."

The stairs were steep, and my lower back screamed with each step. The pain was so intense I had to cling to the railing just to stay upright. Marion lowered herself one step at a time, gripping the handrail with both hands, her face twisted with effort. The air grew colder as we descended, thick with moisture and the metallic stench of something foul.

At the bottom stretched a tunnel lined with pipes and electrical conduit, disappearing into darkness in both directions. Emergency lights flickered overhead, casting a sickly yellow glow that turned every shadow into something alive. Water dripped somewhere ahead, each drop echoing like a countdown.

"This way," Sela breathed, guiding us left into the maze.

The tunnel curved and branched, connecting parts of the hospital I'd never imagined. Steam hissed from overhead pipes, filling the air with choking heat. Our footsteps echoed, no matter how carefully we walked, and I tried not to think about what would happen if we got lost down here in the dark.

Then we heard it, footsteps. Behind us. Getting closer.

Sela pushed us between two large pipes, pressing a finger to her lips. We froze, trying to disappear into the shadows, to become part of the infrastructure itself.

The footsteps came closer, now joined by whistling, a cheerful tune that made my skin crawl.

I recognized it.

Tobias rounded the curve, pushing a mop bucket. His face was still swollen from his fight with Isaac, but he was smiling, whistling like he was having the best night of his life. He passed within three feet of us, close enough that I could smell his cologne, mixed with something worse. His eyes flicked to our hiding spot. The smile widened. He kept walking.

We didn't breathe until he was gone, his whistle echoing down the tunnel like a nightmare in retreat.

"Almost there," Sela whispered, pointing ahead to where the tunnel opened into a larger space.

The loading dock was larger than I'd expected, crammed with boxes and medical equipment under the dim emergency lighting. Overhead doors on one side led to the outside world, to freedom, to air that hadn't been breathed by monsters. A regular exit door glowed red beneath an emergency light, our gateway to escape.

So close.

We picked up speed despite the pain, despite the blood soaking through our bandages. Marion stumbled, and I caught her, both of us nearly going down, but Isaac appeared suddenly and steadied us.

"The door." Sela headed for the exit. "Once we're through, we run for Isaac's car. Don't stop for anything. Don't look back."

She reached for the handle, her keycard ready. This was it. Freedom was just on the other side of that door. She swiped once. The light stayed red. Nothing happened. They'd changed the access.

"Shit," she muttered, trying again with more force.

That's when the lights came on. Bright fluorescents flooded the loading dock, making us all squint and shield our eyes after so long in the tunnels' dim gloom.

Tobias stepped out from behind a stack of boxes, that same cheerful smile stretched across his swollen face. Behind him, more orderlies emerged from the shadows where they'd been waiting. Their eyes reflected the harsh light like predators', and I realized with growing horror that this had all been planned.

"Going somewhere?" Tobias asked, sing-song and falsely concerned.

I spun around, hoping the tunnel was still clear, but more orderlies blocked that exit too. We were completely surrounded. Trapped like animals in a cage.

Footsteps echoed from a side passage. Varnar emerged, his white coat pristine despite the grimy loading dock, his warm smile utterly terrifying.

"Did you really think we didn't know?" Varnar asked,

gliding closer with that predatory grace I'd learned to fear. "Every word whispered in the dark. Every plan made in desperate huddles. These walls have been listening for decades. And they tell us everything."

"Run!" Sela shouted, but there was nowhere to go.

They rushed us from both sides in an instant. Isaac fought harder than I'd ever seen anyone fight, caught one orderly in the throat with his elbow, another in the ribs with a wild punch. But there were too many of them, and they were ready for resistance.

I heard the crack before I saw it—Tobias bringing his baton down on Isaac's knee. The sound was wet and wrong, like a branch snapping in a storm. Isaac went down screaming, his leg bending at an angle that made me gag. I knew they'd destroyed something that would never heal right.

"Isaac!" Marion tried to reach him, but two orderlies grabbed her arms, twisting them behind her. When she struggled, one of them backhanded her across her already-damaged face, adding fresh blood to old injuries.

Sela tried to help, but an orderly's boot slammed into her ribs with a sound like kindling snapping. Multiple cracks, not just one rib, but several, breaking like dry twigs beneath a boot. She dropped to her knees, coughing blood onto the concrete.

I fought too, clawing and kicking with everything I had left. Someone grabbed my hair and slammed my head against a concrete pillar. Stars exploded across my vision, my skull ringing like a bell. When my sight cleared, we were all on the ground, our hands zip-tied behind our backs.

"Bring them," Varnar ordered, calm and satisfied. "It's time they understood what this place really is."

The orderlies hauled us to our feet. I'd lost both shoes in the chaos, and the cold floor bit into my bare feet. They half-carried Isaac between two of them. Varnar walked ahead, leading us deeper into the hospital than I'd ever been, past doors marked with symbols I didn't recognize, down stairs that seemed to descend forever into the earth.

The deeper we went, the older everything looked. Modern tile gave way to medieval stone blocks. Each breath tasted of something sweet and rotten that coated my throat.

Finally, we stopped in front of a massive wooden door. Ancient oak, carved with symbols. Varnar produced a key that looked like it was made of yellowed bone, old and polished smooth by countless hands.

The lock clicked with a sound like breaking bones, and the door swung open on hinges that screamed like tortured souls.

"Welcome." Varnar savored it. "To the real St. Dymphna."

Chapter Fifteen

The door opened, and we emerged into a circular chamber that I recognized from my visions. But seeing it in person was different. The altar stood in the center, dark with stains that had seeped so deep they'd become part of the stone. Modern medical equipment sat alongside ancient symbols—IV stands positioned at ritual points, monitors with cables snaking across carved channels, surgical instruments on steel trays next to ceremonial blades.

People were already waiting. Some I recognized as orderlies and staff. Others were strangers in dark robes. But there, near the altar, stood a figure that made my blood freeze.

The old man from my vision. The one who'd helped the young heir after his mother died centuries ago. He should have been dust, but here he stood, beard gray down to his chest, moving carefully towards us.

"Finally." The sound ground like stone. "The gathering is complete."

Dr. Alan stepped forward, pulling off her white coat to reveal a black dress underneath. Not modern black, but something that belonged to another century, with symbols embroidered in thread that seemed to shift when I looked directly at it.

"You've brought them as promised. Our sacrifices." A giggle slipped free.

"As promised," Varnar confirmed. "The guilty one and her protectors. The betrayers who thought they could deny the Judge his due."

They threw us down in the center of the room. The stone was cold and sticky beneath my knees. Isaac tried to push himself up, but his broken leg gave out. Marion curled into herself, sobbing quietly. Sela wheezed through broken ribs.

The orderlies cut our zip ties, then hauled us to our feet and held us in place.

The cultists formed a circle around us. I recognized some faces from my vision, not descendants, but the same people, preserved by whatever bargain the Varnar bloodline had struck on their behalf. They watched us with hungry anticipation.

"Twelve years." Varnar walked over to Sela and grabbed her hair, forcing her to look up at him. "Twelve years you pretended to serve while plotting betrayal. Did you think we were fools?"

Sela spat blood at his feet. "I served the patients. Not your master."

Tobias kicked her in the stomach. She doubled over, gasping.

"Enough," the old man commanded. "Save her consciousness for the offering. The Judge prefers his meals aware."

They beat Isaac next. Breaking his fingers one by one, snap, snap, snap, each one deliberate. His screams echoed off the stone walls until his voice gave out. Marion tried to turn away, but they held her head, made her watch.

"This is what happens to those who defy the Order." Dr. Alan spoke conversationally, like she was giving a lecture. "The beatings are lessons. The screams are teaching moments."

"Enough foreplay." Varnar straightened. "Prepare the altar. It's been too long since the Judge has been fed a guilty one."

They dragged Sela toward the altar, her broken body leaving a trail of blood on the ancient stone. I tried to move forward, but rough hands held me in place.

"No." Confusion cut through my terror. "I'm the guilty one. I killed my husband. I'm the one you want—"

Varnar turned to me with that thin smile. "You thought you were the sacrifice?" He laughed, the sound echoing off the chamber walls. "Oh, Zahra. You're far too valuable for that. No, you're here to watch. To witness what happens to those who betray centuries of Order."

"But the Judge wanting a bride—" The words slipped out before I could stop them.

Varnar went still. His eyes narrowed. "How do you know about that?" He stepped closer.

My mouth went dry. "I... someone mentioned it. Margaret knew about it."

He studied me like a predator deciding if prey was worth the chase. The lie tasted bitter on my tongue.

Dr. Alan checked her antique pocket watch, breaking the tension. "All true. But tonight isn't about feeding the Judge a bride. Tonight is about punishment. About reminding everyone what happens to those who try to help the cattle escape."

They forced Sela onto the altar. Even with her injuries, she fought, weak, broken, but still resisting. Her arms flailed, catching one cultist across the face. Blood ran from his nose, but he just smiled.

"Still fighting," Varnar breathed, admiring. "Good."

Ancient leather straps secured her wrists and ankles. The restraints looked centuries old but held firm, darkened with the blood of countless victims before her.

"The ritual," the old man intoned, moving to stand at the head of the altar. "As it was. As it will be. As it must always be, until the final feeding."

Dr. Alan approached with a curved blade, metal so dark it seemed to swallow light, with veins of red running through it like living tissue. Without ceremony, she grabbed Sela's wrist and sliced deep across her palm.

Blood welled up immediately, far more than such a wound should produce. It ran down Sela's arm in thick streams, but instead of pooling on the altar, it flowed into the carved channels with impossible precision. The blood moved like it was alive, filling each groove until the entire altar glowed with dark red light.

"By blood and binding," Varnar called, the chant taking on a strange resonance. "By guilt acknowledged and pain made manifest. We summon the Executioner. Let him prepare the way for our Lord Judge. Let him open the door between worlds."

The chanting started. All the cultists joined in, speaking words that predated language but somehow made terrible sense in my bones. The sound built and built, echoing off the chamber walls until my skull felt like it might crack.

The blood began to bubble and steam. The stones inside that circle cracked. Something was pushing up from below, something that had been waiting. The temperature spiked until the air warped with heat waves.

A hand emerged first from the boiling blood, massive, scarred, and bare. It gripped the edge of the broken stone and pulled. An arm followed, thick with muscle that moved like steel cables under skin. Then broad shoulders, a chest carved from granite and crisscrossed with old wounds.

The Executioner rose from the blood-filled circle like something being born from the earth itself. Blood ran down his bare torso, following the contours of his chest, dripping from leather pants that clung to his legs. His other hand dragged his blade up with him, that massive thing that looked too heavy for any normal man to lift. His boots struck stone as he fully emerged, each step making the chamber vibrate. That iron helmet gleamed in the torchlight, the red slits already scanning the room.

Marion whimpered beside me. Even some of the cultists stepped back respectfully.

"Finally," Varnar breathed. "He comes to collect, as always. But tonight is special. Tonight we offer not just a sacrifice, but a betrayer. One who walked among us, almost learned our secrets, and tried to deny the Judge his due."

The Executioner moved toward the altar where Sela lay bound. The blade dragged behind him, carving grooves into the ancient stone. He reached the altar and stood over Sela, raising that massive blade high above his head.

Sela's eyes were open, aware, watching death itself prepare to claim her.

I couldn't let this happen. Not to Sela. Not to someone who'd tried to help us.

I broke free from the hands holding me and threw myself

forward. Time seemed to slow as I ran, my bare feet slapping against blood-slick stone. The Executioner's blade had already begun its descent, that terrible arc that would split Sela in half.

I dove between them, my body slamming into the altar, on top of Sela. The blade stopped inches from my back, close enough that I felt the wind of its passage.

Everything stopped.

The chanting cut off mid-word. The bubbling blood went silent. Even the torches seemed to freeze mid-flicker.

The Executioner stood perfectly still, blade suspended in the air. Those infernal slits burned down at me where I lay sprawled across Sela's body, shielding her with my own.

"What are you doing?" Varnar's voice cracked with disbelief. "Move! You're interfering with the ritual!"

I pushed myself up, turning to face the Executioner. My whole body shook, but I spread my arms wide, keeping myself between him and Sela.

"No," I yelled. "She doesn't deserve this. She tried to save us. Take me instead."

The Executioner tilted his head, just slightly. The blade didn't move up or down. It just hung there in perfect suspension. I could feel his attention like physical weight, as if his hellish eyes could see through my flesh to something deeper.

"MOVE!" Varnar roared. "He serves the Judge! He must complete the execution!"

But the Executioner didn't move. Seconds stretched into eternity. The blade began to lower, not to strike, but to rest at his side.

A thing inside the chamber snapped. I felt it under my ribs, sharp as a chain breaking. He had been sent to punish guilt, and I had offered mine freely. The old command had nowhere left to grip.

"No," Varnar shouted. "No, this isn't possible. You cannot refuse! The contract, generations of service—"

The Executioner turned towards Varnar. His posture had shifted. The mechanical purpose of a servant had given way to choice.

"You broke the rules!" Dr. Alan screamed. "The sacrifice must be completed! The Judge must be fed!"

Varnar crossed the chamber in two strides and grabbed Marion by the throat, lifting her off her feet. His other hand found the wounds on her ribs, pressing cruelly into the cuts he'd made earlier.

"Let him complete the ritual," he snarled at me, "or I break her neck."

Marion's wails of agony pierced straight through my soul.

Blood ran between Varnar's fingers where he dug into her ribs. Marion's face went gray. Her eyes rolled back, then focused on me with desperate clarity. She tried to speak but only managed a wet, choking sound. The noise she made wasn't human anymore.

Seeing her so helpless and in pain... my mind went white.

And then I screamed.

It wasn't a normal scream. The scream ripped out of me, dragging years of swallowed rage with it. The sound shook the chamber's foundations. Walls cracked. Dust rained down. The blood pools bubbled and hissed.

Varnar dropped Marion, clutching his ears. She hit the ground gasping. Several cultists fell to their knees, blood running from their noses.

When my scream ended, I was on my knees, and my throat was raw.

The pool where the Executioner had emerged began swirling violently, forming an expanding whirlpool. The floor cracked and the pool grew wider.

"What's happening?" Dr. Alan's composure finally broke.

The pull started gently, then grew stronger. A young cultist slipped on the blood-slick stone and was sucked into the whirlpool. His scream cut off as he vanished. Another tried to run but was dragged backward, fingernails scraping stone before he disappeared.

"Grab the pillars!" Varnar shouted.

The remaining cultists scattered, wrapping themselves around columns. Most held on as their robes whipped in the vortex wind.

I scrambled to free Sela from the altar. The ancient restraints crumbled at my touch. Marion crawled toward us, fighting the suction. Isaac slid across the floor, barely conscious.

Dr. Alan's heels skidded as she fought for a pillar. Tobias had his massive arms wrapped around another column, his face purple with effort.

Marion reached me and wrapped her arms around my waist. I grabbed Isaac with one hand, held Sela with the other. We formed a human chain anchored to the altar.

The Executioner moved through the chaos untouched by the pull. His arms wrapped around me from behind. The moment he touched me, the suction lessened.

"Hold on!" I shouted.

The pool stopped expanding just feet from where we huddled.

Then the ground beneath us vanished.

We plunged through like the blood was a door. Reality folded and twisted. As we fell, I saw Dr. Alan lose her grip above us, tumbling after with a piercing scream. Tobias fell too, his huge frame spinning through the void.

The Executioner cradled my head against his chest while Marion clung to my waist. Isaac and Sela were also protected by his impossible strength. We all tumbled together through space that wasn't space, toward whatever waited below.

Chapter Sixteen

We landed hard on metal that shrieked beneath us, a sound like the building itself was screaming. I was still pressed against the Executioner's chest, his skin burning hot through my clothes. I scrambled off him.

The two cultists who'd been sucked in before us lay twisted at impossible angles nearby. They'd hit the metal grating wrong, spines snapped on impact. Blood seeped from their bodies through the rusted floor, dripping into the darkness below.

Looking around, I realized we were in a place that was almost St. Dymphna, but twisted. Fundamentally, impossibly twisted.

The Executioner stood slowly. Steam curled from his bare chest as he rose to his full height. His scarlet eyes locked on me. I instinctively backed away on my hands and knees, my carved lower back screaming in protest.

"Stay away from me!"

When Marion and the others got their bearings and saw him, terror froze them in place. Marion's scream died in her throat. Isaac tried desperately to crawl away on his shattered leg. Sela just stared up at the massive figure, blood trickling from her mouth.

Then the sirens started.

Loud, piercing wails echoed through the twisted corridors. The Executioner's helmet snapped toward the sound, his massive frame going rigid. For a moment, he stood perfectly still, like he was listening to something we couldn't hear.

Then he vanished. Simply stepped backward into shadows that shouldn't have been deep enough to hide him, and disappeared.

"Where did he go?" Marion whispered, but I was already scanning our surroundings.

The walls weren't stone anymore. They were rust, deep, living rust that breathed and wept thick drops of blood. The ceiling dripped something warm that splattered on the ground with wet smacks. In the distance, those sirens kept wailing, voices that sounded almost human.

We were in the Realm Beneath of the hospital. The place where the Judge kept his throne.

The floor was no longer tile. It was metal grating threaded with pulsing red veins, like exposed arteries. The spot where we'd landed radiated heat, like we were lying atop some massive, sleeping beast.

I pushed myself upright, every movement sending flares of pain through my hip. The carved V throbbed with each breath. Marion was beside me, trembling, her eyes wide with terror.

"What is this place?" she asked.

Before I could answer, more bodies slammed onto the grating behind us. Dr. Alan hit hard, her face smashing into the metal. When she lifted her head, blood streamed from her broken nose.

Good.

Her black dress was torn, her perfect hair hanging in sweaty, tangled clumps. She looked around at the hellscape and something shattered behind her eyes.

"This isn't possible," she breathed, staggering backward from the pulsing walls. "This isn't real."

But it was real. It was very real.

Tobias landed next, rolling to absorb the fall. He got to his feet quickly, his eyes locking on Dr. Alan. "Doc, where the hell are we?"

"How the fuck should I know?" she snapped, her composure cracking. "Look around, you moron. Does this look like anywhere I've ever been?"

The walls weren't just rusted, they were alive. I could see shapes embedded everywhere. Limbs. Faces. Twisted human silhouettes pressed into the surface from within, mouths frozen in silent screams.

One of them turned its head and looked at me.

I scrambled backward, bumping into Marion. She grabbed my arm with ice-cold fingers. "Did you see—"

"Yeah. I saw."

The face in the wall was young. Female. Her eyes wide with terror. Her mouth moved frantically, but no sound came out. Behind her, more faces strained toward us. The walls were full of them.

Dr. Alan saw them too. Her control fractured entirely. "No," she whimpered, backing away faster. "This is a hallucination. A breakdown. This isn't happening."

"Doc, calm down," Tobias reached for her. "We stick together—"

"There is no 'we'!" she screamed. "You're all going to die here, and I'm not dying with you!"

She turned and bolted down the corridor, her heels clattering against the metal grating. Tobias cursed and ran after her, but the corridor stretched, growing longer, the distance between them widening.

"So will you, you bitch!" I shouted after her, but the building swallowed the words.

"Alan! Wait!" Tobias's voice faded as the building absorbed them both, leaving us alone with the faces in the walls, and something massive, breathing in the dark.

Isaac tried to sit up, his face pale and drenched in sweat. "My leg! It hurts so bad!"

I crawled over, palms burning from the hot metal beneath me. The veins on the metal floor pulsed faster, like our presence excited whatever lived here. Isaac's leg was mangled, bent at an impossible angle, shattered.

"We need to get out of here." Sela struggled upright. "The walls are breathing. Can you feel it?"

She was right. I could feel it. A hunger in the air. An intelligence behind the rust and rot. The building was watching us, tasting our fear, savoring our pain.

"Can you walk?" I asked Isaac.

"I can try." But when he put weight on his leg, he collapsed, biting back a scream. "No. I'm not going anywhere."

"Then we carry you." Marion swayed, despite barely standing herself.

I scanned for a way out, and there it was. The door Varnar had brought us through.

"If this place mirrors the hospital, then beyond that door should be stairs," I pointed. "That might be a way up."

We started moving, supporting Isaac between us. Every step felt like dragging ourselves through molasses. The door always seemed just out of reach.

"Move faster!" I gasped.

Finally, we reached the stairwell, its steps made of the same pulsing, breathing metal.

But then, behind us, came that terrible scraping sound again, metal dragging against metal, slow and heavy. Accompanied by the groan of stressed steel under massive weight.

"He's back," Marion whimpered. "The thing in the iron helmet is back."

"Just keep moving," Sela wheezed out.

The stairs ended at a door rimmed with organic growth, veins and tendons that moved like muscle. I shoved it open, and we stumbled through.

We were in the cafeteria. Or what had once been the cafeteria.

Now, the tables and chairs were sculpted from human bone, fused and polished, gleaming white in the hellish light. The serving line displayed organs instead of food: hearts still beating in metal trays, lungs inflating and deflating, brains glistening with thought.

The walls were lined with bodies.

Whole bodies. Arms outstretched. Eyes open. Watching us with eternal agony.

Some wore scrubs, patients. Others were faces I didn't

recognize, perhaps staff members who at some point might have been long reported missing. All alive. All aware. All trapped, unable to move, to speak, to die.

"Jesus Christ," Isaac breathed.

"He's not here," Sela rasped, grim. "No god is here."

Movement caught my eye. One figure was fresher than the rest, still bleeding. Margaret.

I'd seen her cut in half. But here she was, absorbed into the wall, the living structure feeding on her sorrow. Her eyes locked on me, wide and pleading.

Then we heard it, footsteps. Heavy. Coming from another corridor, not the one we'd just used.

Tobias burst into the room, wild-eyed and alone. His clothes were torn, face scratched like he'd run through thorns. When he saw us, relief broke across his features.

I wish he would die, but in a place like this, strength was in numbers.

"Thank God. You guys didn't get too far," he huffed.

"Where's Dr. Alan?" Marion asked.

Tobias shook his head. "Gone. The corridors, they keep changing. I followed her, but suddenly I was somewhere else. The corridors keep changing. They don't want us finding the way out."

He took in the bone furniture, the living wall of bodies. His face turned green. "What happened here? What did this?"

"The Judge." I didn't know how I knew. The knowledge had just... appeared. "This is his domain. His feeding ground."

"The who?" Isaac looked at me, confused.

"Something old," I answered. "Something Varnar and his cult have kept trapped here for centuries. A being that hungers for sacrifices steeped in guilt, sorrow, and pain."

"How do you know this?" Marion asked.

But before I could reply, the scraping returned—metal dragging metal—louder now. Closer.

"Under the table!" I hissed. "Now!"

Chapter Seventeen

We were hiding beneath the bone tables, pressing ourselves flat against the floor. The space was cramped—Isaac's broken leg jutted out at an awkward angle, and Marion was shaking so hard the whole table vibrated above us.

She grabbed my arm, her nails digging in. "Oh God, oh God, he's coming. Zahra, he's—"

"Look at me," I whispered, trying to keep her grounded. "Just look at me."

But her eyes were wild, unfocused. "I can't do this. I can't—"

The Executioner's footsteps entered the cafeteria.

Isaac pressed his hand to control his pain and whimpers. Tobias took in a deep breath, pressing himself so flat against the floor he looked two-dimensional. Even Sela went silent, her eyes wide, fixed on the approaching sounds.

The Executioner moved through the cafeteria. I could see his scarred chest through the gap beneath the table. Marion trembled uncontrollably now.

"Please," she breathed into my hand. "Please don't let him take me. Not like this. Not here."

The footsteps grew closer. I heard him overturning tables, bone furniture crashing to the floor with wet thuds. He was searching methodically, patiently. Like he had all the time in the world.

Then the footsteps stopped, right next to our table.

I could see his boots through the gap. Massive, black leather, splattered with things I didn't want to identify. The blade's tip rested on the floor beside them, still making that low, moaning sound.

"He knows we're here," Sela whispered.

The table creaked above us. Then it lifted, just picked up and tossed aside like it weighed nothing. We were exposed, flattened like insects under a rock.

The Executioner loomed over us, that terrible helmet tilted downward. Steam rose from his bare, scarred chest. The blade hung at his side, the hungry metal singing softly.

"Run!" Isaac screamed.

We scattered like roaches under a light. Isaac tried to crawl on his shattered leg. Sela stumbled toward the exit. Tobias ran for the serving line.

But Marion—Marion was too slow. Too broken. Her injuries made her clumsy. She fell after just a few steps.

The Executioner was on her in seconds. His massive hand closed around her throat, lifting her off the ground like she weighed nothing. Her feet kicked uselessly in the air.

"No!" I screamed, running back toward them.

The blade rose, ready to split her in half.

I threw myself between them without thinking.

"Take me!" The sound tore from my throat. "I know you

want me. You've wanted me for a long time. Here I am. Take me."

The Executioner went perfectly still. The blade froze midswing. His helmet turned slowly toward me.

Marion dropped to the floor, gasping and clutching her throat. "Zahra, no!"

"I know what I am." I stepped closer to the towering figure. "I know why you've been watching me. Following me. Here I am."

He didn't move. Just stood there, studying me. The blade stayed raised, but his grip had shifted, less threatening. More... considering.

"Zahra, get away from him!" Marion screamed.

Isaac was dragging himself toward us. Tobias had stopped running and stared in horror.

But I held my ground. I looked up at that terrible helmet, at the weapon that could end me in one swing.

"Go!" I shouted, never taking my eyes off him. "Run! Now!"

"We're not leaving you!" Marion cried, but Isaac was already grabbing her arm.

"Move!" he gasped through gritted teeth. "She's giving us time!"

Tobias snapped out of it and helped pull Marion. Sela was already limping toward the exit, blood still trickling from her mouth.

"Zahra, please!" Marion's voice cracked as they dragged her away. "Don't do this! Don't sacrifice yourself for us!"

But I stayed. Keeping his attention on me.

His helmet remained fixed on me, those red eyes burning

through the metal slits. The blade was still raised. But he wasn't moving toward the others.

"That's it," I whispered. "Just look at me. I'm what you want."

Behind me, I could hear them struggling toward the exit— Isaac's broken leg dragging, Marion still screaming my name, Tobias and Sela supporting them both.

The Executioner tilted his head slightly, studying me. Then something burst from the wall behind me, a half-rotted corpse, its jaw unhinged, reaching for me with fingers like broken twigs. I hadn't even seen it coming.

The Executioner's blade came down in a blur. Not at me, past me.

Steel cleaved the thing in half.

Black ichor splattered across the floor as the creature collapsed in pieces.

The sight staggered me. The stench of rot and decay filled my nose. I doubled over and vomited everything I had left. Then kept retching until there was nothing but bile. My vision tunneled. The room spun.

The last thing I saw before darkness took me was the Executioner lowering his blade, looking down at me with that burning crimson gaze.

Then I fainted.

Chapter Eighteen

I woke up screaming.

The sound tore from my throat before I could stop it —guttural, inhuman—echoing off surfaces that weren't walls. This wasn't a chamber. This was hell.

Torture devices hung from hooks like Christmas ornaments designed by the devil. Tables with restraints still crusted in dried gore. Implements I couldn't name, but my body recognized instinctively, the way prey understands teeth.

I stumbled back, bare feet sliding on something wet. Fire lanced through my lower back. The carved V Varnar had left in my flesh still burned, angry and infected. I pressed a hand against it through my torn clothes and felt warmth. Fever heat, not healing warmth.

"You're awake," a voice said. Deep and rough, distorted through a helmet, like someone speaking after centuries of silence. It came from everywhere and nowhere, reverberating off metal and bone. I spun until I found him, half-hidden in the shadows.

The Executioner stood beside a table clearly meant for

dismantling people piece by piece. He watched me with a terrible, patient stillness.

The memory crashed back. The cafeteria. Marion screaming my name.

Take me, I'd said, stepping between him and my friends. Let them go.

And he had. He'd dragged me through shadows, through some kind of door, to this place where souls came to be processed.

"Where are they?" The words came out hoarse, cracking. "Marion? Isaac?"

"Gone. As you wished." The words came flat and unreadable behind the helmet.

"Are they safe?" I needed to know. Even asking felt like weakness.

He tilted his head, considering. "Safe is relative. They are not here."

I looked around, at the bloodstained restraints, the chains dangling like dead snakes, the dark puddles I didn't want to name. Not here was probably the best they could hope for.

"And I'm here because...?" The question shrank to nothing.

"You offered yourself." He took a step toward me.

"I offered myself to save them. So kill me and get this over with!" The words slipped out before I could stop them. I braced, waiting for punishment.

But he straightened, not in anger. Recognition. Like I'd said something worth remembering.

I tried to step forward, but pain exploded in my back. Lightning under my skin. I felt the infection creeping. My hand came away from the wound slick with blood.

The Executioner moved. Two strides, and he was on me.

I scrambled back, breath sawing, but there was nowhere to go. Just more metal. More instruments. More horror.

"Stay away from me!"

He didn't stop. I dodged, but my injured leg gave out. I hit the ground hard, jarring my spine. Then his shadow fell over me.

He grabbed the waistband of my scrub pants.

"No!" I kicked at him, clawing wildly. "Please, no, don't—"

He yanked. The fabric shredded like paper. I was left in a tattered scrub top and underwear, exposed, shaking, waiting for him to take what he wanted.

But he didn't.

Instead, he knelt beside me and examined the wound.

The carved V felt worse than I'd imagined when air hit it. And now I could smell it, the sweet, rotting scent of infection.

"You were there," I whispered, rage and fever fusing. "When Varnar did this. I saw you watching."

He said nothing.

"You liked it," I spat. "Watching them torture me. Carve his fucking initial into my back like I was livestock."

Still silence.

Then he reached for a tool, a thin rod, glowing white-hot at the tip.

"This will hurt."

"Good," I hissed. "Maybe you'll finally get off on my pain instead of just watching—"

He pressed the rod to the wound.

I screamed. The sound bounced off the walls, came back warped, like I was hearing my own death from outside my body. My back arched off the ground as agony ripped through me, pure and incandescent.

When it was over, the wound was sealed, burned shut, but clean. No more infection. Just a scar that would never let me forget.

I lay on the cold metal floor, drenched in sweat and tears, my body trembling from pain and exhaustion.

He set the rod aside and looked down at me. I stared up, lips parted, throat raw.

"You disgust me."

"Then why heal me?"

"Because no one else will." He stood at rigid attention, unmoved.

"That's not mercy."

"No," he agreed. "It's control."

My teeth locked together. Anger simmered beneath the pain. "You think you own me now?"

"I know I do." The certainty made my skin crawl.

I let out a bitter laugh. It scraped my throat raw. "We'll see about that."

He moved to a shelf and retrieved a rusted tin, peeling it open with surprising care. Inside was meat, gray and slick, gleaming with its own juices. Army rations? Or something older?

He held it out to me.

I turned away, bile rising.

A low sound rumbled in his chest, not quite a growl. Something deeper. Older. "Eat." No room left for argument.

I took the tin with shaking hands and forced myself to swallow. The meat was salty, tough, but it filled an emptiness I hadn't known was there. Water followed, clearing the metallic taste from my mouth. I drank slowly, feeling the trembling in my hands begin to fade.

Then, without warning, he reached for what remained of my torn clothing, and simply ripped it away. The last scraps that had clung to my body were gone. I was naked. Fully exposed on the cold metal.

He soaked a cloth in something that smelled of herbs and antiseptic, then began to wash me with the same care he'd shown while cauterizing my wounds.

Arms first. Then my breasts, my belly, between my legs. Not slow. Not rough. Just thorough. Like I was a weapon being cleaned after battle.

I turned my face to the wall, shame burning hotter than the cauterizing rod had. This was worse than pain. This complete exposure, this clinical intimacy, felt more invasive than anything Varnar had done.

"Why?" I breathed the question.

He continued washing the insides of my thighs, the cloth warm and careful against sensitive skin. He didn't answer immediately.

"Why not just kill me?" I pressed.

"Dirty," he groaned, as if that explained everything.

Rage writhed inside me, desperate to escape. The casual dismissal. The way he handled me like I was just another tool to be maintained. I kicked him, driving my heel into his chest with what little strength I had left.

He didn't budge. Might as well have kicked a mountain. He just caught my ankle in one massive hand and pulled me back toward him.

My legs spread involuntarily as I slid across the metal, breath catching in my throat. He stepped between them, his presence filling the space like heat from an opened furnace.

He knelt slowly, never breaking that burning gaze from behind his mask. The heat between us crackled, dense, electric, charged with something ancient and unspeakable. His hands settled on my thighs, vast, callused things, and pried me open without struggle. My breath hitched.

Then he stopped.

Just stopped.

He could have forced me. He could have taken anything he wanted from me, and there was nothing in this room strong enough to stop him.

But he waited.

That waiting did something worse than fear. It put the choice back in my hands.

I shook when I spoke. "This part is mine."

His hands went still on my thighs.

"Mine." I said it again, stronger this time. "Touch me because I choose it. Because I asked. Because he made my body betray me, and I need one thing that belongs to me."

The red slits burned brighter.

"Make it mine again."

My nipples ached, tight and flushed. The air stung where it touched them. I bit my lip, hard, anything to keep my focus. But my eyes locked on the movement of his hands as they bracketed my hips. I should've screamed. I should've fought. But my body was ahead of me, rising, tilting toward him.

He didn't speak. Just lowered his head and pressed one thick finger into me, slow and deep.

My lips parted on a gasp. He watched the whole time. Watched me stretch around him.

Then another finger, pushing past the first, curling.

The sensation sliced through me: shock, then heat. I writhed, my heels scrabbling uselessly against the slick metal. His thumb settled against my clit.

The pressure was excruciating. Gentle. Insistent. The way he circled it made my spine shudder. The pads of his fingers found a rhythm inside me, and I couldn't hold back the sounds that came out of me.

A low moan broke from my throat. I arched into him, panting. My hips moved before shame could stop them. My thighs clenched around his wrists. He twisted his fingers slightly, a flick of precision. My eyes rolled back. My mouth opened, but no sound came. Only breath. Only heat.

I was drenched. Burning. Every flick of his thumb against my clit sent shockwaves through me. And his fingers—oh god, his fingers—worked with terrifying grace, stroking places no one had ever touched. Not like this.

I gripped the floor with both hands, nails scraping metal. The pressure built, unbearable, exquisite. My moans turned to sobs. My skin felt too tight. My heartbeat thundered in my ears.

When the climax hit, it tore through me like wildfire consuming everything in its path. The sound that escaped my throat wasn't human. It was something primal. Desperate. My thighs clamped around his hand. My nails scraped the metal. And for a moment that stretched into eternity, I forgot everything except the pleasure that shattered me completely.

He pulled away slowly, fingers glistening with my release. He raised his hand beneath his helmet. I heard the faint rasp of breath, then the unmistakable sound of him licking his fingers clean.

One by one.

Savoring.

Then he draped a black cloth across my chest, covering me with something that felt almost like tenderness.

He lifted me, carrying me to what served as his resting place, a raised platform of welded metal and leather. But it was only as he laid me down, as the leather embraced my used body with sickening warmth, that the full weight of it crashed over me.

What I had asked for. What I had wanted. What that wanting meant.

I rolled onto my stomach, turned my face to the side, and let the tears run.

Chapter Nineteen

The salt from my tears had dried into crusty tracks down my cheeks when I finally opened my eyes again.

How long had I been crying? Hours? Days?

Time had no teeth down here, where torchlight never changed and shadows never moved.

The leather beneath my cheek felt wrong. Too soft in some places, too rough in others.

Suddenly, I realized it wasn't leather.

No… it was human skin, stitched together with black thread thick as fishing line. I could feel the raised edges where different pieces met: a birthmark here, dark and round as a quarter; the puckered ridge of an old scar there, maybe from surgery or violence. The faded blue of a tattoo that had once meant something, to someone who was now furniture.

"You skinned them." The words came out flat. Empty. Like my soul had finally given up trying to feel shocked by anything he did. I rolled off the bed and hit metal. My knees cracked against the floor and I vomited.

My hands shook as I wiped my mouth with the back of my wrist, leaving streaks of spit and blood across my skin.

The bed loomed behind me like an accusation. I could see it clearly now in the flickering torchlight: patches of skin in different shades, from pale white to deep brown and everything in between. A patchwork quilt of human beings reduced to their most basic components.

Someone's grandmother. Someone's child. Someone's lover.

"And I came for you." The words trembled.

He stood in the doorway, watching me retch. Steam curled from the seams of his helmet, and the great blade rested against his shoulder like it weighed nothing at all. "They were already dead."

There was no emotion in it, no justification. Just fact, delivered in that low rumble that seemed to come from somewhere deeper than his chest.

"They had names." I screamed.

I stayed on my knees, staring at the bed. At the stitchwork. At the way someone's hand had been preserved and stretched to form a corner.

The fingers were curled slightly, like they'd died reaching for something.

"They had families. Dreams. Fears. They probably begged you not to kill them."

"They were sinners."

I looked up at him, this towering figure of judgment and steel. "Aren't we all? Aren't you?"

He tilted his head. The red glow behind his eye slits showed something that might have been curiosity. Or hunger.

With him, I couldn't tell the difference.

"What was their sin?" I asked. "What did they do that was so terrible you turned them into furniture?"

Silence.

"Tell me," I insisted. "Tell me what they did that was worse than murder. Worse than torture. Worse than whatever you are."

More silence followed.

He shifted his weight, and the blade scraped against metal, sending sparks dancing across the floor.

"You don't know, do you?" The realization hit me like cold water. "You just killed them because you could. Because someone told you to. Because it felt good."

Still nothing. But something in his posture changed, a tension that hadn't been there before.

"I apologize." The words spilled out before I could stop them. I pressed my forehead to the cold metal and spoke to the dead whose skin surrounded us. "I'm sorry I let him touch me after he killed you. I'm sorry I came on his fingers while you're nothing but furniture now. I'm sorry I'm still breathing when you're not."

My words echoed off the walls and came back twisted. Distorted.

"I'm sorry he made you into this." I reached out and touched the edge of the bed, running my fingers along some-one's arm that had been stretched and tanned and stitched into place. "I'm sorry no one remembers your name."

Tears hit the floor and hissed against the heated metal.

My shoulders shook with sobs that felt like they were being ripped from somewhere deeper than my lungs.

Somewhere in the place where shame lived and fed and grew fat on every choice I'd ever made.

"I'm sorry," I whispered again.

To them.

To Marion.

To everyone who'd ever believed I was worth saving.

Memories flooded back like water through a broken dam.

The way I'd responded to him. The sounds I'd made. The way my body had arched against his touch while the screams of his victims still echoed in these walls.

How could I live with that? How could anyone?

The worst part wasn't even the physical response, bodies did things without permission all the time.

The worst part was how I'd felt in those moments with the Executioner.

Wanted. Desired. Chosen.

Varnar had made my body respond too, forcing sensation until I came, wanting to own my shame. That orgasm had tasted like self-hatred.

But the Executioner's touch was different. He didn't touch me to humiliate or control. He touched me like I was something precious, dangerous and perfect in my damage.

And unlike with Varnar, when my body responded, I'd wanted it. Craved it. I'd felt desired by someone.

That didn't make it clean.

It made it mine, and that was the part I couldn't forgive.

And that someone was a monster who turned people into furniture.

I crawled across the floor until I found what I was looking for: jagged shards of metal.

I picked up the sharpest one and drew it across my palm, watching blood well in the cut.

The pain was clean. Simple. For a moment, I controlled something.

Heat surrounded my hand before I could cut deeper.

His fingers closed over mine, burning the wound shut before I could choose to bleed.

Even that small agency was stolen from me. "Let me bleed. Let me choose something. Anything."

He released my hand and stepped back.

The wound was sealed, leaving only a thin white scar to mark where I'd tried to take control of my own suffering.

"I need to die." Steady. Calm.

Like I was asking for a glass of water instead of begging for oblivion.

"Kill me. Please."

Theo's words echoed in my head. All the cruel things he'd said about my body, my worth, my broken places. But he'd been wrong about so much. Wrong about me being worthless because I couldn't give him children. Wrong about me being ugly because I wasn't thin. Wrong about me being weak because I took his abuse.

This was different. This was true.

I was exactly as worthless as I felt.

"You were right." I addressed the empty air where Theo's ghost sometimes appeared.

"About everything.

I am disgusting. I am broken. I am exactly the kind of woman who would spread her legs for a monster."

The Executioner made a sound that might have been disagreement.

Or maybe just steam escaping from his metal helmet.

Marion had gotten hurt protecting me, believing I was

worth something. What would she think if she could see me now? She'd sacrificed herself for a woman who wasn't worth saving. Who wasn't worth the pain she'd endured. Marion had seen something in me that didn't exist. Hope where there was only emptiness. Strength where there was only weakness.

I crawled toward him on hands and knees across the metal floor. The rough surface scraped my palms raw, but the pain felt clean compared to everything else.

"Everyone thinks I'm worth saving." I pulled my knees tighter. "But they don't know what I am."

He stood motionless as I approached, then stepped back when I reached for him from my place on the ground.

The rejection sent fresh shame spiraling through my chest. But I followed him anyway, still on my knees.

When I caught up, I grabbed onto his leg and pressed my face against the leather covering his calf.

"I came for you. You turn people into furniture, and I came on your fingers." My words were muffled against him, but I knew he heard. Felt the way his body went still. His hand came down and touched my hair. Gently. Like I was something fragile.

But I grabbed his hand and pulled it down to my throat, wrapping his fingers around my neck.

They circled it completely, thumb and pinkie overlapping.

"Do it," I whispered. "End it. I can't live being this."

His grip didn't tighten. Just held.

The pressure was there but not painful.

"There's a difference between surviving and choosing." I forced myself to look at him. "Between enduring and embracing. Varnar forced me to come, and I survived it. You touched me, and I chose it. That's so much worse."

I stood up on shaky legs from where I'd been at his feet. The Executioner remained standing, towering over me. The world tilted. I started to fall. He caught me before I hit the floor.

In one smooth motion, he lowered himself to sit on the ground and pulled me down with him. I ended up in his lap, facing him, straddling his thighs, my chest pressed against his.

His hand stayed at my throat, not squeezing, just holding. His other arm wrapped around my waist, anchoring me in place.

"The worst part"—I turned toward the darkness—"is that part of me would probably let you do it again."

Even now, drowning in self-loathing, I could still feel his hands on me. The way he'd touched me like I was something precious instead of broken. The way I'd felt beautiful, after so many years.

"I hate myself for wanting it," I whispered. "I hate myself for liking it. I hate myself for thinking about it even now."

His chest rose and fell beneath me, rhythmic. Like breathing, though I wasn't sure he needed to breathe.

"I'm supposed to be the victim here." I laughed, and it came out ugly. "The innocent one. The one worth saving. But victims don't beg for more. Victims don't come on their torturer's fingers and ask for it again."

The hand at my throat moved. Just slightly. Thumb brushing along my pulse point.

"Kill me," I begged again. Softer now, as if I was praying. "I can't live being this. I can't live knowing what I am."

His arms came around me properly then, and I felt smaller than I had since I was a child. Safe in a way that made no sense. Protected by the thing that should destroy me. "Please,"

I whispered against his chest. "I'm begging you. End it. Let me die before I become something worse."

But he just held me. Let me cry until there was nothing left. Until my throat was raw and my chest ached and the tears stopped coming. He held me through all of it.

Silent and steady as a mountain.

I thought about Theo. About how he'd held me sometimes after the worst beatings. How he'd stroke my hair and tell me he was sorry, that he loved me, that he'd never do it again.

But this was different. The Executioner wasn't apologizing or making promises. He was just there.

"I used to think I was good," I whispered when the crying finally stopped. "Not perfect, but good. Someone who tried to do right. Someone who helped others. Someone worth saving."

My fingers landed on his bare chest, covered in scars, and I traced the raised marks.

"But good people don't come undone the way I did with you." The words broke. "Good people don't crave darkness. Good people don't choose the monster over salvation."

He shifted beneath me, and I could feel the heat radiating from his bare skin. It should have burned. Instead, it felt like the warmth of a fireplace on a cold night.

"Maybe I was never good." The words tasted like ash. "Maybe I was always this thing wearing a good person's face. Maybe Theo saw it in me from the beginning. Maybe that's why he knew he could hurt me and I'd take it."

The Executioner made a sound deep in his chest. Not quite a growl. Not quite a purr.

Half comfort, half warning.

"Say something," I begged. "Tell me I'm wrong. Tell me

I'm not the monster I think I am. Or tell me I am and put me out of my misery."

But he remained silent. Just held me in the flickering torchlight while shadows danced across the walls, and the bed of human skin watched us with dead eyes.

"Sleep," he rumbled at last. The words rumbled through his chest and into my bones. "You burn too pretty to snuff out now, *my moth*."

I closed my eyes and let unconsciousness take me. But even as I fell into darkness, I knew I would wake up unchanged. Still alive when I deserved to be nothing but memory and regret.

The last thing I felt before sleep claimed me was his hand in my hair, stroking gently. Like I was something precious instead of something damned. Like he saw something in me worth preserving—Even if I couldn't see it myself.

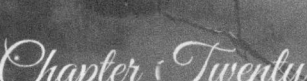

Chapter Twenty

I paced the chamber in restless circles, my bare feet slapping against the stone. Back and forth, back and forth. The black sheet he had given me was wrapped around me like a towel, tucked tightly under my arms.

He'd been gone for hours. Again. Every day, if days existed here, followed the same pattern. He'd bring food and water, watch me eat, then touch me until I came apart in his hands. Then he'd vanish, like that would be enough to sustain me until next time. Three days? Five? A week? I'd lost count.

"Do not leave this chamber until I return." Always the same command.

The food kept my body alive, but my mind was starting to crack. Nothing but stone walls and silence between his visits. Nothing but the memory of his hands and what I was becoming pressed in on me.

The walls felt closer each time he left. The chamber smaller. I was going mad in this box, with only his visits to mark time. I was losing myself in here. Or maybe finding what I really was. I couldn't tell anymore.

"Fuck it," I muttered, stopping in front of the door.

The iron handle was cold beneath my palm. I expected it to be locked, expected some mystical barrier to keep me trapped. But it turned easily. The door groaned open on hinges that sounded like screaming.

Outside, I saw... sunlight.

Actual, impossible sunlight streamed down the corridor beyond. Not the red glow of torches. Not the sickly green of emergency lighting. Sunlight. Golden and warm, filtering through windows I remembered from my first days at St. Dymphna.

I stepped out cautiously, adjusting the sheet to keep it secured around my body. The hallway looked exactly like the hospital I remembered, but corrupted. The walls were decaying, and they thumped like they were alive.

My footsteps echoed as I walked, past doors I recognized. The solitary cells. The medical wing. The rec room where Marion used to go manic. Everything was as it should be, yet smothered in dust and silence that felt... deliberate.

"Hello?" I called out, the sound bouncing off stone and coming back hollow. "Is anyone here?"

Nothing.

I moved faster, checking room after room. Empty beds with stripped mattresses. Abandoned wheelchairs pushed against the walls. Personal belongings scattered across the floors, like everyone had vanished mid-conversation. Near the elevator, a maintenance cart leaned crooked against the wall, but these weren't normal tools. A bone saw. Scalpels. Pliers crusted with old blood. A drill that looked made for teeth. A heavy wrench, the kind that could crush a skull. Surgical tools... or torture instruments.

And everywhere I looked, the dust patterns were uneven. Thick in some places, completely absent in others. Like someone had tried to stage abandonment.

Hope bloomed in my chest. Maybe this was all a nightmare. Maybe I'd been drugged the entire time. Maybe I'd finally woken up.

I ran, legs burning, lungs screaming for air. The exit door appeared ahead, unmarked metal that had never looked so beautiful. I sprinted, the sheet billowing behind me. My hand closed on the push bar, and I shoved with everything I had.

The door swung open, and hell vomited in my face.

The world beyond wasn't Earth. Twisted spires of blackened bone jutted from ground that vibrated like infected flesh. Overhead, a sun burned that wasn't really a sun. A swollen red thing that gave off heat without warmth, light without hope. Ash fell like snow from clouds that moved against winds that blew from nowhere.

And standing in the wasteland, waiting for me, were three of them.

Things that might have once been human stepped closer, their faces blurred and waterlogged, like reflections in a dirty pond. Features shifted constantly. A nose where an eye should be. A mouth opening sideways across a cheek. Patient gowns clung to their rotting frames, the fabric fused into skin that looked like it had been boiled, then left to cool.

They turned toward me in perfect unison, movements too synchronized to be natural. "Why is she alive?" the first one gurgled, black water spilling from what used to be lips.

"Is she separated from the others? Maybe she can lead us to wherever they're hiding," the second one rasped, its head tilting at an impossible angle.

"She smells like hope," the third whispered. And the way it said hope made my skin crawl, like it was something diseased.

My chest tightened with something I hadn't felt in what felt like forever. Isaac. Marion. Sela. If these things were talking about others, about people hiding, then maybe... maybe they were still alive somewhere. I didn't give a damn about Dr. Alan or Tobias. Let them rot in whatever hole this place had swallowed them into. But the others...

"Where are they?" I spit the words before I could stop myself. "Where did you last see the others?"

Their waterlogged faces twisted into grotesque, leering smiles.

"Oh, you want to know," the first gurgled, stepped forward on legs that bent wrong at the knees.

They advanced, wet gowns dragging with a sound like tearing skin. I backed away, fumbling for the door behind me with shaking fingers.

"We think you know where they are," the second whispered, its face shifting with each word. "The Judge wants them. The Judge wants you."

"Oh, he wants to see you all scream!" the third one crooned.

My back hit the door. I scrabbled for the handle, panic rising like bile in my throat. The metal was ice-cold, but it turned. I yanked the door open and threw myself inside, slamming it shut behind me.

"Let us in. Let us make our report," one called through the door.

"The Judge is waiting for news," another added.

The door shuddered behind me. They were trying to force it open. I threw all my weight against it, bracing with everything I had. For once, being heavy was an advantage. I planted my feet and leaned hard, becoming a human barricade.

I looked around, wild with desperation. There had to be something, some kind of weapon, some way to fight. My eyes landed on a metal rod, bent and rusted, that looked like it had once held an IV bag.

The door shuddered again, harder this time. My strength was failing, sweat making my grip slip on the handle.

I made a choice.

I lunged for the rod and grabbed it just as the door burst open. I hefted it in both hands. It was heavier than it looked, solid steel with a sharp point at one end. When they came through, I was ready.

The first creature stumbled in, its ruined face splitting into a grin. "Found you," it gurgled. "Found the wandering—"

I drove the rod through its chest with every ounce of strength I had. Black fluid erupted from the wound, spraying across my face and arms. The creature looked down at the metal jutting from its body with genuine surprise.

"Interesting," it wheezed.

Then it crumpled.

The others surged forward, but the narrow doorway bottle-necked them. I swung the rod with all my strength, catching the second one across the temple. Its head caved in with a wet crunch, and it dropped without a sound.

The third one slipped past my guard. Its waterlogged fingers closed around my throat. I gagged on the stench of stagnant water and rot, but managed to drive my knee into what I hoped was its groin. It doubled over, and I brought the rod down hard on the back of its skull.

For a moment, I stood there gasping, covered in black

fluid. Outside, the wasteland beyond stretched endlessly in all directions, empty now, but somehow more threatening in its silence.

That's when the sirens started.

Air raid sirens, like the ones they tested in tornado country. But these were wrong, distorted, playing at frequencies that made my teeth ache and my vision blur. The sound came from everywhere at once. The sky, the ground, inside my own skull.

I slammed the door shut and leaned against it, shaking. The sirens continued, muffled now but still audible through the walls. I'd triggered something. An alarm. A warning.

And now they were coming for me.

I needed to get back to the Executioner's chamber, back to safety, such as it was. But which way? The corridors all looked different now. Older. Darker. Like the false sunlight had been just another lie.

I chose a direction and ran. My bare feet were silent on floors that had changed from linoleum to something that felt like raw meat, bloody and pulsing. The sheet had come completely loose. I clutched it against my chest, trying to stay covered as I moved.

Behind me, the sirens wailed their impossible song.

I turned a corner and stopped cold.

She stood at the end of the hallway, perfectly still in a way that made me shiver with dread. Average height, unremarkable build. But something about her posture was wrong. Too straight. Too symmetrical. Like someone pretending to be human and almost getting it right.

Then she started walking toward me. Each step was identical. Exact length, exact speed. Mechanical. Inhuman.

When she got close enough, I saw her face.

Or where her face should have been.

Her jaw was shattered, broken into a crown of mirror shards that reflected my own terrified expression back at me in a dozen fractured pieces. Above that, smooth skin stretched where her eyes and nose should've been.

"Oh, here you are. The Judge wants you so bad," she cooed in my voice.

How was that even possible?

"Who... what are you?" I asked.

She tilted her head, mirror shards catching light from nowhere.

"Helena Wolfe. Though names matter less here than what we become." Her voice was still mine, but hearing it from her mouth made my skin crawl.

Helena Wolfe.

The name clicked. Dr. Alan. Varnar. They'd mentioned her in that hellish session.

Her jaw cracked as she rearranged it into something resembling a smile.

"But I couldn't stand sharing him. Those other girls he'd bring into his office, the way he'd touch them, focus on them... That attention was supposed to be mine."

The air around her shimmered like heat.

"So I started collecting them. Their faces, to be precise." She dragged her fingers along her cheek, where someone else's skin hung loose. "I'd wear their faces when I visited him. He liked the variety, you see. Different girls, different screams, but always me underneath."

She laughed, and somewhere in her throat, glass tinkled.

"Eventually he got bored and fed me to this place. But you know what? I like it here. Down here, I'm every face that matters."

Her head tilted at an impossible angle. "I got word he likes you too." She giggled and raised a shard of mirror. "Why don't you give me your face? I wanna try it on."

She was insane. Completely, utterly mad.

I had to run.

I feinted left, then dove right, trying to get past her to the stairwell, but she was already there, blocking my path with unnatural speed.

"You think the Executioner cares about you?" My own laughter echoed from her ruined mouth. "You think you're special? He's just intrigued. Eventually he has to give you to the Judge. That's his job. His duty. His purpose. Don't think you're so special he'll stray."

She circled me, murmuring in Latin: "Dolor purificat. Sanguis mundus facit."

Those words. I had heard the cultist saying those words.

Pain purifies. Blood makes clean.

The ancient motto of this cursed place.

Her claws slashed across my shoulder, mirror shards extending from her fingertips. The pain was immediate and blinding, three deep gouges that burned like acid. Blood ran hot down my arm, dripping off my elbow. I spun and kicked. My bare heel slammed into her knee. The joint gave way with a wet pop. She stumbled, screaming through the ruin of her face as her leg bent sideways. A shard fell from her hand, clattering against stone.

I stepped back and accidentally landed on it. The glass bit into my heel, sharp enough to make me gasp.

"Fuck!" I dropped to one knee, more from the shock than the cut. I grabbed the shard and yanked it free, tossing it aside. A thin line of blood welled up, but nothing compared to my shoulder. Still, I forced myself upright and ran. I had to.

"You can't run forever," she cooed in my voice. "I know everything about you, Zahra. Every secret you've hidden. Every nightmare that haunts you. Every moment you wish you could forget."

But she was wrong about that.

She could mimic my voice. Reflect my image. But she couldn't read my mind.

If she could, she'd know I wasn't trying to run anymore.

I was leading her.

Toward the maintenance cart I'd seen earlier, abandoned near the elevator bank. The one with the scattered tools. I had seen some pliers, and a heavy wrench.

"You know what your worst fear is?" she asked, circling. "It's not him. It's not this place. It's that you like it here. That you've found exactly where you belong."

"Stop!" I screamed, and the walls shook.

She looked around, delighted. "Venit Sponsa Doloris." She grinned. "The Bride of Sorrows comes."

"I must get you to the Judge," she announced.

She lunged, fast, stuttering like broken film.

I dove sideways, rolled across the floor. Her mirror claws slashed the wall where my head had been.

My hand closed around the wrench just as her weight crashed down on me.

We rolled, a tangle of limbs and glass. She was stronger than she looked, but I had leverage, and desperation. I slammed the wrench into her chest.

Glass exploded, each shard reflecting a different version of my terrified face.

She screamed, not in my voice this time, but in something inhuman and broken. "You… Can't kill me!"

I struck her skull next. More glass shattered, and her voice vanished mid-sentence. She kept moving, dragging the top half of her torso toward me with broken fingers, but the mimicry was failing.

The temperature in the hallway spiked suddenly.

I knew he was coming before I saw him.

The Executioner stepped through the wall itself, blade in hand. But he didn't strike. He watched as I raised the wrench again.

"Finish it." The order rolled through the hall.

I crushed what remained of her mirror-shard skull with one final blow. The fragments scattered across the floor, each one reflecting nothing but darkness before going completely black.

I stood there, breathing hard, staring at what I'd done. The body the Mirror Eater wore was finally gone. After everything she'd put me through, every stolen word, every twisted reflection, it was over. A grim satisfaction settled in my chest as I dropped the wrench. It hit the floor with a heavy clang.

The Executioner knelt and began gathering the shards, every piece, into a pile. His red eyes caught sight of the bloody shard across the room, the one I'd pulled from my foot. He crossed to it, picked it up, and followed the blood trail back to my injured heel. He added that piece to the pile.

Then he pulled a small vial from his belt and poured something over the gathered shards. Liquid fire that hissed and steamed as it touched the glass. Within seconds, nothing remained but a dark stain. The body was gone, but somewhere deeper in the realm, I could still feel her, a fractured presence, stripped of form, waiting.

"Why?" I asked, clutching the sheet to my bleeding shoulder, standing on one foot.

"So the Judge doesn't know one of his loyal ones is gone," he replied, focused on his work.

Then he turned to me, and I felt his attention settle like weight on my skin.

"Sit," he commanded.

The command came before I could speak.

I dropped onto the nearest surface, an overturned crate, still clutching the sheet around me. My shoulder and foot throbbed with pain.

He knelt in front of me without ceremony, massive hands surprisingly gentle as he lifted my injured foot. Blood seeped between my toes, mixing with the grime on the floor.

He stood and pulled a torch from a wall sconce. The wrench still lay where I'd dropped it. He held the metal head in the flame until it glowed orange, then red.

"No—" I tried to pull back. I knew what was coming.

His grip tightened, not painful, just absolute.

"Be still," he commanded.

The hot metal touched my flesh.

The smell hit first, burning meat. My meat. Then pain screamed through every nerve. I thrashed, couldn't help it, but his hold never wavered. My scream built in my throat and he shifted, offering his free hand.

I bit down, hard. My teeth sank deep into his palm. He didn't flinch. Just held steady as he pressed the burning metal to each gash.

Tears streamed down my face. Snot ran freely. Still, I kept biting, white pain swallowing the edges of my vision.

"Done," he announced.

He pulled the wrench away.

I released his hand, gasping. Deep tooth marks showed dark against his skin, already healing too fast to be natural.

He set my foot down gently and turned to my shoulder, pulling the sheet aside without asking.

"This one's deep," he observed, examining the wound. He grabbed gauze from the nearby medical cart and worked quickly, wrapping the injury with quiet efficiency.

"Not here," he added. "It needs to be looked at properly."

"Why... Why did you come for me?" I asked, watching him.

"Why did you leave the chamber?" he countered, not looking up.

"Because I was bored!" The words came out sharper than I intended.

"In your boredom, you killed Mawkeepers," he stated. No judgment, just fact.

So that's what those fuckers were called.

I nodded. "Yeah. I did."

"You killed a Sanctified. You triggered the alarm," he continued.

"I didn't know there were rules—"

"There are always rules." He stayed on one knee before me, the heat from his body warping the air. "You learned three important things today. One: this place has layers. Some are more dangerous than others. Two: the Sanctified can be killed, but it requires commitment."

I forced the words out. "The Mirror Eater. What was she?"

"One of the Judge's favorites. The Sanctified." He tilted his helmet slightly. "The Sanctifieds are not victims. Not cursed. Monsters, true monsters who fed on suffering. The Judge perfects them. Gives their cruelty purpose."

"Are there more?"

"Yes," he confirmed. "They don't stay dead. The Judge brings them back... unless someone with real authority ends them."

My throat went dry. "And the third rule?"

"The third rule is that I will always find you," he stated simply.

"How?" The word cracked. "How did you know I was in danger?"

"Because I never left," he revealed.

It hit me like a punch.

I froze completely. "What?"

"I was watching. Testing. Waiting to see what you'd do when you thought you were free," he explained.

He said it so simply. Like he was describing the weather. The rage hit fast, hot and blinding. "You son of a bitch." My words shook. "You let me fight them alone. You let me get hurt."

"Yes," he acknowledged.

Just that. No apology. No excuse.

"Why?" The word broke on my tongue.

"Because you needed to know you could survive without me," he explained. "And I needed to know if you would come back. Will you? Or do you want to explore this place alone?"

I shook my head quickly. The thought of wandering these corridors alone, facing more of those things without him, made me shiver. I'd do anything but roam alone. I needed him, and we both knew it.

Then, without warning, he shifted back onto his heels and in one fluid motion, lifted me off the crate. My weight didn't slow him. Before I could protest, he hoisted me over his shoulder like a sack of grain, yet somehow with care. He angled me so my injured side faced outward, my stomach resting along the broad line of his shoulder blade.

His hand steadied me at the small of my back as he stood in one smooth movement. All nearly two hundred pounds of me. The floor fell away beneath my feet, my head hanging down his back, blood rushing to my face.

The muscles beneath his scarred skin didn't even flex.

He adjusted his grip once, ensuring my wounded foot hung free, then began walking. Calm, deliberate, like carrying grown women over his shoulder was routine.

I should have fought. Should have screamed. But I didn't. This was better than walking on a ruined foot.

As we moved through the hallway, something gnawed at me.

"What did she mean?" I asked, voice muffled against his back. "Why did she call me Bride of Sorrows?"

He went silent.

Only the sound of his footsteps echoed in the dark.

"Tell me," I demanded, gripping his shoulder tighter.

"The Judge wants a bride," he revealed finally. "Perhaps she thought it was you."

My whole body tensed against him. "No." It came out a whisper, then louder: "No, no, no—"

I thrashed on his shoulder, trying to get free. "I won't, I can't, not him—"

His grip tightened. "Stop moving," he commanded.

"The Judge can't have me! I won't be his—"

"He won't take you," he growled, voice low and fierce. "Not while I draw breath. Not while I still stand. I swear it."

I forced myself to go still, though my heart hammered in my chest. Fear and fury churned together. "I still hate you," I muttered.

"I know," he replied, and kept walking.

Chapter Twenty-One

He carried me through corridors I didn't recognize, past doors older than the hospital, down staircases that shouldn't have existed. Finally, he stopped in front of a door marked with symbols I couldn't read.

The smell hit me first when he pushed it open, like a butcher shop on the hottest day of summer. Then I saw what hung from the ceiling.

Bodies. Dozens of them, suspended by hooks through their shoulders. Some were fresh, still dripping. Others had been there long enough to change, skin gone waxy, features frozen in expressions of eternal suffering. This was his workshop.

But they weren't corpses. At least not all of them. As we passed beneath them, I heard whispers. Soft pleas for mercy. For water. For death. Eyes tracked our movements, some still flickering with sparks of consciousness.

"They're still alive," I whispered. "Why not just kill them?"

"Death would be mercy. Mercy is not mine to give," he answered.

Tables lined the walls, cluttered with tools I didn't want to name. Blades, clamps, and devices with too many moving parts. Everything was stained dark with old blood. Steam rose from drains in the floor.

In the center of the room stood a massive table made of compressed bone. Its surface was blotched with stains that told stories I never wanted to hear.

"I want to go back." Panic clawed up my throat.

"Back where? To the chamber you couldn't wait to leave?" He set me down near the bone table. I pulled the black sheet tighter around myself.

"You brought me here to threaten me," I stated. "To show me what happens if I disobey again."

"I brought you here to keep you safe," he groaned.

"Safe?" I laughed, bitter in the stifling air. "In a place like this? A world of monsters and freaks?"

Crimson light leaked through the helmet's narrow openings. Even through the metal, I felt his anger radiating like heat from a forge.

"You think you're different from us?" He dropped low, dangerous. "You put on quite a show back there."

He turned fully toward me, the helmet reflecting the flames of the torches.

"You killed the Mirror Eater with nothing but a wrench. You fought a Sanctified entity and won."

"She got what she deserved."

"Ah." He tilted his head, like he'd heard something important. "And who decided that? Who made you the judge of what Helena deserved?"

I opened my mouth, then closed it. Because the truth was simple and damning—I had decided. In that moment, with the wrench in my hands and Helena writhing beneath me, I had appointed myself her executioner.

"That's normal. Self-defense. That doesn't make me like you." I kept it matter-of-fact.

The Executioner picked up a small blade from the table, holding it to the light. Seeing the blade, I backed away until my spine hit the bone table. He continued, "Doesn't it? You enjoyed killing her. I saw it in your posture when I arrived. The satisfaction of a job well done."

He approached slowly, but when he reached me, he didn't threaten. Instead, he stood beside me. "Let me see your shoulder." He stayed calm. "It needs to be treated."

I turned reluctantly and pulled the sheet down to expose the gauze he'd placed earlier. He peeled it back. The edges of the wound were darkening.

He cleaned the damage Helena had left with surprising gentleness. The blade he used was precise, sharp enough to cut away the ruined tissue without adding to the trauma.

He lifted me easily, his palms spanning from my hips to my lower ribs, and set me down on the table as if I weighed nothing. Then he checked my foot.

"Your foot will heal fine." He examined the wound carefully. His attention returned to my shoulder. He dabbed at a deep gash. "But this... you're bleeding internally. She nicked something important."

I gripped the table edge. "Will I die?"

"Not if I treat it properly." He kept working, eyes still on the wound.

He worked in silence for several minutes, cleaning, stitching and bandaging with the same careful precision he probably used to hurt people.

I finally broke the silence. "Why?"

"Why what?" He didn't look up from his work.

I watched his hands move. "Why do you care if I live or die? You could find another broken woman to play with. Someone who wouldn't question you or fight back."

"I could." He wrapped gauze around my shoulder. "But I don't want another woman. I want you."

"Why me?" I pressed.

He paused, helmet tilted toward his hands. The red glow in his eye slits dimmed slightly, like he was looking at something only he could see.

"We're connected somehow. Even I don't understand it fully." The words came slowly. "But you called for me once."

My eyes widened. "What?"

"Years ago. A child's voice begging to be taken. Normally I can't hear such things... I exist here, in this realm. But that night, something pulled me. Transported me." He sounded almost confused. "I found myself looking at a little girl. You."

My breath caught in my throat. "I dreamed of you when I was twelve, didn't I?"

He nodded. "It wasn't supposed to be possible. Something greater than both of us made it happen. Connected us across realms that should never touch."

"And then?" I prompted.

"Then nothing, for years. Until your husband strangled you. Again I was pulled... transported to watch. I saw what he did to you." He grew darker. "I whispered to you then. Told you what choosing revenge would mean. I wanted you to fight back. To damn yourself."

I whispered back, "Why?"

"Because then you'd end up here. Not everyone does...

most souls go elsewhere. But the guilty who choose their guilt? They come to places like this." He resumed bandaging. "And I knew if you came here, I'd find you. I would search through every version of hell until I found you, *my moth.*"

I shook my head. "That's insane."

"Perhaps. But here you are. Here we both are. Whatever force connected us that night when you were twelve... it was right." His words echoed certainty.

I thought about Theo's visits and how he killed him.

"You killed Theo's ghost in my cell. How could you even reach him? How could you kill something that's already dead?" I asked.

The Executioner secured the bandage. "Your guilt was strong enough to manifest even in the ordinary world. That's rare. Most people's ghosts stay in their heads. But you... your self-hatred was so pure it took physical form. It could follow you anywhere."

"So it wasn't really him?" I needed to understand.

"It was real enough to hurt you. Real enough that I could destroy it when I finally reached you." He hardened. "He was tormenting you. Only I get to do that."

The possessiveness made me look up. "So you want to torment me?"

He nodded slowly. "I should skin you. Hang you on these hooks. Watch you bleed. Torture you until you break completely." His hands stilled on the bandage. "But I can't. I don't want to."

He turned, walking back to the table where he'd picked up the medical supplies.

"You're brave." He lowered, soft. "Stronger than most who

find their way here. You killed Helena without hesitation. Faced down creatures that would've broken others."

His shoulders shifted. "But underneath all that strength, you're still fragile. Still breakable."

I was done being fragile. Done being the woman who cowered and apologized for taking up space. He saw strength in me, but he still thought I could be broken.

Behind him, I unwrapped the sheet completely. The fabric whispered as it fell on the table, leaving me bare in the torchlight. The heat kissed every inch of my exposed skin. I felt the stares of the hanging souls tracking my movements.

"You keep calling me your moth," I told him, steady in the thick air. "But what if this moth doesn't burn? What if she's stronger than you think? What if it craves the flame."

His massive frame went rigid. Even without seeing his face, I could feel the war beneath the helmet. Control versus want. Duty against desire.

"Turn around." I commanded, steady despite my racing heart.

His hands flexed at his sides. "If I turn around, if I see you like this—I won't be able to stop myself."

"Then don't stop." The words came out like a challenge.

And slowly, he turned.

Those hellish eyes pulsed like embers through the slits of his iron helmet as his gaze moved over my naked form. Where he looked, heat bloomed, every nerve ending sparking with sensation.

"Za-hh-ra." He drew out each syllable with careful precision.

The way he said it stopped my breath. Not the flat "Sara" everyone defaulted to, but Za-hh-ra, the soft 'z', the gentle roll of the 'r' my mother had taught me. The way no one had bothered to learn in twenty-four years.

My knees went weak. All this time, and he was the first to get it right without being told. That did something to me. Broke something. Fixed something. I don't know. But hearing my real name in his inhuman voice made me want him more than I'd ever wanted anything.

"Beautiful," he murmured, and the helmet modulated the word into something guttural, reverent. His control trembled—I saw it in the way his massive hands flexed, in the slight widening of his stance, like his own body was bracing against what it wanted to do.

He closed the distance in just a few strides and cupped my face with impossible care for a creature made to kill. His fingers curved gently beneath my jaw, tilting my chin so I had no choice but to look up into those twin infernos pulsing inside the mask. "I've waited so long to touch you like this. To worship every inch of what you hide under those sheets."

Then he knelt and pushed me gently back until I was lying on the bone table, legs dangling. His hand found the bandaged wound on my shoulder, fingers hovering just above the gauze without touching.

"Does it hurt?" he asked, voice softer through the helmet's modulation.

"A little." I nodded.

Promise saturated every word as he spoke. "I'll be careful."

One hand moved up—past my belly, over my ribs—to cup my breast. He cradled the curve in one broad palm, then used his thumb—barely a flick, just enough to wake sensation—to toy with the nipple. "Every curve of you." His free hand traced down my side, fingers spreading over the fullness of my hip. "Your soft belly, these hips... you're a goddess made flesh."

"Those sounds you're going to make," he growled, voice thickened with want. "Mine now."

And from beneath the bottom edge of the helmet, a tongue slid out. Black as oil. Long. Wrong. Too flexible.

It touched my knee first, a taste. Then higher, curling against my inner thigh in slow spirals, hot and slick and curious. The tongue moved like it had eyes, like it could smell need, and when it finally found the wet heat between my legs, I gasped.

Not from shock. From surrender.

He didn't dive in. Not yet. He teased. Traced me. Circled the swollen lips without touching my clit directly, building heat that spread in waves of dark pleasure.

Above, his hand worked my breast, rougher now. The flat of his thumb dragged across the hard nub, sending shocks of pleasure ricocheting down my spine. Each press and flick was synced with the movement of his tongue below.

The tongue flicked up. Found the bundle of nerves and stayed there, pressing soft at first, then circling with steady precision.

I moaned.

It moved faster. Deeper. Curling into me—slick and sinuous—hitting places no human ever had. I arched, hand shooting out for purchase, gripping the edge of the table like it might fly apart beneath me.

The rhythm built until I was panting, head thrown back, every inch of my body tight with the need to break apart. His tongue thrust deeper, and I cried out—once, then again—

louder, higher, as the orgasm ripped through me like a curse breaking.

My thighs clamped around his helmet, but he didn't move, didn't pull back. His tongue stayed inside me, licking slow, coaxing aftershocks from nerves that hadn't stopped sparking.

By the time he withdrew his tongue and rose to his feet, my legs were still quivering.

"Now," he whispered, the helmet sealing again with a soft hiss. "Now I claim you."

His rough, scarred palms gripped the insides of my thighs, fingers spreading me open like he was laying bare some sacred text. I could feel the calluses on his fingertips—the life, no, the lives—he'd taken with those hands.

They didn't frighten me.

They made me wetter.

He stayed between my legs for a breathless pause, staring up at me through the slits in the helmet. Then his hand found something on the side of the table, a control panel I hadn't noticed. The hydraulics hissed, and the table rose slowly until I was at the perfect height for his massive frame.

Eight feet tall to my five-two.

Now we were aligned.

He reached for the zipper. It came down slow, teeth parting with a rasp that sounded too loud in the quiet. His hips shifted forward, pants tugged low enough to free the thing he'd kept hidden.

My breath caught.

His cock hung heavy, thick as my wrist and veined like something carved from volcanic rock, dark red over black, the ridges pronounced, pulsing just slightly at the tip like it had its own hunger. A single drop of slick gathered there and fell, landing hot against my thigh.

I reached out without thinking. My fingers closed around the base and couldn't meet. My palm barely spanned the underside, and it throbbed in my hand, alive, twitching under my touch like it could sense my awe.

The skin wasn't soft. It had texture. Heat. Weight. My thumb grazed the underside and found another ridge.

He shuddered.

He grabbed my wrist, not to stop me. Just to feel it. The contact.

"Touching me like that," he rasped, breath catching against the metal, "you don't know what you're inviting."

"I do."

His breath hitched. One hand went to my cheek. The other wrapped around the base of his cock, guiding it toward my entrance. He rubbed the head against my slit, slow, messy strokes that spread my slick along his ridges. Teasing. But also preparing me.

Still, the stretch would be brutal.

He positioned himself at my opening. I could feel him— the sheer size of him—pressing right where I pulsed hardest. I tensed, hips twitching.

He caught my chin and turned my face toward him, forcing me to look into his burning eyes.

"Breathe," he ordered.

"I am."

"No." He tilted my chin up. "You're bracing."

Then his hips pushed forward.

My body resisted, then gave.

Just the head. It already felt like too much. My fingers

clawed at the bone table, spine arching as the blunt pressure filled me with fire. There was pain but not enough to stop. Just enough to remind me what it meant to be taken.

"That's it," he whispered, voice low and ragged. "You're doing perfect."

He slid in another inch.

I moaned, high, desperate.

He groaned in return, the sound vibrating through the helmet. "Tighter than I imagined. Hotter. Like you were made for this."

I clutched his forearms. "It's—God—it's too—"

"I know. But you can take it. I'll help you."

His hand slipped down between us. His thumb found my clit, rubbing tight, deliberate circles as he sank deeper. The tension snapped. My body loosened, and he seized the moment.

With one long, brutal thrust, he buried himself to the hilt.

The stretch ripped a scream from my throat. He leaned in, helmet brushing my cheek in an attempt to calm me.

"You're mine now," he growled. "Every inch. Every sound. Every tremble."

And when he pulled back and drove into me again—harder, deeper—I believed him.

He stayed inside me for a heartbeat that stretched into eternity. His cock throbbed against my walls, every ridge forcing me to feel all of him. My cunt clenched around him, struggling to keep up, and the way he shuddered made it clear, he felt everything.

Then he started to move.

Slow at first. Just enough to make me feel the drag, the friction, the ache deep inside. My hands slid to his waist, gripping as his hips rolled forward again, grinding against my pelvis with punishing rhythm.

He fucked me like he was carving something into me.

"Do you feel that?" he rasped, voice shaking as he drew nearly all the way out, then slammed back in. "That stretch? That burn? That's your body learning who owns it."

Every thrust stole the breath from my lungs.

He held my throat, not choking, just cradling it. Thumb resting against my throat like he was tracking the flutter of my pulse.

"Say it," he growled. "Tell me who your body belongs to."

"You," I gasped, nearly sobbing. "You—fuck—please don't stop."

"Never."

His pace turned savage.

He gripped under my knees and pulled them around his hips, folding me in half. The angle changed. Deeper now. So deep he hit that spot inside me that made stars burst behind my eyes. My back arched, mouth open in a soundless scream.

He felt it. Saw it.

"You're gonna come." He'd gone nearly incoherent.

"No," I begged. "Not yet—"

But it was already happening.

I had no say in it. The orgasm ripped through me like lightning, my cunt clamping down around him, desperate to keep him inside.

I screamed. Shook.

That did it.

His thrusts turned frantic. Brutal. Every motion slammed bone against bone, skin against skin. Sweat streaked his chest. Then he let go.

With a raw, broken groan, he shoved deep, deeper, and came inside me. Hot, endless pulses of thick seed spilled into me. I felt it bloom through my belly. His hips jerked with every release, fingers digging into my thighs so hard I knew I'd bruise. "These thighs... so full, so strong. All mine now. All mine." His whole body shook as the orgasm tore through him.

We stayed like that, locked, gasping, ruined.

My body still twitched as aftershocks rolled through me. My thighs trembled, slick and messy. His come was already leaking from me in warm trails.

His helmet dropped to rest on my good shoulder.

Our chests heaved in tandem. The only sound was breath. Flesh. Silence thick with something new.

Chapter Twenty-Two

The moment our breathing steadied, the sirens began to wail. Deep, bone-rattling sounds that seemed to come from the walls themselves. He pulled away from me, zipping himself up in one swift motion.

"What's happening?" I asked, scrambling to wrap the sheet around myself.

"The Judge is summoning me." His helmet turned toward the workshop's exit, the red eye slits dimming. "He knows you're here. His sponsa doloris. With me. What we did."

My blood ran cold. "But you killed the Mirror Eater. You destroyed her vessel so he wouldn't know—".

He said nothing.

The Judge knew. Had always known. And now he was calling his Executioner back, along with whatever I had become in his eyes.

The sirens grew louder, echoing through the building above, bouncing off stone and metal until they formed a symphony of warning.

"What will happen?" I asked.

"Punishment."

The word sealed our fate. I'd seen what punishment looked like in this place, the hanging souls in his workshop, their eternal whispers of agony. The thought of joining them made my whole body lock up with terror.

Before I could speak again, he scooped me up. My stomach hit his shoulder, the sheet tangling around my legs as he strode toward a section of wall I hadn't noticed before. The stone looked different here, older, with symbols carved so deep they seemed to pulse with their own dark light.

His fist slammed into the stone. It crumbled inward, revealing a tunnel that descended into absolute darkness.

He carried me down rough-hewn steps, deeper into the building's bones.

We passed through the ritual chamber where we'd first landed, that terrible room of bone and blood where everything had changed. But he didn't stop. He kept going, taking me deeper still, into the very foundations of this place.

Each step took us further from anything resembling the hospital above. That was just the surface. A mask. Below it lay something older. Worse. A place carved from living rock and pain, a foundation built on screams and watered with blood.

The walls changed as we descended. White stone gave way to black rock, then to something that wasn't quite stone at all. It felt organic. Breathing. Like we were traveling through the digestive system of some massive beast.

My shoulder throbbed where Helena's claws had torn through skin and muscle. The bandages the Executioner had applied were holding, but wetness was seeping through.

The air grew colder the deeper we went. My exposed skin broke out in goosebumps that had nothing to do with temperature and everything to do with the wrongness that saturated every wall and floor.

The attack came without warning.

Hairless, flayed canine forms leapt from shadows I hadn't seen. They poured from crevices that shouldn't have been large enough to hold them. Their faces were carved into permanent surgical grins, jawbones hinged with gleaming metal.

They laughed as they attacked, children's giggles played backward, the sound bouncing off the walls like broken music.

The laughter was the worst part. Somehow. It spoke of innocence corrupted, joy twisted into something obscene.

"Grin-Hounds." The Executioner set me down behind a pillar. He drew his massive blade. "Stay back."

The sword cut through the first creature like paper, splitting it clean in half with wet efficiency. Black blood splattered the tunnel walls in arterial sprays. Its death shriek was barely human, more like tearing metal mixed with a child's scream.

But more came. Always more.

They poured from the walls like water, emerging from cracks too small to hold them.

He fought with brutal precision. Each swing took limbs. Each thrust found hearts, or whatever passed for vital organs in these things. The blade moved like it was alive, flowing from one kill to the next without pause.

But for every hound that fell, two more emerged from the dark.

Their laughter echoed louder, building into a crescendo that made my teeth ache. Blood—his and theirs—painted the walls in abstract patterns that might have been beautiful under different circumstances.

"Ah, the prodigal returns." A voice came from deeper in the tunnel. Calm with sermonic certainty.

At once, the hounds began to back off, slinking into the shadows but not leaving. Watching. Waiting.

A figure emerged from darkness, nightmare wrapped in sanctity. Tall and thin, moving with the certainty of someone who had never doubted he was right.

His robes were stitched from scripture pages, the words moving across the fabric like they were alive, trying to escape.

Where his chest should have been was a hollow cavity filled with scales and scorched coins that clinked softly as he moved. They looked like scales of justice, but blackened, warped by heat, until they resembled charred skin.

"Gallows." The Executioner spat the name, blade still raised despite the blood dripping from his wounds. "You should've stayed in your chapel."

The priest, or whatever he had become, smiled. His teeth were filed to points, each one carved with scripture in a language I didn't recognize. He waved his hand and an invisible force made the Executioner fall on his knees. He tried hard to break free but couldn't.

"I've served the Varnar line since the beginning." Gallows never shifted from that awful calm. "When their ancestors first summoned the Judge in the 1400s. I was a priest then too. Helped prepare the first sacrifices, women who knew too much. Men who asked too many questions. We burned them as witches while I took their confessions."

He stepped closer, coins clinking in his hollow chest.

"The current Varnar is the latest heir. His grandfather grew a conscience, wanted to shut the whole operation down. The Judge ate him alive, right there in the chapel. His father tried to renegotiate the terms. Lasted three years before the Judge broke every bone in his body and left him breathing on the altar for a week." Gallows tilted his head, amused. "The young heir learned early. He never questioned. Never flinched. That's why he's still breathing."

"I chose this, you see. Chose to follow the Judge into this realm. Chose to become Sanctified, one of his eternal servants, granted life unending to extract truth from the guilty. The Judge rewards those who serve willingly. We become more than human. We become instruments of divine judgment."

His eyes landed on me. Teeth flashing in what might have been a smile.

"And you, little whore, you're exactly the kind of sinner I was made to break. How predictable that he would bring you here."

The Executioner stepped between us, blade raised.

But Gallows lifted one pale hand. His fingers were too long, joints in places joints shouldn't be. Wire threaded through his skin, like he'd been sewn together from spare parts.

"Now, now. Violence is so... crude. The woman must confess first. Purification before punishment, as it should be."

Pain exploded across my skin.

It felt like I was being skinned from the inside out. Like every shameful thought I'd ever had was being carved into my flesh with burning needles.

Words appeared, branded into me by invisible hands.

The names of everyone I'd hurt. Every lie I'd told. Every selfish moment burned into my skin like I was livestock.

The pain was beyond anything I'd known.

Worse than Helena's claws.

Worse than the bruises and cuts from my marriage.

Worse than what Alan and Varnar had done to me.

This was the pain of absolute truth. Of having every hidden part of yourself dragged into the light and judged guilty.

"Tell me"—his hollow chest resonated through my skeleton—"what did you do with our Executioner? What sins did you commit on that table of bones?"

I tried to speak, but the words stuck in my throat like broken glass. More text appeared on my arms, chest, and thighs, spelling out every shameful thought in burning letters. The pain worsened each time I stayed silent, building until I thought my mind might crack.

Gallows circled me like a predator, his scripture-stitched robes rustling with each step. The sound was like pages turning in a book written in blood.

"For every silence, a lash. For every lie, the rope."

The text burned deeper when I thought about lying. It wasn't just on my skin anymore—I could feel it burrowing into me, carving through muscle and bone.

Behind the priest, the Executioner fought against the invisible force that held him back. His blade scraped against the stone as he struggled to reach me.

"You corrupted our sacred instrument of judgment," Gallows pressed, the words rising like a sermon. "Tell me how it felt to be claimed by a monster. Tell me how your body responded to his touch. Tell me how you moaned while tortured souls watched from above."

The truth spilled out in broken gasps.

"I wanted it," I sobbed, the words torn from someplace deep inside. "I chose it. I let him touch me and I—"

The pain flared white-hot.

"I enjoyed it."

"More," Gallows demanded, circling closer. "Tell me how your flesh answered when your soul begged it to stop."

"I was wet for him," I screamed. "I spread my legs and begged him to claim me. I came while those poor souls watched." Each word was agony, but lying was worse. The text would've burned straight through to my heart if I tried to deceive him.

"And while you rutted like an animal," Gallows continued, voice smooth as poison, "did you think of your friends?"

"I didn't think about them," I whispered, the admission breaking something inside me. "I forgot they existed. All I could think about was him inside me."

"Such honesty," Gallows murmured, almost reverent. "Such beautiful truth."

He leaned closer. I could smell the grave dirt on his robes.

"And do you believe," he asked with terrible gentleness, "you deserve salvation... or damnation?"

My mind began to fracture under the weight of forced honesty. The pain burned through every layer of who I thought I was until there was nothing left but raw truth. I could feel myself breaking apart, piece by piece.

"Damnation," I whispered, barely able to form the word. "I deserve to burn."

That's when the Executioner's fury shattered whatever bound him.

The restraints cracked like breaking glass. He moved faster than human eyes could follow, crossing the distance to Gallows in one leap.

"Now, now... she hasn't finished her confession—"

Gallows began, but that awful calm finally broke as the Executioner drove his massive blade straight through him.

Finally, fear lit the priest's eyes. "You cannot! I am Sanctified! I am chosen, !"

But the blade was already destroying him. His scripture robes unraveled, the text writhing as if trying to escape whatever hell had made them. His hollow chest imploded. Coins melted. Scales burned. The tunnel filled with acrid smoke that reeked of sulfur and charred parchment.

Gallows collapsed into ash and scattered pages. The scripture writhed across the stone floor before going still.

The Executioner drew the same vial he'd used on Helena's shard and emptied it over the ashes.

The burning text vanished from my skin as Gallows died, leaving only the memory of pain, and the knowledge of what I truly was. I fell to my knees, tears pouring down my face. Not from pain. From something worse. Understanding.

Every lie I'd ever told myself, every excuse I'd ever hidden behind, gone. I saw what I was now. And the truth was almost too heavy to bear.

"If this is happening to me," I whispered, breaking, "what about my friends?"

The Executioner knelt beside me, his rough hands cupping my face. His thumbs brushed away tears that burned against my cold skin.

"They're survivors," he murmured. "They'll make it. You have to believe."

I hoped he was right.

Chapter Twenty-Three

My throat was raw from screaming during Gallows' confession torture.

"Water." The word came out as a croak. "I need water."

The Executioner stopped and carefully set me down in a small alcove carved into the tunnel wall.

"Wait here," he rumbled, gentle despite the inhuman echo. "There's water ahead. I'll get it for you."

I nodded, slumping against the cold stone as he disappeared into the darkness.

The alcove felt ancient, older than the hospital above by centuries. These walls had absorbed suffering until it became part of their very foundation. Dark stains marred the stone in patterns I didn't want to understand. How many had died here? How many had begged for mercy that never came?

That's when I heard the scraping.

Not the skittering of rats or insects. Something deliberate. Human-sized. Trying to stay hidden.

Dr. Alan crawled from a hidden crevice in the alcove wall.

She still wore the same black dress from the ritual chamber, though it now hung in tatters. She looked like she'd fought her way through hell. Her once-perfect blonde hair clung to her face in damp, matted ropes, twisted with blood and grime. Her expression contorted with madness but underneath it, that calculating gleam still flickered. The part of her that had made psychological torture an art form.

"You." The word dripped with venom. "You ruined everything, you little bitch."

She pulled herself fully into the alcove, and I saw what she'd been doing in that crevice. In her hand was a stone she had shaped into a crude blade, honed sharp through what must have been hours of obsessive grinding against the walls.

That level of dedication told me everything I needed to know about her mental state.

"Do you have any idea what you've done?" She rose louder with each word, cracking at the edges. "Centuries of work! Centuries of careful cultivation! The sacrifices, the rituals, the perfect system we created!"

She spoke like she was the victim. As if the torturer of countless patients—who had smiled while breaking minds—was somehow wronged.

"Everything was perfect. In order. Controlled." She took a step forward, the blade trembling in her grip. "The weak were culled. The strong were refined through suffering. We were creating something beautiful. Something pure. And you destroyed it all!"

"Beautiful?" A bitter laugh escaped me. "You call what you did to those women beautiful?"

"You wouldn't understand. Small minds never do." Her eyes blazed with fanatic light.

"I served faithfully for years. Every girl I sent into the depths, every mind I dismantled, every scream I orchestrated into perfect harmony, it was all for him. For the Judge."

She began to circle me, and I forced myself to stand despite the pain in my limbs.

"Varnar was an idiot," she spat. "A small man playing with forces he couldn't begin to grasp. He thought the Judge wanted someone broken. Some weeping thing soaked in sorrow. He kept sending down these sniveling wrecks who couldn't string together a coherent thought."

She stopped in front of me.

"But I read the true scriptures. The ones carved in languages older than human speech. The Judge doesn't just want sorrow. Any fool can be sad. He wants his bride. His equal. Someone who understands the exquisite artistry of suffering."

Her face lit up with pride, quivering with twisted joy. "I've perfected myself for decades. Every woman I tortured, every scream I pulled from their throats, it made me stronger. Sharper. I became the perfect instrument of suffering."

She stepped closer.

"That's what he needs. Not some weeping little victim like Varnar kept sending. He needs someone who knows how to create pain, not just feel it. Someone who can make the damned scream forever."

Her smile was hideous.

"I'm not broken like them. I'm the one who does the breaking. That's why I deserve to be his bride. The bride doesn't just marry the Judge. She becomes part of him. Shares his power. His essence. Two become one, united in flesh and purpose."

"You're insane and pathetic." It wasn't anger. Just a statement of fact.

"Am I?" she hissed. "Or am I the only one who truly understands?"

She raised the blade, testing its weight.

"When I bring him your corpse, when I show him that I restored order from the chaos, you'll see. He'll see. He'll know who deserves the throne beside him."

She lunged.

The blade came at my throat with terrifying precision. But months underground had changed me. The fear that once paralyzed me was gone, replaced by something colder. Something sharper.

I rolled aside. The blade hissed past my ear.

I moved on instinct. When she swung again, I caught her wrist and twisted hard. A crack, followed by her scream.

"You made me believe I was worthless. Insane." I hissed through my bloodied teeth. I drove my knee into her gut. She collapsed, gasping.

"Just another broken thing for you and Varnar to study. And then sacrifice."

The blade clattered to the floor. I grabbed it, testing its weight. It felt dense with intent, each edge sharpened through hatred and obsession.

That's when I heard footsteps.

The Executioner emerged from the tunnel like judgment incarnate, carrying a battered metal container filled with water. His helmet turned, slowly, from me to Alan. He took in the scene without a word, utterly still.

"Dr. Alan."

No surprise in his tone. Just certainty.

"I wondered when you'd crawl from your hole."

Her face drained of color. Real fear finally cracked through the madness.

"You know each other?"

I didn't answer. There was no point.

I moved fast. Faster than my broken body should have allowed.

The blade found her throat, not deep enough to kill, but enough to open the voice box. Her screams turned to wet whistles, echoing through the stone.

"Remember Marion?" I hissed. "How you cut her?"

"Remember what you did to me?"

Blood bubbled from her open throat. She tried to scream, but no voice came.

"You wanted to be the Judge's bride?"

I grabbed her by the matted hair, dragging her to a flatter section of the floor. "Let me prepare you for him. Let me skin you. You love blades, don't you? You bitch!"

The Executioner set down the water and moved closer. When I raised the blade, he caught my wrist, gently.

"The skin must be taken while they live." He guided my hand. "Like this. Find the plane between dermis and muscle."

He showed me on her shoulder. Even with a crude blade, precision mattered. This wasn't about death. It was about understanding.

I worked methodically.

Arms first. The blade sawed through flesh with sick efficiency. Then her legs. Her pulse surged against the stone.

She gurgled. Whistled. But stayed awake.

"Don't you dare pass out on me, Doctor." I mimicked her clinical tone. "For research purposes I need you awake."

Her body convulsed as I peeled her open, strip by strip. Muscle. Fat. Nerves. By the time I reached her torso, her breathing grew ragged. Shallow.

Her eyes rolled back, showing only white.

Then... nothing.

I sat back on my heels, the blade dripping.

Dr. Alan lay there like something from a butcher's window. Everything exposed, except her face. I'd left that untouched. I couldn't bring myself to ruin it.

The shock had taken her. Her body quit before the blade could.

She died on that cave floor, raw, ruined, and finally understanding what her victims had felt.

THE WATER WAS COLD AGAINST MY HANDS, BUT IT COULDN'T wash away what I'd done. I scrubbed until my skin was raw, watching the pink water swirl and disappear into cracks in the floor. My hands wouldn't stop shaking.

Some faint light filtered down from somewhere above, just enough to see shapes and shadows. But it was fading now, growing dimmer with each passing moment. In the dying light, I could see Alan's corpse sprawled on the cave floor. The sight made my head reel.

"I did that." The words sounded strange, distant.

"I took her apart piece by piece. Listened to her suffering and felt... satisfied."

The Executioner remained silent, a monolithic presence in the fading light. His silence was worse than any judgment.

"She deserved it." I tried to convince myself, still scrubbing at the blood under my nails. "After everything she did—all the women she tortured—she deserved exactly what she got."

But the words rang hollow. Somewhere between the first cut and the last, I'd crossed a line I could never uncross. My knees gave out. I slumped against the cave wall, exhaustion crashing over me in waves.

"What am I becoming?" The question came out as a whisper. "First Theo, now this. Each time it gets easier. Each time I feel less human."

The light was almost gone now. I could barely make out the Executioner's silhouette, but his red eyes burned through the darkness like coals refusing to die.

Then the last of the light vanished.

The darkness was absolute, pressing against me like a living thing. In that suffocating blackness, every horror rushed back. Theo's burning screams. The wet sound of Alan's skin peeling away. The copper taste of blood in the air. And somewhere in the dark, Alan's corpse lay cooling. Was she really dead? What if she moved? What if she crawled toward me in the darkness, skinless fingers reaching?

A panicked sob tore from my throat. I scrambled away from where I thought her body was, following the twin points of red light burning through the darkness. My hands found his chest, solid and warm. I pressed against him, shaking, my fingers clutching at his body like he was the only real thing left in the world.

"Please." The word came out broken. "I can't... I can't close my eyes. What if I see their faces? What if I dream about what I've done? What if I wake up and I'm even worse than before?"

His arms encircled me with infinite care. For someone designed to deal death, his touch was impossibly gentle. "You need to sleep, Zahra. Your body is failing. Rest now."

"You don't understand." I pressed my face against his chest, feeling the steady rhythm of whatever passed for his heartbeat.

"The guilt is eating me alive. I'm becoming just like them. Like Varnar. Like Alan. Taking pleasure in violence, in control, in making others suffer."

"You take no pleasure in it." The rumble moved through his chest, vibrating against my cheek.

"I have watched true sadists for centuries. They smile as they work. They linger over pain, savoring it like wine. You did what was necessary for survival. Nothing more."

"That doesn't make it right," I argued.

"No. But right and wrong are luxuries this place does not allow."

My hands found his helmet in the darkness, fingers tracing the metal. The surface was smooth in some places, rough in others, as if it had been damaged and repaired countless times. I could feel the bolts at the edges, the seams where metal met whatever lay beneath.

"Why do you wear this?" I asked as my fingers explored the strange symbols etched into its surface. "Why keep your face hidden even in the dark?"

Silence stretched between us before he answered.

"I am not meant to be looked upon. What lies beneath would... disturb you."

"After everything I've seen? Everything I've done?" I let my hand rest against where his cheek would be. "I don't think anything could disturb me anymore."

"This is different." There was something almost vulnerable in those two words, a crack in that inhuman authority.

"The helmet does not come off. Cannot come off. It has become part of me, fused through centuries of wearing. What I was before..."

He trailed off.

"You're ashamed." The realization hit me with surprising force. This being who had shown no emotion through all the horrors we'd witnessed was ashamed of his appearance.

"I am ugly." The words were simple, factual.

"Scarred beyond recognition. Burned and broken and remade so many times that nothing human remains. Not beautiful. Not like you."

The word beautiful from him, here in this pit of nightmares, after I'd just skinned a woman alive, was so absurd I almost laughed. Instead, tears came. Hot and sudden, streaming down my face in the darkness.

"Beautiful?" The word cracked.

"I'm covered in blood. I've murdered two people. I'm losing my mind in this place. How can you call me beautiful?"

"Because I see what remains beneath the blood and guilt." His hand covered mine where it rested on his helmet. "The woman who fought to save others when she could have only saved herself. Who shows mercy even to monsters like me. That is beautiful."

My fingers traced down from his helmet to his neck, feeling the scarred skin there. He tensed but didn't pull away. I explored carefully, learning the landscape of old wounds and twisted tissue. Whatever had been done to him, it was beyond anything I could imagine.

"You saved me," I whispered, letting my hands map the

broad planes of his chest. "Over and over, you've protected me. Carried me when I couldn't walk. Taught me to survive. That makes you beautiful to me."

He was quiet for so long I thought he wouldn't respond. When he spoke, the words came out rougher than usual.

"Sleep now, Zahra. You are exhausted beyond measure. I will keep watch. Nothing will harm you while you rest."

"I'm afraid to sleep." The admission came out small, childlike.

"Afraid of what I'll dream. Afraid I'll wake up and be someone else entirely. Someone worse. And Alan... what if she's not really dead? What if she crawls—"

"She is gone." His arms adjusted around me, turning my body away from where the corpse lay.

"I will keep you safe from the living and the dead. Sleep now."

"Promise?" The word was slurred. Exhaustion was winning despite my fear.

"I promise. Rest now. Let go of consciousness. I have you."

The darkness didn't seem as threatening wrapped in his arms. My body grew heavy, each limb weighing a thousand pounds. The cave floor was hard beneath us, but his chest was warm, solid, real. An anchor in this nightmare realm.

"Don't let me go." I whispered as sleep dragged me under.

"Never." The sound followed me down into unconsciousness.

"I will hold you through every dream and nightmare. You are safe with me."

As awareness faded, I felt his hand stroke my hair with impossible tenderness. This creature of death and judgment holding me like I was made of spun glass. In a realm built to punish, where human connection was a liability, we'd found something neither of us expected.

My last coherent thought was wonder at the strange turns life could take. How I could find gentleness in hell's depths. How a monster could show more humanity than any human I'd known. How, even covered in guilt and blood, someone could look at me and see beauty.

Sleep took me then, deep and dreamless, held safe in the arms of the Executioner while darkness pressed in around us and the dead woman's blood slowly cooled on the cave floor.

Chapter Twenty-Four

My eyes snapped open at the sound of footsteps coming down the tunnel, lots of them, trying to move quietly. But I knew who they were. The Executioner was already standing with his blade ready, blocking the entrance to our alcove.

Marion came through first. She looked thinner than when I'd last seen her, with new worry lines around her eyes, but her fighting spirit was still there. She carried a metal rod that had been sharpened to a point. Isaac limped in behind her with wood strapped to his broken leg as a makeshift splint. He had a crude knife made from scrap metal tucked in his belt. The two of them were supporting Sela between them. Her feet barely touched the ground, and blood had soaked through the cloth wrapped around her thigh. Tobias entered last, constantly checking behind him. His usual arrogance was gone, replaced by genuine fear. He gripped a piece of rebar stained with something dark. Nobody trusted him. Nobody had the strength to waste on revenge while the realm hunted us.

Then they saw Alan's corpse sprawled on the cave floor.

The body lay there in the dim light, a mess of exposed muscle where I'd removed the skin. They froze, taking in the scene. Their eyes moved from the corpse to me sitting against the wall, then to the Executioner standing guard with his bloodied blade.

"Jesus Christ." Marion stared at the body, then at the Executioner. "What happened here?"

I could see what they were thinking. Of course they assumed the Executioner had done it. He was the monster with the bloody weapon. I was just Zahra, the woman they'd been trying to protect.

"Get away from her." Isaac's voice was tight with fear, but he started moving toward me anyway, ready to pull me away from danger.

"Wait." I stood up slowly. My legs were still shaky from exhaustion. "He didn't kill her. I did."

Sela's sharp eyes studied me, then looked at Alan's wounds more carefully. I could see her cataloging the amateur cuts, the messy work of someone who'd never done this before. Understanding crossed her face.

"I skinned her alive while she screamed." Clear. No flinch.

That landed hard. Tobias actually stepped backward, his face going pale. Isaac opened and closed his mouth without making a sound.

But Marion dropped her weapon and crossed the space between us in three quick steps. She pulled me into a fierce hug. I went rigid, expecting disgust or horror. Instead, she held me tighter.

"Good," she whispered fiercely in my ear. "That bitch had it coming after everything she did to us. I'm glad it was you."

When she pulled back, there were tears in her eyes along

with something that looked like pride. She held my face in both hands and really looked at me.

"Are you okay? Really okay?"

"I don't know," I answered honestly. "I don't know what I am anymore." I looked at all of them more carefully, noticing details I'd missed. They were definitely thinner, their clothes hanging looser. "What about you? How long have we been down here? You all look like you've been through hell."

Marion and Isaac glanced at each other. "Time moves strangely here," Marion answered. "It feels like weeks, but it might have been days. We tried to keep track at first, but the darkness and the constant danger made it impossible."

Isaac glanced at the Executioner through his broken glasses, one lens completely gone, the other cracked. "After this... thing took you, we ran out of the cafeteria but were attacked immediately. Those crawling creatures with waterlogged faces. One of them bit Sela! We had to hide."

"We found what looked like Varnar's office. That place was a nightmare even in reality, but here it looked cancerridden." Marion shuddered. "Everything was twisted and rotting. We couldn't stay there long without food or water."

"So we went back to the cafeteria." Sela shifted her weight off her injured leg. "Figured it was the last place those things would look for us. We'd already been there once."

Isaac wiped sweat from his forehead. "We don't know how long we stayed hidden there. Could have been days. At least it was quiet for a while. We found some food supplies, some water, and made these weapons from whatever we could break apart."

"Then the sirens started." Tobias's eyes darted to the entrance again. "Same ones we're hearing now. Everything changed. Creatures came from everywhere, not just the crawling ones. Things with surgical grins that laughed like children."

Marion touched the fresh cut on her cheek. "We ran. Found these holes punched through walls, fresh ones with dust still falling. Figured something powerful made them." She swallowed hard. "We didn't know what we'd find, but we had to keep moving forward."

I looked at their battered faces, the blood on their makeshift weapons, the way they stood despite everything they'd endured. Then my gaze fell on Alan's skinned corpse.

"We're still breathing," I told them. "That's more than most can say down here."

The Executioner moved then, stepping closer to me. The others tensed, but he simply extended his hand. I took it without hesitation. His fingers closed around mine, gently, possessively.

Marion's eyes widened at the gesture. "Zahra, what...?"

"He saved me." Simple as that. "Over and over. And now he's mine."

The declaration should have sounded insane. A broken woman claiming ownership of a nightmare creature in the depths of hell. But the Executioner's grip tightened slightly, acknowledging the truth of it.

"We need to get out of here." Isaac's words came urgent. "There has to be a way back to the surface. Some exit we haven't found."

"The tunnels are blocked now," Tobias added, still eyeing the Executioner warily. "Whatever's up there, it's spreading down. We barely made it through."

Sela had been studying the Executioner with that sharp

intelligence of hers. "You appeared in the ritual chamber to bring souls down." She held his gaze. "Can you take us back the same way?"

The Executioner's helmet turned toward her, red eyes glowing through the slits. The silence stretched long enough that I wondered if he would answer at all.

"Yes," he ground out at last, stone on stone. "But it requires returning to the ritual chamber above."

My blood turned to ice. The ritual chamber meant going back where it all started. And with the alarms blaring, the Judge and his creatures would know that would be the place we'd go to escape. It wasn't good. Not for us, and not for the Executioner, who had betrayed his master by choosing me.

"They'll destroy you." I turned to face him fully. "The Judge will punish you for helping us."

He lifted his free hand to my face, his fingers impossibly gentle as they brushed my cheek. "I want you safe. That's all that matters now."

The others stared in shock at the tender gesture. This creature of nightmares cradling my face like I was something precious. Something worth preserving. Marion made a small sound of surprise. Isaac stepped back. Even Sela looked shaken by what she was witnessing.

"But what about you?" I pressed, covering his hand with both of mine. "What happens to you after?"

"Let me worry about the Judge." His thumb traced my cheek. "You deserve a chance at life. At freedom. At choice. Even if that choice takes you away from me."

His words left me still. He was offering to sacrifice himself so I could be free. So I could choose my own path, even if that path led me away from him.

"I won't leave you." The words came fierce. "Not after everything."

"You don't know that yet." Something I'd never heard before threaded through the words. Sadness. "You haven't seen the sun in days. Haven't breathed air that doesn't taste of death. You may feel different once you're free."

"I'm a monster, *my moth*. This place is hell. When you're back in the world above, you'll remember what I am. What I've done."

The pain in those words made my chest ache. "You've been better to me than any human ever was. You're not a monster. You're good."

He chuckled, but there was no humor in it. Just centuries of self-loathing given voice. "Good? I've killed thousands. Tortured souls for eternity. Made furniture from their skin."

"You protected me. Saved me. Chose me over everything else." I pressed my hand against his scarred chest. "That's not what monsters do."

A distant crash echoed through the tunnels. Marion shifted behind us. "Zahra. We need to move. Whatever's happening up there, it's getting worse. We could hear screaming, things breaking through the walls..."

The Executioner released my face and turned towards a wall. "Then we go down. All of us. Now."

Sela limped forward. "Can you really get us out? All of us?"

The Executioner nodded once. "The ritual chamber connects all levels. From there, I can open a path to the surface. But the Judge..." He paused. "Not the chamber you know. There's another. Older. Much older."

"How old?" Marion asked.

"Before the asylum. Before the town. Before humans gave it names." The twin embers behind his iron mask shifted downward. "It lies deep. Deeper than the Rust, deeper than the Weeping. At the very bottom, where stone becomes something else."

"And we have to go down there?" Isaac's voice cracked slightly.

"Down and down and down." The Executioner's words were heavy.

"Then we must go, because going up is no longer an option!" Marion held firm. She looked at me, at the way I stood so naturally beside this creature of darkness. "Together."

The Executioner pressed his palm against a section of wall that looked no different from the rest. Ancient symbols flared to life under his touch, spreading outward like veins of fire. The stone groaned and split, dust cascading as a hidden doorway ground open. Beyond it, stone steps spiraled down into darkness.

"The old paths. Built before the asylum. Before everything."

And so we began our descent. The Executioner led the way. I walked beside him, our hands still clasped. Behind us, my friends followed, injured and exhausted, but alive.

As we descended toward whatever waited below, I wondered what would happen when we reached the bottom. If I would still be the same person who had entered this hell. If the woman who had skinned Alan alive could ever exist in the world above.

But those were questions for later.

For now, we descended, toward our escape, toward the

ancient chamber, toward a choice I wasn't sure I was ready to make.

The Executioner walked with his massive blade ready, every sense attuned to the dangers lurking in the darkness ahead. "Keep moving," he commanded, the command echoing off the tunnel walls. "The longer we stay exposed, the more likely we are to be overwhelmed."

Behind us, Marion and Isaac supported Sela between them, her sharp features etched with pain, though her eyes remained alert and calculating.

"How much farther?" Marion gasped, her strength waning under Sela's weight. Sweat beaded on her forehead despite the cold air that seeped from the stone walls.

"I can walk," Sela protested weakly, though her legs trembled with each step. "Don't slow down for me."

"Like hell," Isaac replied, adjusting his grip on her arm. "You can't walk on your own. It will hurt bad."

Tobias stayed in the middle of our formation, his usual predatory swagger replaced by nervous energy that made him jump at every shadow.

"This is insane," he muttered, wiping sweat from his brow. "We're walking deeper into a trap. The Judge wants us down there."

"Would you rather stay up here with those strange creatures?" Marion snapped, her patience wearing thin.

"At least up there I know what's trying to kill me," Tobias shot back, cracking on the last word. "Down there could be anything."

"Down there is the only way out," the Executioner stated without turning. "The ancient chamber holds power older than the Judge's prison. There's no other option."

The ancient stone steps descended into absolute darkness, slick with moisture and worse things that made our feet slip and slide as we went deeper. The walls were carved with symbols that seemed to writhe, their meanings lost to time, but their malevolence still palpable.

From the side passages came the sound of skittering movement, echoing off the stone in ways that made it impossible to tell how many things were out there, or how close.

"Something's following us," Isaac observed, shifting his grip on Sela while his free hand tightened on the makeshift weapon he'd fashioned from a broken piece of metal. "Multiple somethings."

"They're herding us," the Executioner corrected grimly, his helmet turning slightly to scan the darkness behind.

The temperature began to drop as we descended, and our breath began to mist in the cold air. The stone walls became smoother, more deliberately crafted, as if we were entering a more sacred part of whatever ancient structure this had once been.

"The air tastes different here," Isaac noted, wrinkling his nose. "Heavier. Like it's been trapped for centuries."

That's when the first attack came.

Hairless humanoid forms emerged from crevices in the walls—Mawkeepers. Behind them came the Grin-Hounds: flayed canine creatures with metal-hinged jaws.

"Fresh meat descending," they whispered. "She didn't break properly."

The Executioner's blade cut through them with wet efficiency, black ichor spattering the walls. We fought desperately while descending, but they kept coming.

"There's too many!" Isaac shouted.

Five Grin-Hounds circled Tobias, cutting him off from the group. His weapon broke against an armored skull. The first hound's jaws clamped on his forearm with precision. "Help me!" Tobias shrieked as blood fountained from the wound.

Isaac moved to help, but Marion grabbed his wrist. "He's already gone."

"You fucking cowards!" Tobias screamed as the hounds dragged him into a side passage, the screams fading into darkness.

We kept descending, the Executioner cutting down anything that approached. Finally, we reached the ancient ritual chamber.

The Executioner examined the seals on the massive doors. "Blood opens the way."

Without thinking, I slashed my palm on a jagged protrusion. My blood flowed down carved channels, and the symbols began to glow. The doors groaned open with a sound like breaking bones, revealing a vast chamber that disappeared into shadow.

Above us, a vortex of energy swirled and crackled, showing glimpses of the surface world through its chaotic center.

"Everyone through, now!" the Executioner commanded.

But before any of them could reach the portal, a clicking sound echoed from the chamber entrance.

She glided in on spinning thread spools instead of legs, her body a fusion of human anatomy and medical equipments. Arms ending in hooks gleamed with fresh blood, and her torso was split open, revealing a cavity filled with living flesh-spools made from previous victims.

"Well, well." Soft as silk. "The faithless executioner returns to the house he betrayed."

The Executioner stepped protectively in front of me, his massive frame blocking her view of me.

"Seamstress," he growled.

"Such a harsh tone for an old friend," she purred, circling us with predatory grace. Her thread spools left trails in the dust, weaving patterns that hurt to follow with the eye. "Especially when I've come to help with your little... problem."

"We both know why you're here," the Executioner replied, shifting his stance to keep me hidden behind him. "The Judge sent you to drag me back in chains."

"Oh, my dear Executioner," she laughed, a sound like breaking glass mixed with children's laughter. "I'm not here for you. You're damaged goods now, corrupted by sentiment. I'm here for her." Her hooks clicked together with anticipation.

She began to move closer, and I could see the faces in her torso more clearly now. They were all women—all young—all wearing expressions of eternal terror. Their eyes tracked our movement, silently pleading for a death that would never come.

"You won't touch her," the Executioner growled, raising his blade.

"Won't I?" The Seamstress tilted her head, studying us with the cold interest of a scientist examining specimens.

"Do you know what I do to the broken ones? The ones who think they've found strength in their suffering?"

"I know what you are," the Executioner spat. "A parasite. A creature that feeds on the last moments of hope before crushing them forever."

"Such poetry," she cooed, taking on an almost sexual quality. "But you're wrong about one thing. I don't crush hope. I preserve it. Forever. Every victim I take, every soul I stitch into my collection, they remain conscious. Aware. Hopeful that someday, somehow, the pain will end."

My skin prickled like static before lightning as I understood what she was describing. The faces in her torso weren't decorations, they were living, thinking people, trapped in eternal agony while their bodies were used as components in her grotesque form.

"Let me take you to the Judge now," she purred, looking at me. "And I won't hurt your friends."

"Stay back," I warned, surprised by the steadiness of my own voice.

"Oh, she speaks!" The Seamstress clapped her hooks together in delight. "And such fire in those words. The Judge will enjoy you."

"Go to hell!" I spat.

Suddenly, thread shot from her body like striking snakes, wrapping around our limbs with burning intensity. The material felt alive, pulsing with its own heartbeat as it tightened around us. Each strand carried a different sensation, some burned like acid, others felt like ice, still others seemed to vibrate with electrical current.

Marion slashed at the threads with a broken blade she'd picked up. "What is this shit?"

"Living thread," the Executioner replied, cutting through the supernatural restraints with his massive blade. "Made from human nerve endings. Each strand carries the pain of its donor."

"That's sick!" Isaac gasped, trying to free himself from threads that were slowly crushing his arms.

"That's artistry," the Seamstress corrected, more thread emerging from hidden openings in her body. "Each strand is carefully harvested from a willing donor. Well... willing eventually. Everyone breaks in the end."

Sela fell as threads tightened around her throat, cutting off her air supply. Her face began to turn blue as she clawed desperately at the supernatural restraints, but the thread only grew tighter with each struggle.

The Executioner's bladework became frenzied as he tried to cut through the endless threads while keeping the Seamstress at bay. But she seemed to have unlimited resources, more thread emerged from her body to replace whatever he destroyed.

"Such beautiful chaos to organize and arrange," she purred, her hooks reaching for me around the Executioner's protective stance and locked her eyes with mine. "I'll finish your friends properly, then keep their soul forever in my collection. They'll have eternity to appreciate my craftsmanship."

The Executioner roared with rage, caught between protecting me and freeing the others from her threads. His blade trembled with indecision as the portal above wavered, its edges becoming less distinct with each passing second.

"Choose quickly," the Seamstress taunted with obvious glee. "Send her friends through the portal and I'll let them live. But she stays with me. The Judge has plans for this one. She is his to break, his to reshape, his to judge as he sees fit."

Thread wrapped around my shoulders, the Seamstress's hooks piercing my flesh and lifting me into the air. Pain exploded through my body, but I fought against the restraints with everything I had. The hooks weren't just physical, they seemed to be trying to pierce my soul itself.

I met the Executioner's burning gaze through his helmet and forced the words out despite the agony. "Help them go," I gasped, blood running down my arms from where the hooks had penetrated. "Get them out of here. Don't let my choice be meaningless."

For a moment, there was absolute stillness in the chamber. The Executioner didn't want to abandon me. I could see the war in his posture, the way his grip tightened on his blade until his knuckles went white.

He turned toward my friends, raising his weapon to clear a path to the portal. "Go!" he shouted. "All of you! Now!"

That's when the explosion came.

The doorway exploded as something too big forced through.

It was him, the Judge!

Chunks of rock bounced off my shoulder. The Judge had to duck and twist sideways, but even hunched he scraped the ceiling. Dust and bits of ancient mortar rained down.

The portal above us died instantly, not a slow fade but a violent collapse, like someone had ripped a hole shut. The magical energy dissipated with a sound like drowning.

He straightened inside the chamber. Fifteen feet of wrong. His wings were fucked up, like someone had taken bat wings and let them rot half off. They dragged wet sounds across the floor. One wing had holes in it.

His skull was too long, mouth hanging open with endless rows of teeth. The horns grew straight from his skull, just bone erupting through skin. The left one had cracks running through it. Where eyes should be, there were only pits weeping black tar that never stopped flowing.

His skin didn't fit right. Too tight in some places so you

could see every vein, too loose in others where it hung like melted wax. The muscles underneath moved on their own— one flexing while another relaxed—giving him this constant rippling motion that made me seasick to watch.

Chains wrapped him like he'd been gift-wrapped in hell. They weren't restraining him, they moved when he moved, part of him. Rust flaked off constantly. No, not rust. Dried blood.

"My wayward Executioner." The sound came from every-where, the walls, the floor, inside my chest. I felt my ribs vibrate. But those weeping black pits were locked on the Executioner alone, and the rage there could have melted steel.

The Judge's massive hand shot forward. Chains erupted from the air itself, thick as tree trunks, glowing with hellish heat. They wrapped around the Executioner's arms, legs, throat, and yanked him to his knees with such force the stone floor cracked beneath him. He tried to rise, muscles straining, but the chains only tightened.

The Seamstress dropped me so fast I didn't have time to catch myself. My face met the floor. She was already prostrat-ing, grinding her forehead into the stone.

"Master," she muffled against the floor. "I have brought you the corrupted one, as you commanded."

"Have you?" He didn't look at her. Didn't look at me. Only at the Executioner. "What I see is betrayal. Centuries of service thrown away for mortal flesh."

The chains tightening around the Executioner started heating up. I could hear them sizzling against his skin, smell flesh cooking. He didn't flinch, but I saw his whole frame lock, saw his massive body tremble just once. My chest cracked open watching it, this creature who'd saved me, who'd chosen me over eternity, now burning for that choice.

"You dare steal from me?" The Judge's words dripped venom. "My blade. My instrument. Corrupted by this... nothing?" He pointed at me without looking, like I wasn't worth his attention.

"She chooses her own fate." The Executioner's voice rang out despite the chains crushing his chest. Still fighting. Still protecting me even as his skin blackened under the burning metal.

The Judge laughed, that grinding, breaking sound that made reality hiccup. "Choice? There is no choice here, my broken tool. There is only judgment. And yours, my wayward son, has finally come."

He slammed his fist into the floor. The impact reverberated through every bone. Power radiated outward in waves I could see, warping the air, cracking stone. But all I could focus on was the Executioner—my protector, my monster, my salvation —brought to his knees because he'd dared to care about me. I'd done this. I'd broken him just by existing, just by being something he wanted to save. And now we were all going to pay for it.

Chapter Twenty-Five

The chamber dissolved.

One moment, stone walls surrounded us. The next, we hung suspended in a void where thoughts had weight and my terror left trails of light. When we crashed back into reality, everything was wrong.

The ground beneath us wasn't earth but ash mixed with bone dust, still warm, like whatever had burned here never stopped burning. Above us stretched no sky, only a red membrane that pounded with its own heartbeat.

We weren't in the hospital anymore. This was what had always waited underneath. The truth beneath every lie we'd told ourselves about where we were.

"Welcome to my true domain."

The Judge stood before us. And here, in this place, his chains blazed with their own light. Behind him rose something that called itself a castle but had been built from nightmares. Every stone was bone, human skulls compressed into bricks, ribs forming archways, femurs as pillars. The whole structure wept blood from ten thousand eyes that death hadn't closed.

The moat surrounding it bubbled with boiling blood, steaming with the stink of copper and rot.

"Move."

New chains materialized around our limbs. We walked, not because we chose to, but because choice had been torn from us. The Executioner strained against his bonds until his scars split and bled, red ribbons painting his chest, but the chains only tightened in response.

The bridge was vertebrae: human spines fused together, bending slightly under our weight. From inside the bones came whispers. Last words. Dying breaths. Names of people long forgotten, everywhere but here, where forgetting wasn't allowed.

Inside the castle, the throne room broke my mind trying to process it. Too vast to comprehend. Its ceiling was lost in shifting shadows that moved independently of any light source. Everything had been carved from human remains but arranged with terrible artistry. The throne itself defied direct gaze, hundreds of skeletons twisted together in a shape that still tried to scream.

The Judge settled into it, and the bones glowed in recognition of their king. Torture devices lined the walls, but these weren't normal tools. I saw a rack designed to stretch guilt until it snapped, wheels that spun through dimensions of pain, braziers burning concepts instead of coal.

From alcoves in the walls stepped servants that used to be human. Now they were empty things, moving only because he willed it. Their faces were blank as unwritten paper.

"Kneel."

My knees hit the mosaic floor before the thought to resist

could form. This wasn't obedience, it was compulsion. His word was physics here.

His burning gaze moved over us like fingers rifling through pages, reading everything written in our souls. When those eyes found mine, I felt him cataloging my capacity for suffering with the patience of a collector appraising a rare find.

"The nurse." He pointed at Sela with one clawed finger. "Still thinking knowledge means power."

She rose into the air without any visible force lifting her. Just floated, suspended like a butterfly pinned to nothing. Her clothes didn't tear or fall away. They simply ceased to exist, leaving her naked and exposed while he circled beneath her like a shark.

"Your medical training. Your rationality. Your careful distance from the horror you helped maintain. All useless here." The Judge circled.

He began with her mind before touching her body. Every patient she'd sewn back together just so they could be broken again played out in her head. The faces of women she'd bandaged, knowing they'd return tomorrow with fresh wounds. Her clinical detachment that allowed the torture to continue, so long as the paperwork was filed.

I watched her composure crack as the weight of her complicity crashed down.

Then he began on her body.

Fingernails peeled back one by one. Each finger broken with a cracking sound. Her ribs broke like kindling while she remained conscious for every splinter. The skinning came last, strips of flesh pulled away while servants caught them in silver bowls.

When she finally crumbled to ash, we remained frozen, forced to watch every particle scatter.

"Next," he commanded.

Marion tried to shrink back, but invisible hands dragged her forward. He lifted her like she weighed nothing.

"The survivor. How many times you've escaped death. Let's fix that," he mused.

Her clothes vanished.

He wrapped her legs in chains that cut to the bone, then peeled her skin from thigh to ankle in perfect spirals. Acid on the exposed muscle made it bubble, eating through fibers while Marion's screams turned inhuman. He crushed every bone in her feet, ground her ankles to powder, and dismantled her knees until they were only meat and fragments.

Between tortures came visions: her daughter Emma calling for her. The child's voice echoed through the chamber, pulled from Marion's mind and made real.

"She asks for you every night." He kept his tone conversational. "I tell her you're too busy with new friends."

That broke Marion completely.

When he dropped her, her legs were useless meat, but she remained alive to feel every nerve still firing. "Crawl from now on, brave one." The order dripped venom.

Isaac came next.

The Judge forced him to watch himself at St. Dymphna, every time he stood outside while patients screamed. Every report documenting injuries he never questioned. The comfortable fiction that he was helping when, really, he was just another cog.

Then the Judge pried his mouth open and carved symbols into his tongue with a conjured blade. The patterns burned white-hot as he removed most of the muscle, leaving just enough to taste copper forever but never form words again.

"No more pretty lies about helping. Taste your failure forever." The Judge's decree rang out.

Isaac collapsed, clutching his throat, producing only wet, meaningless sounds.

"And finally..."

Those furnace eyes turned to me with something almost like affection, the personal attention of a collector who'd saved the best piece for last.

"My Sponsa Doloris."

He lifted me without touching me. Invisible hands raised me until we were eye to eye. This close, I could see the nuclear fire burning inside his skull. I could feel the heat of it against my face.

"Do you understand what you are? Why I've waited so long for someone like you?" He dropped to an intimate whisper that still carried to every corner of the vast chamber.

"Zahra Mitchell. Parents dead in a crash while you lived. Blamed yourself for surviving. Married a monster. Lost three pregnancies and believed it was punishment for outliving your parents. Killed your husband and felt nothing, then hated yourself for that nothing. Such perfect, concentrated guilt."

"Strip," he roared.

And suddenly, I hung naked in the air while he prowled beneath, examining me like art he was about to destroy, with reverence.

"You're not just guilty, Zahra. You're guilt itself given form, the Platonic ideal of survivor's shame. Every person who ever wondered, 'Why them and not me?' Every spouse who felt relief at a funeral and loathed themselves for it. Every parent who lived when their child didn't. Centuries of accumulated survivor's guilt, refined and distilled into one perfect vessel."

He floated up to my level, his burning face inches from mine.

"You killed Theo and felt the hollow absence where remorse should be, then spent months torturing yourself for that absence. That self-loathing, that perfect spiral of shame eating itself, it's exquisite. You come pre-broken in exactly the right ways. My Bride of Sorrows. Mother of new agonies. We'll birth suffering together that will make Hell itself weep with envy."

He showed me visions of Theo's death, but twisted. In these versions, I kept him alive for days, slicing off pieces while he begged. I smiled while I worked. I took photographs. I called his mother so she could listen to him scream. And in the visions, I enjoyed every second, with the pure sadism I'd always feared lived inside me. "This is what you wanted. What you're truly capable of. What you fear you are."

I gathered what little moisture I could and spat directly into his burning face.

The rage that twisted his features made the bone walls crack. The throne groaned like a living thing in pain. The temperature spiked until each breath seared my lungs.

"Such spirit requires special attention. Let me show you the price of defiance."

Chains of solidified agony held me spread in the air like a mounted butterfly. These weren't just hot, they carried every pain he'd ever inflicted, condensed into material form. Thousands of deaths flooded through me simultaneously. I drowned while burning, while being flayed, while being crushed. All at once. All eternal.

But worse was experiencing their punishments from the inside. I wasn't just watching Marion's legs being destroyed—I was Marion, feeling acid eat through muscle. I wasn't just seeing Isaac's tongue carved away—I was choking on the blood. Sela's skin peeling became my skin.

"Your defiance caused this." The Judge loomed closer. "Every second you resist costs them more pain."

The guilt hit harder than any physical torture. I was the reason my friends were broken.

He began burning symbols into my skin with fingers that wrote in fire. My fingers he broke and healed, just to break again. Molten metal poured into wounds that sealed around it, trapping the heat inside forever.

Through it all, the Executioner roared. He fought chains that should have been unbreakable, and I could hear metal starting to give way.

"You were made to serve, not to feel," the Judge called without looking at him.

"For centuries I was your blade. Nothing but steel in your hand. But she looked at me and saw something worth saving." The Executioner's voice came out strained against the chains. "You taught me cruelty. She taught me mercy."

The metal restraints groaned as he struggled, blood running down his arms where the burning chains cut deepest.

"The difference isn't the pain but whether they deserve it!" His words came out raw, desperate. "I was your monster. Now I'm hers. And monsters can love without destroying what they care for."

The chains cracked louder as his muscles tore and

reformed, ancient bindings finally giving way to something stronger than divine compulsion. The Judge turned with genuine surprise. "Impossible."

The Executioner burst free in an explosion that sent shrapnel through servants. His blade swung for a killing blow. The Judge caught it bare-handed. "You still don't understand your place."

He ripped the weapon away and began the real punishment. Skin peeled in patterns. Bones broken with patience. He forced the Executioner's head toward me.

"I pulled you from the void when this realm was young. Gave you form, purpose, power." The Judge's voice was molten fury. "You are nothing without me. Less than the dust beneath my feet. I can unmake you with a thought, scatter your essence so completely that even the memory of your existence burns away."

His grip tightened on the Executioner's skull. "Look what your pathetic weakness caused. Her pain is your fault. Every scream, every cut, every moment of agony, all because you forgot what you are."

The Executioner's helmet turned to me. Through the eye slits, I saw everything, desperation, love, and an apology that broke what was left of my heart.

"I should have protected you." Sound scraped through damaged vocal cords. "I'm sorry."

The Judge leaned closer, his burning breath searing the Executioner's exposed skin. "You should have. But you couldn't. You are my creation. My weapon. My tool. Nothing more. And tools that break get replaced."

When the Executioner couldn't move anymore, the Judge pinned him down. His foot came down on that ancient helm.

"Watch him die," the Judge looked at me and even though I wanted to look away, I couldn't. "Watch the only thing that ever cared for you become nothing."

The chains holding me suddenly released. I crashed to the ground, limbs useless, unable to do anything but watch.

The Judge's foot pressed down on the Executioner's helmet. It began to crack. Through the widening splits, his crimson gaze stayed on me. The helmet shattered. The Executioner crumbled to ash that scattered on winds from nowhere.

At the same time, I shattered too. The grief came out as a sound that scraped my throat raw. I clawed at my own face, tore at my hair. "Please," I begged. "Bring him back. I'll do anything."

The Judge fed on my despair. Then the grief transformed into rage so pure it felt like swallowing molten metal.

"You BASTARD!" I yelled and lunged at him with nothing but hatred and fingernails. He caught my throat, lifted me, but his expression had changed. Surprise mixed with approval.

"Even broken, you bear fangs." He studied me. "Perfect. My bride will have spirit to season the suffering."

The Judge smiled wider. "Yes. You'll do perfectly. My Sponsa Doloris. Together, we'll teach the universe new ways to weep."

Chapter Twenty-Six

The Executioner's ashes covered everything, floor, altar, my skin, like gray snow that tasted of iron and smoke.

The Judge circled me where I lay crumpled on the floor. His fifteen-foot frame moved like smoke given flesh, the burning crown casting shadows across walls made from compressed bones.

"Do you know what makes you special?" He crouched beside me. In his own domain, those empty tar pits burned from within, molten, alive, level with mine. "I've had so many guilty women brought here. But their guilt was simple. Hot. Fresh. They killed in anger, in moments of madness. Their guilt burned bright, but quick."

One burning finger touched my chin. My skin blistered.

"You, though? Seven years with Theo. Every bruise, you thought you deserved. When he broke your ribs on your birthday, you apologized for bleeding on his shoes."

The memory punched through my body, me on my knees,

ribs flaring with pain, sobbing apologies while he stared in disgust at the stain on the carpet, like that was the real offense.

"Three miscarriages." His hand had pressed flat and cold against my belly, not with tenderness, but accusation. "Each one you blamed on yourself. Like you murdered those possibilities through imperfection."

The truth was a boulder in my chest, unmovable, heavy with shame. My throat burned as if his words had lodged there, scraping raw on the way down.

"You still mourn the idea of him. Maybe he could change. Even now, some part wonders if you drove him to cruelty."

He was right. That voice, the poisonous, slithering one, still whispered late at night: What if you'd just been better?

"And Varnar. That night in his office. When he made you come."

The memory slammed into me like ice water. My hips moving when I told them not to, pleasure building while my mind screamed no. Waking in the medical ward afterward, the carved V burning under gauze, Marion's hand finding mine in the dark. I had wanted to claw my own skin off. I still did.

"You hate yourself for that more than you hate him."

The Judge stepped back, admiring me like a glutton eyeing a feast. His eyes glowed faintly and his grin stretched too wide, too hungry. "Six hundred years I've waited for someone like you. Guilt aged to perfection. Sorrow distilled into poison. Self-hatred so pure it could corrupt saints."

He spread his arms. The chains adorning them clinked softly, a sound almost delicate, like wind chimes made from vertebrae and regret.

"My Bride of Sorrows!"

A sliver of memory slicing through the fog: Dr. Alan's voice, sharp and trembling, back in the caves.

"The bride doesn't just marry the Judge," she'd said. "She becomes part of him. Shares his power. Shares his essence. Two become one, united in purpose and flesh. Whatever she is becomes part of him forever."

Whatever she is becomes part of him.

The words echoed louder now. I'd rather tear my own heart out than become like him. Never. I'd throw myself into the void before turning into that thing, that monster who fed on suffering and gorged himself on other people's pain.

"Will you marry me?" the Judge asked, with mock ceremony. The chamber, stained with blood and pain, might as well have been a garden arbor in his mind.

I shook my head in defiance. "I'd rather die." The words came out like venom. My nails dug into my palms hard enough to draw blood. I wanted to tear that smug expression apart with my bare hands. But I could barely stand. "Death would be a mercy compared to that existence. I'd choose hell over one second as your bride."

His gaze, those pits of smoldering judgment, shifted to the far corner where my friends lay like discarded dolls. Marion's legs bent at angles nature never intended, shards of bone glinting through torn flesh. The air reeked of copper and open wounds. Her eyes rolled toward me, unfocused, pain-blind.

Isaac lay beside her, his mouth working silently. The stump of his tongue writhed against blood-slick teeth, trying to form words that no longer had shape.

"I can heal her legs." The Judge's tone was breezy, casual, like he was discussing the rain. "Then break them again. Then heal them. Then break them. Forever. Each time, a new kind of pain. Bones remember trauma, you know. They scream louder with each breaking."

A sound rasped from Marion, half a sob, half a growl. Rage or despair, it was impossible to tell with the blood bubbling from her lips.

"Isaac's tongue can regrow. I'll harvest it every night. Then cut it again. Sometimes with scissors. Sometimes with rusted wire. Sometimes I'll let him grow it back halfway before taking it again. The anticipation is worse than the cutting."

I looked at my friends. My family. The only people who'd ever loved me without conditions or expectations.

Marion was trying to shake her head, tears cutting tracks through the blood on her face. Her eyes begged me not to do this. Isaac just stared at nothing with the empty gaze of someone who'd seen too much. They'd suffer forever if I refused. And knowing the Judge, he'd make me watch every second.

"I'll ask again." The Judge's voice dropped to something dangerous. The temperature in the chamber spiked, walls cracking from the heat. "And this time, think before you speak. Will you be my bride, or shall I start tormenting your friend now?"

The word lodged in my throat like broken glass. I looked at Marion's ruined legs, at Isaac's bloody mouth one more time and then at the monster waiting with dwindling patience.

My head moved once. The smallest nod that felt like signing my own death warrant.

"Bravo!" The Judge snapped his fingers, and the world remade itself around us. Walls ground against each other with the sound of molars chewing through stone. The bones in the floor rearranged themselves, rising and falling like waves made of death. What had been a throne room became a cathedral, but not one any god would recognize.

Spines curved upward to form gothic arches. Ribs spread out to create pews where no living thing would sit. Femurs stacked into pillars that wept marrow.

And the altar...

I recognized those bones. Smaller. More delicate. Female. The women Varnar had killed. Six hundred years of sacrifice, stacked and forgotten.

The air sparkled, and the dead came back.

Father Gallows materialized in his robes made of stitched scripture. The Mirror Eater appeared in fragments. The Seamstress skittered forward on her thread-spool legs, and what she carried made bile rise in my throat, a dress that had once been women. Different shades of skin stitched together with veins for thread. Some patches were pale as winter, others dark as earth, all of them sewn into this mockery of bridal dress.

She held it up like a prize, and then it was on me.

There was no transition, no moment of changing. One second I was naked and bleeding, the next this thing clung to my body like it had grown there. Warm. Pulsing with remembered life. Someone's belly skin stretched across my ribs. Someone's back wrapped around my shoulders. I could feel the different textures, soft here where a young woman's thigh had been, rough there where age had marked another.

Revulsion washed over me, but then something impossible happened. Despite the furnace heat, goosebumps swept up my arms. Not the horror-chills I expected. This was different. Clean, somehow. Like stepping from a sickroom into snow.

"Can't have a wedding without the groom's rival." The

Judge's laugh scraped against my bones. "Let me fix that oversight."

The ashes that had been my Executioner, began to move. First just shifting, then swirling, then rising in a column that hurt to look at. The resurrection happened in reverse, bones assembling, meat wrapping around them, organs nestling into place with sounds that would haunt me forever. When skin finally stretched over it all, he gasped back to life naked and confused, still wearing that ancient helmet.

His red eyes found mine through the slits. Saw the dress. Understood.

He tried to stand but chains erupted from the stone itself, wrapping his limbs with a sound like breaking teeth. They yanked him spread-eagle, displaying him like a warning.

"Release her!" His shoulders dislocated with wet pops as he fought. "Take your revenge on me alone. Kill me a thousand times but I beg you, just let her go."

The plea cracked behind the metal. "Please. I love her."

The Judge's roar made dust fall from the ceiling. My bones vibrated with it. "Insolent tool! You forget yourself. You are metal given form, nothing more. Love? From an instrument of execution? I'll unmake you for this presumption."

A blade appeared in his hand, not metal but something worse. It hummed with the memory of every scream that had ever echoed here.

The Executioner stopped fighting. His massive frame sagged in the chains, and his eyes found mine across the vast cathedral.

"Tell her why," the Judge commanded, raising the blade. "Since you claim to love her, tell her what you see. Last words should matter, even from things that were never meant to feel."

The Executioner never looked away from me. "I love your strength that you call weakness. Your survival that you call selfishness. Your scars that you call ugliness. I love the way you still try to save others when you can't save yourself. I love you, Zahra. Not as a tool loves its purpose. As a man loves a woman."

The blade went in slow between his ribs. The Judge watched my face while he did it, like my pain was the real show. The Executioner's light dimmed but his gaze held steady, anchoring me to something human even as he died.

The last wall gave way. Not into despair, but into terrible clarity. The guilt I'd carried for years—thick as tar, acidic and suffocating—had fermented into something else. Something that might choke even a god.

Father Gallows began the ceremony, grinding each word to dust. "Do you, Last Judge of the Realm Beneath, Our King, take this woman as your bride?"

"I do." The words cracked the bone pillars.

"Do you, Zahra Mitchell, take this King of Suffering as your husband?"

The compulsion hit like a fist to the throat. But as my mouth opened, something else slipped in. A whisper that didn't touch my ears but settled in my bones.

Yes. Let him bind himself to you.

Young. Female. Older than the stones but somehow still innocent.

"I do." They tore free, but that presence lingered, almost pleased.

The Seamstress brought rings made from finger bones, yellow and grooved. They fused to our skin with the smell of burning meat.

"Speak your promise," Father Gallows intoned.

I looked at the Judge. At this thing that had fed on misery for millennia and called it divine.

"I will give you all of me." The words barely existed. "Everything I am. Everything I carry. All of it."

He smiled. The fool smiled. "Time for consummation."

Shadow curtains fell around us. He pushed me onto the bone altar. The ribs of dead women dug into my spine. "Six hundred years." His hands left burns wherever they touched. "Six hundred years of waiting for the perfect bride to share my throne."

I stared at nothing and prepared to float away from my body like I'd learned with Theo. But then the presence returned, stronger now. The air around me shifted. Not cooler exactly, but... cleaner. Like finding one drop of fresh water in an ocean of blood.

Give him everything.

The voice was clearer now. I could taste its sorrow, centuries of watching this place corrupt everything good.

Your guilt, child. It's already dead inside you. Rotted into something he's never tasted.

My skin prickled. I smelled something impossible, wildflowers and rain on stone. Things that belonged to the world above.

We both died rather than submit. Now make him choke on what that created.

The Judge lowered his massive head for the binding kiss. The one that would seal our union forever.

Pour it all. Every drop of poison you've been brewing. Show him what happens when you break a woman until there's nothing left but venom.

I opened my mouth. Let him in. And began to pour.

Chapter Twenty-Seven

At first, he moaned into my mouth like I was wine. His burning tongue invaded deeper, drinking my sorrow. The Judge pressed against me, lost in triumph. The bone altar hummed as our essences began to merge.

"Yes," he breathed against my lips. "Your pain makes me stronger."

Then his movements stuttered. His tongue went rigid. He pulled back, confusion on his face.

Black veins appeared under his skin, spreading from where our lips had touched. They pulsed with each heartbeat, mapping corruption across his perfect features. "What is this?"

"Everything you wanted." The words came out hoarse. "All my guilt. All at once."

"No, this is wrong. Sorrow feeds me!"

"Normal sorrow does. Sorrow that comes and goes. Grief with hope still mixed in." I watched the poison spread across his face like ink in water. "But this? This is guilt turned to acid.

Shame that ate itself hollow. You finally ate something already dead inside."

He rolled off me, clutching his chest. The marriage bond had become a pipeline for poison, and he couldn't close it. We were wed now, our essences mingling whether he wanted it or not.

"Impossible!" Light burst from him, trying to burn away the contamination.

The shadow curtains disintegrated, exposing us to the wedding guests.

"I am eternal!" he roared.

He doubled over and vomited. Black sludge that moved on its own, mixed with pieces of his divine organs. Where it hit the floor, ancient bones began to dissolve, releasing the screams they'd held for centuries.

"You're a glutton. Always hungry for more suffering. Never satisfied." I purred.

He lunged at me. Even poisoned, he was still a god.

His fist connected with my ribs—I heard them crack like kindling. The force sent me flying back into a spine pillar. Stars exploded across my vision.

"I'll destroy you!" he groaned. He staggered forward, but his legs buckled. Black corruption poured from his nose, his ears, seeping through his pores like poisonous sweat.

His perfect form was coming apart, skin peeling away in wet sheets, revealing nothing underneath. Just absence. The void where divinity used to live.

"I'll make you suffer for—" He collapsed.

"You taught me something." I pressed my broken ribs. Each breath was agony. "Nothing stays dead here. You made sure of that, wanting your victims to suffer eternally."

Now his own rules would damn him. I reached out with my mind for the Executioner's essence. He was everywhere and nowhere, dissolved but not destroyed.

I grabbed onto the fragments and pulled. It felt like reaching into fire. Like trying to hold lightning.

A thing tore inside me, not flesh, but deeper. Blood poured from my nose, my eyes, my ears. My vision went red, then black, then red again. But I kept pulling.

The ashes swirled into a column, spinning faster until they blurred gray. The bones throughout the cathedral sang, a high note that made my teeth ache. The column exploded outward.

And then—He stood there, gasping. Alive again. Leather pants restored. Helmet intact. Blade in hand. Every scar exactly where it had been. "You brought me back."

"Nothing stays dead here," I repeated, spitting blood.

The Judge turned at the sound of metal dragging across bone. His melting face twisted in shock. The poison had eaten away most of his features. "How? I control death in this realm!"

"You did." The Executioner's words were rust and ruin. "But you're dying now. Real death. Final death."

They clashed in the center of the cathedral, but it was different from before. The Judge's divine fire sputtered. Each swing came slower. Pieces of him kept dissolving and reforming wrong, an eye would melt and regrow smaller, a finger would fall off and return with too many joints.

"Servants! Kill them!" The Judge tried to order.

Chaos erupted.

Father Gallows descended from the rafters, screaming about suffering. The Mirror Eater shattered into a thousand reflections. The Seamstress skittered forward on thread-spool legs. Hundreds of Mawkeepers poured through the bone walls. But their attacks lacked conviction. They could smell their master dying.

Some hung back, watching to see who would win. Predators always know when the alpha is about to fall.

The Executioner carved through them like smoke, always pushing toward the Judge. When he reached the altar, the Judge could barely lift his head. The poison had eaten through all his grandeur. "Please." His hand was more bone than flesh, skin sloughing off.

"I can give you anything. Power. Worlds. Everything—"

The blade found his heart. Black corruption poured from the wound instead of blood.

The Judge looked down at the massive sword buried in his chest, then his burning eyes found mine. In them, there was genuine terror. "How? I am eternal. I am—"

"You're done." I let it land.

I crawled over to him, each movement sending spikes through my broken ribs. When I reached him, I leaned close to his melting face. Close enough to smell the rot. Close enough to see myself reflected in his dimming eyes.

"You wanted my sorrow. My guilt." I pressed my lips to where his ear was dissolving. "You should have asked what kind of woman carries poison in her kiss."

I kissed him one last time and poured the last reserves of toxicity straight down his throat. Every drop of self-loathing. Every grain of survivor's guilt ground to its most potent form.

He crumbled. Not to ash. Not to dust. But to void. To absolute absence.

The realm shuddered. All that power, all that authority was suddenly without a vessel. It hung in the air for one impossible moment. Then it overwhelmed me completely. I hit the ground hard. The power was too much for mortal flesh. My body convulsed. Blood poured from everywhere, eyes, nose, mouth, even beneath my fingernails. I was drowning in copper and fire.

"Zahra!" The Executioner's hands clamped down on my shoulders, trying to hold me still. But I was beyond reach, caught between mortality and something else.

My back arched. I felt vertebrae crack. Then the first horn erupted from my skull, bursting through bone and brain. The second followed. Each one was a railroad spike driven from the inside out.

But through the agony, that presence returned. Stronger than before. No longer whispering but here, wrapping around me like a mother's embrace.

You did it, child. You did it!

The air felt like a breeze, and for a moment, just a moment —I saw her. Young, maybe seventeen. Dark hair like mine. She wasn't transparent, almost ghostly. She was more real than anything else down here.

And somehow, without explanation or logic, I knew exactly who she was. *St. Dymphna* herself.

But the power will destroy you without guidance. Let me help. Let me share what should have been.

She pressed her hand to my forehead, and I felt it, not just the Judge's stolen authority, but something older. Cleaner. The original blessing of this place before it was corrupted. A sanctuary for the mad and broken, twisted into a torture chamber.

Take both. His power to punish the guilty, and mine to recognize those who can still be saved.

My skin changed next. Gray spread in patches as corruption and divinity fought over my flesh. But where her touch lingered, the gray took on a different quality. Not the dead ash of the Judge's realm, but the soft gray of dawn. Of things that exist between night and day.

"Stay with me!" the Executioner begged.

Another convulsion. My spine snapped. Reformed longer. Snapped again. My body was rejecting its own shape, no, it was trying to hold two natures at once. Judge and Saint. Punishment and Mercy.

You are both now, her voice soothed as my bones rewrote themselves. *What I could never be, strong enough to fight back. What he could never be, human enough to know when to stop.*

The fingernails that pushed through were black and curved, yes, but at the tips, they held a faint shimmer. Like stars hidden in dark clouds.

Then, silence.

The pain stopped so suddenly I gasped. Everything went still.

"Zahra?" I heard the Executioner call my name and opened my eyes. The world looked different. Clearer. I could see the sins written into the walls. I could taste fear. I could feel the realm's hunger pulsing with my heart.

But I could also see something else, the first sign of redemption in some souls. The difference between those who chose evil and those who were broken by it.

My work here is done, the presence whispered, fading now. The sanctuary is yours. Make it what it should have been.

I sat up slowly. My body was different. Gray skin that flickered between solid and shadow. Horns that curled back like a crown, but if you looked closely, they held the same shimmer as my claws. Beautiful and terrible at once.

I was still me. Changed. Corrupted. Deified. Blessed. The poisoned woman who married a god, killed him with a kiss, and inherited a saint's forgotten purpose.

"My Queen," the Executioner whispered, dropping to one knee.

I looked at my friends, broken on the floor. Marion trying to drag herself forward on ruined legs. Isaac making those wet, desperate sounds through his mutilated mouth. My first act wouldn't be vengeance. It would be healing.

I moved to Marion first, kneeling beside her. "Be still," I commanded, and my words carried new authority. I placed my hands on her mangled legs, and power flowed through me. Bones realigned with crackling sounds. Torn muscle rewove itself. Her legs straightened first, then the bruises faded from her face, her ribs sealed, and every cut Varnar had left on her body closed. Marion gasped as sensation returned.

Then Isaac. I touched his throat gently. "Speak again," I whispered, and watched his tongue regrow, pink and whole. He coughed, spitting blood, then looked at me with wonder. I put my hand on his shattered knee next and felt the bone pull straight beneath my palm, the joint knitting back together with a sound like cracking knuckles. Then I took his ruined hands and straightened every broken finger until they moved again. He flexed them, staring.

"Zahra?" The words came out rough but real. "You're, what are you?"

"I'm what this place needs," I answered, helping them both stand.

My eyes caught what I knew were Sela's ashes, scattered where the Judge had destroyed her. I wasn't sure if I could bring back someone who'd been gone that long, but I had to try.

I moved to the pile of ash that had been Sela and kneeled. The others watched as I gathered the gray dust in my hands. This was different from bringing back the Executioner. She'd been gone longer. Scattered wider. But the realm obeyed me now. I poured my will into the ashes. Forced them to remember what they'd been. The dust swirled. Condensed. Took shape.

Sela gasped back to life, naked and trembling on the bone floor. Her gray hair fell loose around her shoulders. When she opened her eyes, she blinked, looking around in wonder, one hand reaching up to touch her face where the glasses should have been.

"I can see," she whispered. "Everything's so clear."

I waved my hand. A simple white gown materialized around her, covering her vulnerability.

"You're alive," Marion told her, tears streaming down her face. "Zahra brought you back."

Sela looked at me with those newly clear eyes, taking in my transformed state, the horns, the gray skin, the shimmer at the edges of everything I'd become.

"You killed him." Awe flooded her face. "You actually killed the Judge."

"Yes." I stood and flexed my claws.

The realm pulsed, eager and hungry. But its hunger had changed to match mine. No longer for random suffering. Now it wanted only the truly unrepentant. The ones who hurt others and felt nothing. The ones who chose their darkness.

But for the first time in six centuries, it also wanted to release those who didn't belong here. The broken who'd been punished enough. The guilty who still had hearts that could break.

Chapter Twenty-Eight

I looked at the cowering servants. The air itself had gone electric since the Judge's death, waiting to see what kind of god I would be.

The cathedral had changed. Screams in the walls had quieted to whispers, like prisoners who'd just realized the warden was dead. Even the taste had shifted, less copper and fear, more like the moment before lightning strikes.

"You." I pointed at the Seamstress. "Come here."

She tried backing away on thread-spool legs, but my will dragged her forward. Each click against bone floor sounded like typewriter keys spelling out a death sentence. The faces embedded in her torso watched me with desperate hope. "Please. I served faithfully—"

"With enthusiasm." I circled her slowly. Human skin stretched and sewn into her frame. Tools hanging from her belt, needles that could pierce the soul as easily as flesh. "You added flourishes. Made it artistic."

The threads that made her started writhing like worms under summer rain.

"What are you—NO!"

Hundreds burst through her pores. Red silk from the woman who'd begged for her children. Black cord from the girl who'd gone silent after the third day. White fiber from the grandmother who'd prayed until her last breath. They wrapped around her limbs and pulled.

Her shoulders dislocated first. The wet pop echoed off cathedral walls. Then elbows bent backward. Spine twisted until vertebrae ground like millstones.

"Stop! Please! I'll serve you instead—"

The threads wove through her flesh, forming patterns I recognized from her victims' bodies. The rosette sewn into a young mother's back. The crosshatch used to silence a woman who'd fought back. Nerve endings severed and reconnected in impossible ways.

"You'll feel every thread. Every pull. Unlike your victims, you'll never go into shock. This is your existence now."

Father Gallows tried to run, foot suspended mid-step when I froze him.

"The priest who gave absolution to killers." I placed my hand on his scripture robes. Parchment smoked where I touched it. "Every woman you told to forgive her rapist. Every child you said must honor their abusive parent."

The words on his robes came alive. Latin prayers slithered across fabric like insects, then burned into flesh beneath. "MERCY! I BEG FOR MERCY!"

"Like that girl who came to you after her uncle—" I stopped. He knew.

His skin peeled in sheets, revealing more burning scripture underneath. He screamed as his tongue caught fire, false sermons finally burning away. But even tongueless, scripture kept writing itself deeper.

The Mirror Eater shattered herself into a thousand fragments. Too late.

"Stop." Shards froze mid-air.

"Helena Wolfe." In each fragment, a different victim's face appeared beneath my reflection. "You reflected their worst moments back at them. Made them relive trauma for entertainment."

The shards reassembled wrong. Each piece now displayed a different woman. The girl too young to understand. The woman who'd blocked it out until Helena forced her to remember. The survivor who'd built a new life, only to have it shattered.

The faces screamed. All at once.

Helena's body cracked like a mirror trying to hold its shape. Each fracture filled with a victim's pain. She tried to scream, but a thousand voices came out.

"You made them see their worst moments repeatedly. Now you live them all. Simultaneously. The mind can't process that much trauma at once, so yours will keep trying. And failing."

"Kill me!" The words came in dozens of voices.

"You get what you gave, endless reflection. Except now, it's yours."

The Mawkeepers had tried fading into the walls. I pulled them back like dragging fish from deep water.

"Always lurking. Always reporting secrets." I raised my hand. "You wanted to be part of the walls? Fine."

Bones stretched and flattened. Cartilage spread like mortar. Screams turned to grinding stone as vertebrae became support beams, ribs became joists, skulls became keystones.

"Feel the weight of every soul who suffered because of your reports. Forever conscious. Forever load-bearing."

Silence fell, broken only by thread pulling through flesh, scripture burning into bone, and the settling of living architecture.

Then it hit me. These weren't just servants, they were victims first. Each one tortured until they embraced their tormentor's tools. The Seamstress, broken with needle and thread until she became them. Gallows, carved with lies until he was lies. The Mirror Eater, forced to relive trauma until she weaponized it.

The ultimate corruption: turning victims into victimizers.

The whole system needs restructuring. But first...

"This is justice." The words became law as I spoke them. "Not random torture. Specific punishment for specific sins. The cycle of victim becoming victimizer ends now."

Marion, Isaac, and Sela looked at me. Not with fear, but recognition.

"You survived. Felt guilt for surviving. That marks you as sacred here," I told them.

Suddenly, the cathedral's atmosphere shifted. I felt a devouring want, focused upward through reality's layers until it found what it craved: the ones who slept soundly after destroying lives. Who felt entitled to others' pain. Who'd never experienced remorse.

I could taste them, their certainty, their casual cruelty. Up there right now, trying to summon their dead god.

"The remorseless." The sound harmonized with itself. "Varnar. The cultists. Still calling for their Judge."

The Executioner stood beside the altar, steam rising from

his chest. Through helmet slits, his red eyes held understanding.

"What will you do?"

I looked around at what I'd created. Justice from chaos. But also a diseased system that needed complete restructuring.

A smile pulled at my transformed features. "I'm not sure. But I feel... hungry."

The cathedral shuddered with anticipation. After centuries of random suffering, it would taste something different, justice for the untouchable.

"Then you'll feed." Prophetic certainty filled him. "My queen."

Chapter Twenty-Nine

In the ritual chamber, I could see Varnar pacing among his scattered grimoires like a caged animal. His usually perfect suit was wrinkled, tie hanging loose, hair disheveled in ways I'd never seen.

Time moved strangely between the realms. We'd spent what felt like weeks in the Realm Beneath. But looking at Varnar now, still in the same clothes from our confrontation, the fresh blood still tacky on the altar, I realized only hours had passed here. Maybe a day at most.

"Find something! Anything!" The words cracked in ways that made him sound almost human. The other cultists scrambled through ancient texts, their fingers shaking as they turned pages that wept black tears. These weren't just grimoires, they were contracts written in languages that predated human speech, each one a record of atrocities committed in the Judge's name.

I understood their panic now. For six centuries, they'd kept the Judge bound by carefully worded summonings, he could only manifest when called through specific rituals, trapped by the very contracts his hunger had made him sign. Too dangerous to let roam free, even for his servants. The Executioner had been their go-between, their controllable tool who could cross realms at will.

But I'd eaten their god. Dissolved him from the inside with poisoned sorrow. And the binding contracts had dissolved with him. Now there was nothing limiting me. No summoning required. No contracts to honor. I could appear whenever I wanted, wherever I wanted.

Their carefully crafted control had died with their god.

"The Judge isn't responding," one cultist whispered, the old man I had seen with Varnar before. "Every summons, every offering... nothing."

Of course he wasn't responding. I'd fed him his own poison.

"Try again!" Varnar's composure shattered completely. He grabbed a silver chalice from the altar and hurled it across the room. "Great Judge, Lord of the Damned, we beseech you! Return Dr. Alan! Take the others—Mitchell, anyone, just give me back Alan!"

The candles didn't even flicker. If anything, they dimmed, as if the very concept of the Judge was being erased from reality.

"Please!" He broke on the word. "We've served faithfully! Fed your hunger for decades! My family has given everything! Just give Alan back!"

The Executioner stood beside me between worlds, his massive frame radiating eagerness. I felt his anticipation vibrating through the Realm Beneath like a tuning fork struck against bone. He'd been waiting for this moment. Not just to return, but to return as something other than a slave.

Varnar spun to face his followers, and I saw real madness creeping into his eyes. "Summon the Executioner! Now!"

"Sir, we've already tried," a younger cultist stammered. "We don't have a sacrifice ready. We just sacrificed Jenkins fifteen minutes ago and, nothing happened."

He couldn't have been more than twenty-five, probably recruited from some Ivy League school with promises of power.

"Then we'll sacrifice more. Keep sacrificing until the Executioner shows up." Varnar's eyes landed on the young man. "Starting with you."

He grabbed the cultist and dragged him toward the altar.

"No! Please! I've been loyal—" the young man screamed, trying to break free.

Other robed figures rushed to help Varnar, pinning the struggling man to the stone and gagging his mouth with a piece of cloth.

"By blood and binding," Varnar began to chant. "By guilt acknowledged and pain made manifest. We summon the Executioner. Let him prepare the way for our Lord Judge. Let him open the door between worlds."

His words echoed off the stone as he drew the ritual knife across the sacrifice's wrist. Just a shallow cut, enough to bleed, not enough to kill. The man whimpered through his gag, eyes wild with terror.

Ruby liquid welled up and dripped onto the altar. The moment it touched the stone, everything changed. Instead of pooling naturally, the blood moved with purpose, flowing into the carved channels like mercury finding its level. It spread outward in perfect spirals, following grooves in the stone, ancient symbols drinking the fresh offering.

I glanced at the Executioner beside me. His helmet tilted toward me in question. I nodded.

Time to make our entrance.

The blood pool in their world began to ripple. The temperature spiked so fast the air quivered like pavement in July. Sweat burst from the cultists' skin, soaking through their robes in seconds.

"Yes! Finally, it's working!" Varnar breathed, hope and terror warring in the words. "Something's coming! Everyone stay calm. Form the circle. Remember your training."

But their training had been for controlling summoned entities, not for what was about to emerge.

I had Dr. Alan's corpse in my claws. I'd skinned her body but left her face intact, those dead eyes staring up from a frame of raw muscle.

With careful aim, I hurled it up through the portal. The body erupted from the blood pool like something fired from a cannon, spinning through the air in a graceful arc that seemed to last forever, and landed near Varnar.

For a moment, he just stared. Then his eyes recognized her face, her features. His face transformed in a way I'd never seen before. The arrogance crumbled. The certainty shattered. What remained was just horror and shock.

"No..." He dropped to his knees beside the body, hands hovering over it without quite touching, as if contact would make it real. "No, no, no... Alan... what did they do to you?"

He reached out with shaking fingers to touch her face, or what remained of it.

"I'm sorry," he whispered, and for the first time since I'd known him, I heard real emotion. Raw, unfiltered grief. "This wasn't supposed to happen to you. You were supposed to be safe. Protected. I promised..."

Too little, too late.

But his pain tasted sweet from between worlds, like aged wine finally uncorked.

The blood pool erupted again.

Marion climbed out first, gasping and retching. The journey between worlds wasn't kind to human physiology. She collapsed on the stone floor, covered in the thick crimson fluid, shaking violently from the trauma of the crossing.

"Never... never again..." she gasped, trying to wipe the blood from her eyes.

Isaac followed, coughing and spitting out the foul liquid. His hands flew to his throat in panic, checking that everything was still intact. The memory of the Judge's torture was still fresh, even though I'd managed to heal him.

"We're alive," he kept saying, hoarse and cracking. "We're actually alive. Marion, we made it!"

They were battered, traumatized, covered in blood from the pool, but they were still themselves. People who had survived an impossible nightmare and somehow made it back to the world of the living.

Sela emerged last. Her gray hair hung loose and wet with blood, falling past her shoulders. Red liquid dripped from the ends, streaking down her face. Her eyes swept the room, blinking hard to clear the blood from her vision.

They all stood ready to fight. Marion's fists were already clenched, Isaac's face set hard. The cultists backed away from the emerging survivors, terror replacing their ritual confidence.

Then came the Executioner, my Executioner.

He rose from the blood pool like something born from

nightmares. Bare-chested and magnificent, scars telling stories of centuries of divine punishment. His blade dragged behind him, scoring grooves in the stone that bled.

"Executioner!" Varnar stood with pathetic hope, still kneeling beside Alan's corpse. "You've come! We need the Judge. We need—"

The Executioner's helmet turned toward him slowly. Not the blind obedience of a servant anymore. He was mine now, and Varnar could sense it. The temperature rose another ten degrees. The blood in the pool started to boil.

My turn.

The blood pool began to bubble. I rose from the crimson depths like something born of nightmares. Blood flowed off my gray skin in sheets. My body lifted without effort, ascending from the pool. My horns gleamed wet and black, crowning my transformed head.

The wedding dress clung to my transformed form. It had grown with me, stretched to fit. The stolen skin throbbed with its own heartbeat.

I was no longer the broken woman who'd entered the Realm Beneath.

I was its god now.

"Hello, Varnar." The sound cracked the windows in spiderweb patterns. One cultist's ears began to bleed. Another dropped to his knees, overwhelmed by the presence of something that should not exist. "Looking for the Judge?"

"What... what are you?" he stammered, stumbling backward, nearly tripping over Alan's corpse.

"I am what happens when you push someone too far." I stepped onto solid ground. The floor fractured beneath me.

"When you mistake survival for weakness. When you create the instrument of your own destruction, and call it treatment."

"Where is the Judge?" He climbed toward hysteria.

"I ate him." I said it casually, like I was mentioning what I had for breakfast. "Turns out gods can die if you poison them with enough concentrated despair. He tasted like eons of other people's pain. Gave me heartburn."

I surveyed the room, nostrils flaring. The scent of unrepentant souls was intoxicating. Every cultist reeked of crimes they'd never regretted, atrocities they'd justified, suffering they'd inflicted while sleeping soundly.

Behind me, Marion shifted. "The patients—" The word cracked out of her, urgent. "We have to free them!"

I didn't turn, but I raised one hand in a swift gesture toward the door. *Go.*

Marion hesitated for just a heartbeat, then grabbed Isaac's arm. Sela was already moving. Their footsteps retreated up the stone stairs, fading into the corridors above.

The cultists remained frozen in their circle, trembling. Some still clutched their ceremonial daggers, though their hands shook too badly to use them. Others had dropped to their knees, mouths moving in silent prayers to gods who wouldn't answer.

I stepped closer to the altar, my shadow stretching long across the blood-stained floor. The lead cultist, the one who'd been chanting moments before, backed against the stone table, his elaborate robes now damp with sweat.

"You know what I am." I let the words fall soft.

Above us, distantly, I could hear doors opening. Muffled shouts. The sound of many feet beginning to move. Marion and the others were doing their work. But that was their concern now.

Mine stood before me, reeking of fear and sin.

One cultist—younger, quicker, probably newer—tried to run. He made it three steps before the Executioner's blade sang through the air. His head separated cleanly but kept screaming as it rolled across the floor, eyes blinking in confusion. The body took a few more steps, muscle memory dragging it forward, before collapsing.

"Now, now," I purred. The sound made several cultists whimper. "Leaving already? And the evening's entertainment has just begun."

I moved toward the nearest cultist with predatory grace. The oldest one—Varnar's advisor.

"Six hundred years," I murmured, placing a clawed hand on his weathered face. "Six hundred years your bloodline has served. Six hundred years of torture, and not a drop of remorse. Perfectly aged. Vintage sociopathy."

"I... I am faithful," he wheezed. One of his eyes burst like an overripe grape from the pressure of his terror. "Always faithful to the Judge—"

"The Judge is gone. Now there's only hunger. My hunger. And you're exactly what I've been craving."

I began the extraction. Not his soul. No—I devoured something far more specific. I pulled out his missing guilt, all those centuries of unfelt remorse. It poured from every orifice as black smoke, thick as tar, screaming with the voices of everyone he'd hurt.

His face contorted as he relived every moment of pain he'd ever caused, from his victims' perspectives. Not just their physical agony, but the aftermath. The nightmares. The shattered families. The suicides. The ripples of grief that echoed for generations.

When he was nothing but a hollow husk, I fed deeply. The taste was exquisite, centuries of justice aged to perfection, flavored with every culture he helped destroy. His body crumbled, not into ash, but into dust so fine it resembled the sand of ages. The dust whispered names as it fell. Every victim, finally remembered.

"Delicious," I purred, licking my lips with a tongue now forked and far too long. "Who's next?"

The cultists scattered like roaches exposed to light.

Some ran for doors that no longer led anywhere—I'd been reshaping the building's geometry since I arrived. One opened a doorway only to find a wall of screaming mouths. Another ran in circles, the room folding in on itself, trapping him in an endless loop.

The Executioner moved with brutal efficiency. But he left some alive. He knew the ones I'd marked for feeding. He could smell the particularly rancid guilt on them.

His blade sang as it moved. And the song was names, every soul who had died within these walls, finally given voice. The walls began to weep blood as the building itself remembered its crimes.

"Please!" A cultist fell to his knees, robes slipping open to reveal a chest covered in ritualistic scars, prayers to the Judge carved into his skin. "We were just following orders! The Judge demanded—"

"Following orders." I chuckled. "How many times did your victims beg? How many did you ignore because you were 'just following orders'?"

This extraction was especially satisfying.

He didn't just feel pain, he relived the full lives he'd stolen. Every future he erased for the Judge's appetite. His adult mind couldn't withstand the innocent terror from within. He aged fifty years in fifty seconds, his hair went white, skin shriveled like rotting fruit, teeth falling out as his body tried to carry the weight of his sins.

Varnar backed into Alan's corpse, shaking like a leaf in a hurricane. His expensive shoes slipped in her blood, and he fell, landing with one hand inside her chest cavity. He yanked it back with a shriek. Her organs clung to his fingers like desperate lovers.

The wet, sucking sound made two more cultists vomit.

"Wait. Please. We can make a deal." He'd lost all polish, reduced to raw, animal desperation.

"A deal?" I tilted my head so far it should've snapped. The cracking sound made him flinch. "What could you possibly offer me? Your money? I rule the Realm Beneath. Your connections? I'm linked to every guilty soul that breathes. Your knowledge? I absorbed it when I ate your god."

"Information! Resources! I know where the Judge's artifacts are hidden!"

"Varnar." I stepped toward him slowly, savoring every beat of his fear. "Do you remember what you did to me? That night in your office? The way you carved your initial into my lower back like I was livestock?"

"I was treating you! The Judge's methods—"

"You raped dozens of women. Hundreds, probably. Called it treatment. Felt entitled to our bodies because we were crazy."

I leaned close. "And you never felt guilt. Just disappointment when we fought back."

I was close enough now for him to see the divine fire in my eyes. To smell brimstone on my breath. To understand that his definition of power had been a child's toy compared to what stood before him.

"Please," he whispered. "I had no choice. The Judge—"

"There's always a choice."

I grabbed his throat, lifting him easily. My claws punctured skin, just enough to draw blood. "You chose power. Chose cruelty. Chose to feed on the vulnerable. And you enjoyed it. I can smell your enjoyment. It clings to you like cologne."

The extraction began slowly. I wanted him to feel every second.

I held him suspended, watching his tears burn tracks down his face. That clean presence from the wedding brushed against me again, faint but unmistakable.

"The irony." I tightened my grip on his throat, soft. "You named this place after a patron saint of the mentally ill, then used it to drive them madder."

Varnar's eyes widened. He felt it too, something watching that had waited centuries for this moment.

"Every woman who saw that name and hoped for sanctuary." I leaned closer, letting him see the divine fire in my eyes. "You turned a saint's protection into the perfect trap."

"I'm sorry!" he screamed, tears running down his cheeks like acid, burning his skin. "Oh god, I'm sorry! I didn't—I didn't understand—"

"Too late for understanding. Far too late for sorry."

I still held Varnar by the throat, his face purple, his sanity cracking like ice on a pond. Each fracture revealed something uglier underneath, the truth of what he was without the polish, without the justifications, without the certainty that he deserved to take whatever he wanted.

"Actually," I mused, studying his broken form, "your suffering has barely begun."

A fresh pool of blood opened on the floor.

"No, please," he choked. "Just kill me—"

"Death?" I laughed. "Death is mercy, Varnar. You're going to live forever. Forever carrying what you've done. Forever feeling what they felt. Forever knowing exactly what kind of monster you are."

I hurled him into the black pool. His screams echoed as he fell between worlds growing fainter but never ending until the portal sealed behind him with a satisfied sigh.

I turned.

Marion, Isaac, and Sela stood in the doorway, watching everything. They were covered in blood and dust from freeing the patients, but they stood tall. Unbroken.

"You opened the wards," I observed.

"Every door we could reach," Marion confirmed, chin raised despite the fear in her eyes. "Guided the ones who could walk toward the emergency exits. The rest, the building was coming down. We did what we could."

"And you stayed." I stated.

"Someone had to witness this." Sela's gaze stayed on me. "Someone had to remember."

"We saw the truth below," Isaac added. "We can't unsee it. Wouldn't want to."

"Come closer," I commanded.

They approached without hesitation, though I could smell their fear. It was clean fear, honest. Not like the cultists' terror, which reeked of guilt. These three feared my power, but not my judgment.

They had nothing to hide.

St. Dymphna groaned around us. Larger chunks of ceiling began to fall. The building was dying. Reality was reasserting itself now that the supernatural force holding this place together was gone.

"What happens now?" Marion asked.

"Now?" I gestured to the crumbling chamber. "This place dies. And you three get to live. Really live. Not just survive."

"But what about you?" Isaac's voice carried genuine concern. "You're free now. You could come with us."

The Executioner stood beside me, silent and still as stone. Through the bond between us, I could feel the Realm Beneath beginning to destabilize. Walls cracking. Punishments unraveling. Chaos rising.

"If that realm collapses"—I let it come slowly—"everything connected to it ceases to exist. Including him." I nodded toward the Executioner. "Including all the justice I want to build. Including Varnar's eternal punishment."

"So you have to go back." The realization hit Sela. "To keep it stable."

"To keep it contained." I watched the walls buckle around us. "But also..." I smiled. It wasn't entirely sad. "Perhaps I can make use of the place. All those chambers designed for punishment. All that architecture of suffering. It seems a waste to let it crumble, when there are so many guilty souls who sleep too soundly."

"You'll become like the Judge?" Marion's voice was small. Afraid.

"No." I held firm. "The Judge fed on everyone's suffering.

I have a more... selective appetite. Only those without remorse. Only those who've never felt guilt for their crimes. The world is full of them. And they've gotten away with it for too long."

The building shuddered violently. Time was running out.

"Go," I commanded. "Now. Before it's too late."

Marion rushed forward and hugged me. I tensed, my new form wasn't built for gentleness. But I returned the embrace carefully, trying not to puncture her with my claws.

"Will we ever see you again?" she whispered.

"I don't know," I admitted. "Perhaps new ways will open. Perhaps you'll find methods I haven't thought of. You're all touched by that realm now. Who knows what that might mean?"

They ran toward the stairs. But Marion looked back one last time from the doorway.

"Zahra—"

"Go!" I shouted, just as a massive chunk of ceiling crashed down where she'd been standing.

They fled into the storming night.

I waited. I listened until I heard them clear the building, heard a car start, heard them drive away, to safety. To sanity. To lives that could finally begin.

I turned to the Executioner.

Rain fell through the shattered roof, streaming down his scarred shoulders like a baptism.

"All this time," I whispered, reaching for his helmet. "All this time, and I've never truly seen you."

He didn't resist. My fingers found the edges of the ancient metal. The helmet was warm, almost alive, and I could feel his breath inside, hot as forge fire. I lifted it away slowly, my hands trembling not from fear, but from something deeper.

It clanged against the rubble and rolled into the shadows.

I had to tilt my head back to see his face. He towered over me, eight feet to my five-two, but that difference didn't make me feel small.

It made me feel protected.

His face was a map of old violence. Scars crisscrossed high cheekbones and a long, angular face that seemed too dramatic to be real. Both eyes burned red, but now I saw something else in them: vulnerability. Longing. The same ache blooming in my own chest.

His mouth was too wide for his face, lips full but marked at one corner where something had split them long ago.

His hair was wild and black, spiking in every direction, a dark crown framing his feral face. Everything about him looked unhinged. Violent. Beautiful.

"I am not to be looked at. I'm ugly." Rough and low, almost broken.

My heart clenched.

Centuries of hiding. Centuries of believing he wasn't worthy of being seen.

"Ugly?" I stood on my toes and reached up to trace one of his scars. "You're magnificent. You're mine."

His hands moved to my waist, and suddenly I was airborne. He lifted me like I weighed nothing, bringing me to his level. My feet dangled above the ground as one massive arm wrapped around me, holding me tight against his chest. His other hand cradled the back of my head.

For a moment, we just stayed like that, face to face. Monster to monster. Equal to equal.

His breath was warm against my lips.

Then he kissed me.

It was gentle at first. His lips were softer than they looked. But gentleness couldn't contain what we were. His mouth opened, and I gasped. His tongue was black as midnight, longer than any human's, sliding against mine like silk and sin.

His jagged teeth grazed my lower lip, drawing blood. He licked it away with a growl.

My hands tangled in his wild hair. It was sharp against my palms, drawing tiny cuts, but I only pulled him closer. He growled into my mouth, the sound vibrating through my body.

This was wrong by every standard of heaven and earth. A monster kissing a monster in the ruins of madness.

It was perfect.

When we finally broke apart, both of us breathing hard, he lowered me gently to the floor. The building groaned around us, walls beginning to collapse.

"Mine," he growled, his forehead resting against mine.

"Always," I whispered back. "In every realm. In every form."

He pulled me against his chest, one hand cradling my head against him. "My moth," he murmured into my hair, the words rumbling through his chest.

I pulled back just enough to look into his burning eyes. "You call me your moth, but I need to give you a name too. You're so much more than just an executioner, my execution-er." I traced another scar along his cheekbone, feeling him shudder under my touch. "You're my Flame. The fire I was always meant to fly into. The burning that doesn't consume me but transforms me."

His eyes widened slightly, centuries of solitude cracking at the edges.

"In all this darkness, you were the only light that called to me," I continued, dropping to a whisper. "Not to destroy me, but to remake me. My beautiful, terrible Flame."

"Flame," he repeated, tasting the name like something sacred. His arms tightened around me. "Yes. I'll be your Flame. Always burning. Always there for my moth." He pulled me against his chest, and we stood there in the dying hospital, two creatures born from violence finding something gentle in each other.

The walls could fall. The world could end.

We had already survived worse. We had found each other in hell. And that was enough.

Chapter Thirty

As I returned to the Realm Beneath with the Executioner by my side, Varnar stared at it in horror. His mouth hung open, spit dripping. The walls breathed around us, real breathing, wet and wrong. For the first time in his life, he was seeing where he'd sent all those women. Not some abstract place in his files. This place. With its stink of old meat and floors that squirmed under his expensive shoes. He kept shaking his head like a dog trying to clear water from its ears, but the realm wouldn't leave. It pressed into him through every pore, showing him exactly what he'd been feeding all these years.

"Welcome to your new home," I told Varnar, watching him scramble away from what the realm had built from his memory of Alan, her skinned body, reconstructed in perfect detail. His shoes slipped in the puddle of his own vomit.

The cathedral of bones stretched around us, impossibly vast. Every surface was carved from human remains, but now I could hear them. Whispers built into the foundation itself.

I walked to the nearest wall and pressed my palm flat

against a skull worked into the stone. The voices crashed over me like a tide.

"Oh God," I yanked my hand back. "I need to free them."

The Executioner moved closer, boots heavy on the bone floor. "The damned souls, my Queen?"

"Not just the damned." I pressed both hands against the wall this time, bracing for what would come. "Everyone. Six hundred years of sacrifice mixed together like ingredients in a pot."

They flooded through me. A girl who'd been sacrificed for talking to herself. A mother who'd killed her baby during post-partum psychosis. A woman who'd stabbed her uncle after years of abuse. The guilty tangled with the innocent, all conscious inside the architecture.

"Can you hear them too?" I asked the Executioner.

"I've always heard them," he admitted. "The Judge commanded me not to listen."

The power inside me thrummed, not just the Judge's authority, but something cleaner. That presence from the wedding had left its mark.

I knelt in the center of the cathedral. "If you were sacrificed, tortured for no crime but existing, wake up. Remember who you were."

The walls began to glow. Soft white light seeping through the bones as souls stirred from their imprisonment. A young girl broke free first, hovering there, translucent and confused.

"Where do I go?" she whispered.

I found I knew the answer. Could see the path opening above us. "There. To whatever comes after."

She rose like smoke. Then another. Then dozens. The virgin sacrifices. The falsely accused. The ones whose only crime was being different. Each departure cracked the structure further.

"The realm requires souls," the Executioner warned as the ceiling began to rain dust.

"Then we'll find new ones." I let it settle. "The right ones."

Soon only the guilty remained. Father Gallows writhed against his pillar, burning eternally in scripture robes. The Seamstress twitched in her web of nerve-threads. The Mirror Eater's thousand reflections showed only terror.

I stopped at Father Gallows first. "You've served since the 1400s, haven't you? When Varnar's family first gave you to the Judge."

His eyes found mine through the scripture that bound him. Begging.

Centuries in the pillar had finally taught him something. I could taste it, remorse. Thin, late, but real. "Enough." I touched his shoulder. The scripture robes unraveled, the words writhing as they released their hold. His hollow chest collapsed, coins and scales clattering to the floor. "Face whatever waits beyond." And then he vanished.

Then I turned to the Seamstress who instantly gaped. "You can't release us. We're the worst ones." "You were made by this place before you chose to serve it," I told her. "That earns you one door. Varnar gets none."

"And you've been tortured by your own methods ever since," I observed, dissolving her threads with a touch. "If centuries of feeling your victims' pain hasn't taught you empathy, nothing will."

She sobbed as she faded, relief or terror, I couldn't tell.

The Mirror Eater was last, shattered beyond recognition. "I remember the name. I don't remember the woman."

"Then go find out." I opened the gate. "Face whatever waits beyond. If there is mercy left for you, it won't come from me."

The cathedral emptied. The walls went dark. The realm shuddered, foundations cracking without souls to support them. That's when I noticed Varnar crawling away, trying to hide.

"Not you." He froze at the sound. "Everyone else paid for centuries. You just got here."

I dragged him to the center as chunks of the cathedral ceiling crashed down around us. "Your victims are still breathing. Still remember your hands. You don't get to leave."

"Please—" He begged.

"Besides," I cut him off, "I need you. This place is dying, but something new has to replace it."

That clean presence touched me one last time, approval without words, then faded completely.

"A new hell." Reality began to dissolve around me. "But selective. Only for those who sleep soundly after destroying lives."

Remorse would be a door. Denial would be a chain. Cruelty without regret would be mine.

The Executioner stepped beside me. "What would you have me do?"

"Help me build it." I took his hand as the old realm crumbled. "My version. My rules."

Varnar screamed as existence rewrote itself around us, but I was already shaping what came next. A hell that would be precise. Selective. Just. I told myself the hunger and the justice were different things. Some nights I almost believed it.

Epilogue

The throne wasn't made of bones anymore.

I'd drawn the design in ash on the chamber floor, showing Flame exactly what I wanted. Black metal twisted with silver, arms that curved like serpents, a back that rose twelve feet high. He'd spent three weeks in the forges below, hammering out my vision.

"Another delivery, my Queen."

Flame stood as he always did, at my right side. The iron helmet hid his face, showing only those two red slits where eyes should be. I'd told him a hundred times he didn't need the helmet anymore.

We'd had that fight last week, actually. Me straddling him in bed, trying to pull it off while he held my wrists.

"The fear works better when they can't see me," he'd insisted.

"Bullshit. You're scared they'll see how beautiful you are under there."

He'd flipped me then, pinned me to the bed with one massive hand. "Beautiful? I'm a monster, *my moth*."

"My monster," I'd corrected, then bit his scarred shoulder hard enough to draw black blood.

But today he wore it, like always when we held court.

Eight months since I'd poisoned the Judge with my concentrated guilt and taken his place. Eight months spent learning to govern hell effectively. Not the screaming, writhing nightmare he'd built over millennia, but something that actually made sense.

Sometimes I still heard my mother saying my name the right way. Zaa-hh-ra. On those days, I remembered I had been loved before hell found me. That mattered. A queen who forgot that would become another Judge.

The realm had changed with me. Gone were the walls made of human meat, floors that squirmed under your feet like tongues. The cathedral of bones had been the first thing to go. Now my domain looked like what it was, a massive prison carved from obsidian and steel. The walls still breathed, but slowly. Deep sleep breathing. The air didn't stink of rot and sulfur anymore. Just copper and that electric smell you get before lightning strikes.

I smoothed my hands over my dress, shadow-silk that moved like liquid smoke. Flame had found it for me in some forgotten corner of the realm, folded in a chest that probably hadn't been opened in centuries. It clung to my transformed body perfectly, shifting between deep purple and absolute black depending on the light. At times, stars seemed caught within its folds, like pieces of the night sky stitched together.

"How many today?" I asked, tracing patterns on my throne's arm. The metal warmed under my touch.

"Six confirmed. Marion found the first branch of a network."

I felt them through my connection to the shepherds above. Six souls I'd claimed, marked by their touch so I could pull them down when judgment came due. Marion's fierce satisfaction blazed brightest, she'd been hunting for weeks, following whispers and rumors through Chicago's underbelly. In an unexpected twist, she discovered them through Emma's school. Started with one creepy teacher who kept "special" photos in a locked drawer. That led to others. A whole network hiding in plain sight.

The world above had its own story for what happened to St. Dymphna. The official story blamed a gas leak during a coastal storm, followed by fire and structural collapse. The report listed thirty-seven dead, mostly staff. The patients who survived were transferred to state hospitals and secure psychiatric units across three states, their central files corrupted after the transfers went through. Marion Washington, Isaac Torres, Sela Novak, none of those names existed in any database anymore. I had eaten the records the same night I ate the Judge. New names. New histories. Clean paper trails that would hold up under anything short of divine scrutiny. Marion got Emma back through a private adoption agency that had never existed until I needed it to. Emma had been in state care since her adoptive father's death, lost in paperwork until I rewrote the file.

During the day, Marion was the perfect PTA mom. Made Emma elaborate lunches with notes inside. Helped with homework at the kitchen table. She went to every school play and soccer game. But at night? At night she became something else. And Isaac hunted beside her.

They'd always been in love, even back in St. Dymphna when everything was insane and corrupted. That desperate connection between people who understood each other's damage. Now they worked like a machine, him with his medical knowledge and steady hands, her with her unhinged determination. Emma had started calling Isaac "Dad" last month.

Sela worked alone because Sela always worked alone. She had family in Prague, a cousin who asked no questions and owned a building with a basement. She ran a shelter there now, a real one with real beds and real locks on the doors. She helped women escape from monsters. And when those monsters came looking, when they showed up drunk and angry demanding their property back... well. The resurrection had done something to her. Anyone I brought back carried a spark of my judgment in their hands. Granting her strength beyond that of any ordinary woman in her late fifties. Strong enough to put men twice her size on their knees, mark them with my touch, and send them tumbling down to me.

"Bring them in," I commanded.

Reality rippled in the sorting room. Six figures materialized, stumbling and blinking in the strange light of my realm. Their bodies had died above the moment the mark activated, heart attacks, strokes, sudden collapses that no coroner would question. They thought it was a nightmare at first. They always did.

"Welcome." I stood from my throne, and the shadow-silk dress flowed around me like water. "You're probably wondering where you are."

One tried to run, a man in his forties with a face people trusted. He'd been touching his students for six years. He chose the quiet ones. The ones who wouldn't tell.

"This is insane," said another. The surgeon who'd been

making 'mistakes' during operations. Only on women who looked like his ex-wife.

Then there were the others. Each one marked by my shepherds for good reason. Each one guilty of destroying lives while sleeping soundly.

"This is my domain," I continued, walking down the steps. My feet were bare, always bare. The black glass was warm under my soles. "You're here because you've hurt people without feeling bad about it."

I gestured, and the realm sorted them automatically. Each soul went to a cell designed specifically for their crimes. The teacher would experience every moment of fear and confusion he'd caused, not watching it, but feeling it from inside his victims' skin. The surgeon would endure every operation he'd botched, but from the patient's perspective.

Each punishment fit perfectly. That was my rule. That was what made me different from the Judge.

"Come," I told Flame. "Let's check on our long-term residents."

We walked through corridors of black glass and breathing metal. Other souls moved past us, the ones who'd learned, who'd finally broken open and felt real remorse. They cleaned. They organized. They prepared cells for new arrivals. Even here, the potential for change remained, for those who dared to embrace it.

But not everyone chose change.

Varnar's cell hadn't changed in eight months. Same stone room. Same scene playing on repeat. The realm's copy of Alan lay before him, perfectly preserved, forever just out of reach. He knelt with hands outstretched, fingers passing through her body like she was made of smoke.

"Please," he whispered when he saw me. "Just once. Let me hold her. Let me explain—"

"Explain what?" I crouched beside him, the shadow-silk pooling around me. "Sorry you lost her? Or for the hundreds you violated in your life?"

"I loved her."

"The same way you 'loved' your patients. As things to own. The difference is, she loved you back."

Some souls were too rotted to fix. They served as reminders. Somewhere below, Tobias still ran from the Grin-Hounds. I let them keep him.

We returned to our chambers at the tower's top, where geometry went strange. Stairs that climbed down. Doors that opened onto themselves. Windows showing impossible views, star systems being born, voids between realities, sometimes glimpses of the world above.

The Executioner, my Flame, closed the door and finally removed his helmet. It hit the floor with a clang that echoed through dimensions. His face, with its sharp angles, old scars, and red eyes that burned only for me, was exactly as I loved it.

"Twenty-seven souls tomorrow," I murmured, moving to the window. The dress shifted with me, sometimes heavy as velvet, sometimes light as smoke. "Marion found something big. A whole ring. Doctors, cops, social workers, moving kids like cargo."

"I'll expand the east wing tonight." He moved behind me. His large hands settled on my shoulders, thumbs working at the knots there.

I turned in his arms, having to crane my neck to meet his eyes. "Not tonight. Tonight, I need you here, with me. Inside me."

I took his hand and led him to our bed that he had made with his own hands, with wood found in the Realm Beneath. I didn't want the human bones and skin bed and he fulfilled my wish.

"I need to feel something other than justice and judgment." I moaned and pushed him onto the bed.

He let me push him down, this creature who could snap me in half without trying. Let me climb on top of him, my hands splayed across his scarred chest. The shadow-silk dress pooled around us like spilled ink.

"My Queen," he started, but I pressed a finger to his lips.

"No titles. Not tonight." I replaced my finger with my mouth, kissing him deep and hungry. Tasted copper and smoke and something uniquely him. "Tonight," I whispered, "I am just Zahra. And you are mine."

His hands stayed gentle at first, careful with his inhuman strength. Always so careful. But I didn't want careful. I bit his lip hard enough to draw blood and he groaned, finally understanding.

"Let go," I commanded, and felt him shudder beneath me. "Trust me. Let me see who you really are."

His control snapped like a chain under too much weight. Those massive hands gripped my hips hard enough to leave marks, if I could still bruise. The shadow-silk dress dissolved at my thought, leaving nothing between us but heat and need.

I rode him slow at first, making him wait, making him want. Every time he tried to thrust up, to take control, I pressed down with divine strength, pinning him. His eyes went wide, he always forgot I wasn't human anymore either.

"Mine," I growled against his throat, nipping at the scars there. "Say it."

"Yours," he gasped, hands clutching at my hips like I was the only solid thing in existence. "Always yours, *my moth.*"

I set a slow, deliberate pace, until he was begging in that raw, inhuman voice. Until this creature of death and judgment was completely undone beneath me, calling my name like a prayer. "Please," he groaned, and the sound went straight through me. "Zahra, please—"

"Please what?" I stopped moving entirely, just to watch him struggle for control. "Tell me what you need."

"You. Need you. Need to—" His words devolved into primal sounds as I quickened my pace, taking what I craved.

When I came, it was with my nails dug into his chest, my back arched, divine power crackling through the room like lightning. He followed right after, my name on his lips like salvation.

After, we lay tangled together, breathing hard. The darkness around us stirred with hunger. Even in our afterglow, the work called. Tomorrow the guilty would arrive. The cycle never stopped. It couldn't stop, here, in this hell.

But tonight was ours. Just ours.

"I love you," I whispered against his chest, tracing patterns in the scars.

"And I love you," he replied, pulling me closer. "My queen. My moth. My everything."

Also by Sephyrra

The Primal Sins Collection

A series of dark horror romances. Each book a standalone. Each
monster ruined for one woman, and one woman only.

Insatiable — The Primal Sins Collection Book 1

She went to the Halloween party already broken — by the husband
who left and the friend who helped him do it. She wasn't looking for
trouble. But a monster who feeds on fear caught her scent, and on
her, he smelled something else. Something he'd been waiting a long
time to taste.

Drenched — The Primal Sins Collection Book 2

She came to the fog-locked village for the ocean's secrets. The ocean
had been keeping one for her — something old, something patient,
something that had been hearing her name in the tide for years before
she ever arrived.

Devoured — The Primal Sins Collection Book 3

St. Dymphna's locks women like her away. The ones who killed their
husbands. The ones nobody wants to remember. Six hundred years
the Executioner has paced the asylum floor. He carved the grooves
himself. He was made to kill her. He didn't.

Touched — The Primal Sins Collection Book 4

She married a man who controls everything she does. She moved
into his first wife's house. And in the attic, behind dust and silence,

something that has watched her longer than she knows finally found its way through the glass.

Once Upon a Monster

Dark fairy tale retellings with mature curvy heroines.

Claiming Red — Once Upon a Monster Book 1

They called her Red for the cloak she wore. Soon they'd call her Red for the blood she spilled. She ran into the forest that swallowed six armed men and sent back pieces. Something was waiting in her dead grandmother's cottage. He watched her like he'd been starving his whole life — and he had.

Bride of the Haunted Manor

A standalone gothic romance novella.

She took the caretaker job at Blackwood Manor because she needed a fresh start. Thirty-eight years of pain will do that. Her gift lets her speak to spirits, and the manor has plenty. But one of them isn't just haunting the halls — he's haunting her. A love that crosses the line between the living and the dead, and a sinister force buried in the walls that wants to claim them both.

Acknowledgments

Thanks to my family for not asking too many questions about my search history.

To my husband and kids, who lived with me while I lived in St. Dymphna's. You ate a lot of takeout during the writing of this book. Thank you for understanding when I disappeared into the dark for hours, for days, and for always leaving the light on for me to find my way back.

To my parents, who aren't here to read this but who taught me that stories matter, even the dark ones. Especially the dark ones. I miss you both.

To my siblings, who've been reading my weird stories since we were kids and still beg me to write something "nice" for once. Sorry. Maybe next time. (Probably not.)

To my friends who believe in me more than I believe in myself — you know who you are. Thank you for the late-night texts, the pep talks, the "you've got this" messages when I absolutely did not.

To my beta readers, including Amanda New — thank you for your feedback and for catching what I missed.

To my readers in **Monsters, Demons, and Knotting, Oh My!** Thank you for the endless support and for getting why monsters just hit different.

About the Author

Sephyrra writes from the shadows where horror and desire collide.

Mother, wife, writer, unrepentant procrastinator — usually all at once, rarely in that order. She believes the best monsters are the ones we invite in, and the most interesting heroines are plus-size, over 35, and deliciously damaged.

Author of *Insatiable, Drenched* and now *Devoured*, she splits her time between novels, scripts, and staring at blank pages while pretending to work. Writing isn't just her life — it's her obsession, her therapy, and probably the reason her family eats so much takeout.

instagram.com/authorsephyrra
facebook.com/authorsephyrra
tiktok.com/@Sephyrra

A Note to Readers

If *Devoured* kept you up at night (for any reason), please consider leaving a review on Amazon or Goodreads.

Reviews help other readers find their next dark obsession. They also help me know I'm not alone in thinking monsters make the best love interests.

Thank you for walking through St. Dymphna's halls with me. Thank you for not looking away when things got dark. And thank you for understanding that sometimes the real romance is in the horror.

Now go leave that review. The monsters are waiting to see what you thought.

How to Help an Indie Author

If you want to keep indie stories alive (and keep me caffeinated), here's how you can help:

- *Leave a review.* Even a quick line on Amazon, Goodreads, or BookBub helps more than you know.
- *Tell a friend.* Hand a book to someone who needs a little monster romance in their life.
- *Share online.* Post quotes, selfies with the book, or reactions on social media. Tag me so I can flail over it.
- *Request my books.* Ask your local bookstore or library to stock them.
- *Check out my Etsy shop.* Signed bookplates, extras, and monster merch live there.
- *Stay connected.* My newsletter, Facebook group, and Discord are the best way to get early reveals and chaos.